WHEN YOU WERE MINE

TEACHER CHRONICLES BOOK 2

IDA BRADY

To Team Brida,

For all the love, group hugs and chocolate.

TRIGGER WARNINGS

This book contains the following references (please skip this description if you don't want potential spoilers): mental health/suicide, drugs, swearing, graphic depiction of birth, teen pregnancy, domestic violence, swearing, death of young children.

On the plus, it contains spicy sex.

CHAPTER ONE

*J*ack Davies, international movie star and all-around fuckwit (according to his ex-girlfriend) had spent the past six months running from his problems. Hell, longer than that if he was honest with himself.

Which he wasn't.

Beyond the adrenaline that pumped through his body lay a fear that he didn't dare acknowledge. He was terrified that if he did, he would never be able to rock up to a film set ever again.

Jack closed his eyes against the rambling mess that was his mind and paced the sidewalk outside the busy train station. He wore his cap down low, covering his tell-tale Hollywood blond hair, and adjusted the lapels of his leather jacket.

Deep breaths, Jack. Think of something else.

He glanced at a vibrant poster with a happy, fashionable couple stepping off a tram. 'Step into Spring' my ass.

It may be the middle of September down under, but winter still gripped the city by the proverbial balls.

Christ on a bike, he should still be in sunny Los Angeles right now with a dozen or so women desperate to get their bikini-on and happy enough with a casual thing back at his bachelor pad in the hills.

He *should* be working.

Instead, Jack had lit out, unable to face what had happened. Technically, he hadn't finished filming, but the idea of rocking up to the studio in L.A. on Monday morning brought on a panic attack, which had led him to the airport and on the next available flight to Melbourne, Australia.

Back to his childhood hometown.

Despite his luxurious ticket in first-class, Jack hadn't managed to sleep more than a handful of hours. Insomnia was making more than just a guest appearance on the long-haul flight. It had taken ownership of his life; waiting for him at home every evening, pervading each room like a sinister trail of smoke, until he was choking from the fumes. Tenacious, obstinate, and like the Airbus he had travelled on, it was bloody impossible for him to shift.

Drugs didn't work.

Docs didn't work.

Work didn't work.

After playing pretend for so long, Jack wanted out.

For the first time in his adult life, he didn't give two-shits about his contract, his agent, or even the network. He just wanted to be left alone.

To find peace.

Where once he could bury himself in work to forget, he was now finding ghosts on every set. Behind every scene. He had taken on this film knowing it would bring back those feelings of guilt. But hell, he thought he had a handle on all that shit from his childhood.

He had been so afraid he was going to slip back into his old habits that he did something he hadn't done in a long time. Jack trusted his gut instinct and got the hell out of there.

He kicked at a pebble, focusing on the mist that pervaded

the sidewalk. The clawing sensation crept up the back of his throat. He sucked in the icy evening air, desperate for release.

Not now, you son-of-a-bitch. Not here.

Jack counted to ten then slowly breathed out. The one thing his therapist did help with was breathing techniques. Not that he had seen the woman lately. Or much at all beyond those first few sessions. He snapped the band at his wrist a few times for good measure and walked to the curb.

Just as he was about to check his phone, his brother's shining black SUV pulled up outside of Parliament Station.

And for the first time in nearly forty-hours, the bile settled back down in his stomach and his breathing began to even out.

Thank fuck he was back.

"Tell me again why you won't run away and marry me?" Jack drawled, pecking his soon-to-be sister-in-law on the cheek. "Surely you can do better than this ugly mug?" He clapped his brother, Owen, on the shoulder, careful not to jostle him as he drove.

His fatigue was lifting, replaced by a warmth that only two people in love could emit. Hell, they both radiated romance like some Hollywood blockbuster movie. Without the pretence.

Maybe this was what he needed. A mini break, a chance to clear his head before going back. Jack swallowed the hot ball of guilt at his throat. He wouldn't think about the people he was disappointing in L.A. He couldn't.

"Your proposal wasn't nearly as good as your brother's, I'm afraid." Ally swivelled in the front seat. Her midnight hair had been chopped off and now bounced around the nape of her neck in a stylish, glossy bob. It suited her.

"You didn't appreciate the bouquet of roses, sweetheart?"

"Bouquet!" His brother, Owen, sputtered, shooting him a

glare in the rear-view mirror. "It was a bloody *ocean*. Took up most of the living room."

"See what I mean, Ally? Why would you want this ugly dog, who knows nothing about romance, when you could have me?"

Her lips twitched. "Two hundred roses were quite a bit to handle, Jack. Charlie almost lost her mind."

He could imagine his niece had squealed with delight.

"I've been waiting to thank you, *little* brother, for months now." Owen's blue eyes, a few shades darker than his own, flashed with affection. "Now I don't have to wait."

The laugh that tumbled out felt good. When was the last time he had felt anything other than dread?

He missed being with his family. Hell, the last time he was here, Owen was caught in a vicious custody battle with Charlie's maternal grandparents. Dating Ally, his daughter's sexy schoolteacher had given Owen a new lease on life. He had a kind woman with a spine of steel to help him raise his child. Charlie had even begun to smile again. As cynical as Jack was, he had to admit, their relationship was something out of a Hallmark movie.

It was Jack's legal team that was able to help Owen win his case. He reminded himself of it whenever he began to doubt his character.

When had he done something good and true like that since?

Jack leaned forward between the seats, needing to distance himself from everything but the present. The leather underneath his hands was cool, the car smelled of peppermint, and the motion of the vehicle seemed to sooth his nerves. He could handle this. He *was* handling it.

See? Piece of cake, Jack.

"So where is the little pip-squeak?"

"That 'pip-squeak' has grown another few inches this past

winter." Owen grinned. "She'll lose her shit knowing you're home."

"She's at the De Lotto's place, helping cook up a storm."

Jack frowned. "De Lotto?"

"You remember Sera, don't you?" Ally's eyes were playful. "From way back in the day."

Jack's eyes brightened. "Seraphina De Lotto. Now that *is* a name I haven't heard for—"

"Over a decade. I know." Ally smiled, a teasing glint in her green eyes.

"Do you?"

"I stumbled across the fact that the two of you briefly dated many moons ago."

"We did." Memories belonging to a different man, a different life, slid back into startling focus, as if they had always been there, anticipating his acknowledgement.

Ally rolled her eyes, swatting his hand. "And she was just as forthcoming in her details as you are—honestly, Jack."

"Affairs of the heart, sweetheart." He patted his chest, throwing her a wink.

"You keep your secrets then."

"No secret. We dated before I left for America." *Keep it light, Jack.*

He rubbed at his chest, remembering the brown-eyed girl he had left behind all those years ago.

"To stardom."

"Something like that."

"So why the surprise visit, little brother? We're months out from the wedding. We'd have rearranged our plans this weekend if I had known you were coming." Owen glanced over his shoulder this time. "Everything okay?"

Jack stiffened. Did it show on his face? Could everyone see it?

He lowered his shoulders, assuming an easy grin. He hoped that he pulled it off but these days he couldn't be so sure.

"You mean the ranting 'get-me-outta-here' phone call? Somehow the fucking paparazzi found out where I was staying. There was a nosey photographer waiting for me when I arrived. I usually stay at The Maison, but it was a last-minute trip so they didn't have any availability. Some festival is on. Serves me right for staying in a second-rate place."

"Where'd you book?"

"The Grand."

Ally's mouth opened. "The Grand is hardly second-rate, Jack."

"It *is* in comparison to The Maison. So much for confidentiality. A dodgy concierge let it slip, so I got out of there. I've filed a complaint for that shit."

"Did they attack you?"

"Jesus, Ally. They're paps, not the mafia. Problem was, I was on a call with my agent, and the bastard overheard. I got the memory card out of his camera, but the conversation...well, I can't go all M.I.B on his ass and wipe his memory, can I? It won't take long before the rest of the hounds get a whiff of the story."

And they would be relentless knowing their Hollywood star wasn't so bloody perfect. They'd chase that story until he was in an early grave. He'd seen it often enough when celebs tried to come clean. To get help.

He was fucked.

"Weren't you in the middle of filming?" Owen glanced at him, concern lining his face. "What happened?"

"Some stuff came up and I left. I needed a break anyway."

"Jack—"

"Thanks for the save. I owe you. When my head is clear, we can talk. But right now, I'm just glad to be around a few familiar faces."

Owen nodded, once. "We're glad to have you back, Jack. For however long."

"You never answered my question. Why is the annoying chatterbox at the De Lotto's?"

Ally shifted again. "She's helping Sera's mum with the baking. Once Maryam De Lotto heard how keen Charlotte was in the kitchen, she took it upon herself to take her under her wing and teach her everything she knew. As they're cooking us a dinner feast in our honour, Charlotte wanted a hand at the desserts."

"A belated engagement dinner."

"Holy shit, Owen. Why didn't you say? Drop me off along here and I can get a taxi to your house."

"Too late, I'm afraid. Once Mrs. D heard that we were running late because of a certain S.O.S. from a Hollywood star, she insisted that we bring you over for dinner. Hope that's okay?"

"You know what, sounds perfect to me."

Jack settled back in his seat and stretched out. Maybe this trip to Oz was exactly what he had needed. Might not be so bad after all.

CHAPTER TWO

*S*ome women liked handbags. Others obsessed over shoes. Ever since Sera could utter her first words, her focus and appreciation always resided with food. As a bouncy twelve-month-old, her first words had not been 'mamma' or even 'dadda,' but sitting in her highchair with her three older brothers clamouring around her at the kitchen table, she had turned to her mother, pointed to a bowl of spaghetti and said, 'more.'

Who could blame her?

Since she was little, food was the crux of every family gathering and festivity. It was what they shared when someone got a promotion and what they reverted to for solace at the death of a loved one.

Food was life.

It was also probably handy for her that fitness was her other passion. It was the perfect balance given that she could eat her three brothers under the table.

Sera was her mother's daughter after all.

So it was a no-brainer when she became a Health and Physical Education teacher, combining her love of sports and her desire to work with children.

Shrugging her shoulders, she needed to dislodge the overwhelming sentimentality that had crept up on her of late. Living too much in the past never helped anyone's future.

Sera wasn't one to wallow in the things she didn't have. But as she looked across at her best friend's stepdaughter, Charlie, she couldn't help but acknowledge that quick twinge of longing.

Not jealousy, never of her friend's happiness, but of what she was beginning to realise was a part of her life that she dearly wanted for her own. The lack of which hadn't bothered her much. Until now.

Maybe it was all the wedding planning for Ally. Or the day spent cooking with Charlie, but she was suddenly hyper aware of her own single status.

Maddie's nudge in the ribs brought her gaze into focus. She had been fidgety all morning. From Maddie's pointed looks, it wasn't something she had concealed very well either. But then again, her friend was always shrewd when the occasion suited. Ever since their university days, Maddie had been carefree and happy to play the field. Perhaps she should take a leaf out of her book...

Being back in her parents' house wasn't doing Sera any favours in that department. She was used to living in her own space, but as her water-damaged apartment was awaiting repairs, she would be stuck in her old bedroom for another month, surrounded by childhood memories. Cue her misty-eyed sentimentality.

Sera looked around her at the table that was literally groaning under the weight of all the food. With an Italian father and a Lebanese mother, she was caught in a spell of culinary wizardry, and would be forever trapped in its thrall.

"I'm both delighted and disgusted." Maddie's ivory face was enraptured.

"Disgusted?" Charlotte chipped in before Sera had the chance. Her round face had lost its child-like innocence over the winter. She had shot up past Sera—not that it was a difficult feat —and had morphed in to a willowy thirteen-year-old that would one day reach her father's height. She placed the plate of home-made flat bread in a free corner. "Why? How?"

"Because I know that I'm going to inhale every single thing on this table and feel a level of disgust only reserved for the truly depraved. *Man vs. Food* will have nothing on me."

When Sera's parents held a party, it meant food. Lots of food.

"I'm more starving that you are, so we'll see about that," Charlotte piped up.

"More starving ain't a thing, kid," Maddie countered, lifting another bowl and carrying across to the dining room table. "Didn't your English teacher ever teach you anything?"

"That'd be you." Sera pointed sweetly.

Even though she had known Maddie and Ally in college, it was working together at Woodbury High, that really cemented their friendship. She was lucky to get to see her besties at work every day: they were really more like sisters than friends.

"Where are they anyway?" Charlotte complained, eyeing off the plate of marinated olives. "They're taking aaaaaages."

"Not sure. They had a detour but texted to say they'd be here soon," Sera offered.

When the bell pealed, Sera backed away from the dining room table, wagging a finger at the two girls. "Do *not* inhale all the olives. They're for everyone."

Their twin grins said it all. "We won't!" Maddie and Charlie sang in chorus. She didn't trust them for a second.

Her smile froze in place as she opened the front door. All the air in her lungs seemed to disappear, as if she had been winded.

Jack. Jack Davies.

Sera was unable to do more than gape in confusion. She clutched the door handle, willing her body to action.

How many times had she opened her parents' front door to see his smiling face that summer? How many times had she come to recognise his mood, just by taking in the set of his shoulders? It was an odd sensation. Like looking at the past but through a completely different lens.

It had been a little over ten years. But looking at him, she was transported back into the past.

Sera's heart galloped in her chest, bringing her back to life even as the goosebumps flittered over her skin.

Jack bloody Davies.

Despite the easy smile on his expressive mouth—one that had always seemed ready for a laugh—the hard muscle at his shoulders carried tension. She could sense that energy even before his blue eyes confirmed it.

Jack's black baseball cap sat low but did nothing to mask his devilishly handsome face. A face she knew, whilst altered by the years, as well as her own.

"Seraphina."

His voice. That honey-smooth drawl—now peppered by his time in America—seized her heart. She hadn't a moment to blink before he stepped forward, engulfing her in his embrace.

Sera held on, surrounded by his citrus scent, startled by the hard planes of his body, flush against her own.

She stepped back because she really wanted to linger.

That zing of attraction sparked beneath her fingers, humming under the surface. It was only natural that her body remembered, even when her mind had tried so very hard to forget.

"Jack."

His eyes raked over her face, her body.

"You've let the curls loose."

Sera instinctively shoved back her mass of tumbling, wild hair. She had been going through a hair-straightening phase when she met Jack, which she had abandoned one summer morning when he had seen her out of the shower, loose curls free and unimpeded by chemicals. No man had looked at her with that much longing and pure lust since. Then again, they had been young and…impressionable.

"Takes too long to straighten it these days and I have better things to do with my time. Tell me, why am I having a conversation about hair styling with Hollywood star, Jack Davies, in my parents' hallway?"

Owen walked through the front door with a large bouquet of flowers, Ally in hand. "Sorry, we picked this stray up off the side of the road. Your mother insisted we bring him along."

"They tried throwing me out of the car, but I'm like gum."

"You stick?"

"Stretch. I'm *very* bendy." He wiggled his eyebrows.

"And still inappropriate."

Jack grinned. "It's good to see you, Sera."

The squealing cries from the living room cut off any reply. Charlotte bound into the room, with Sera's mother, Maryam, trailing behind.

"Who's this monster?" Jack cried, hugging his niece before setting her down. "She's grown and eaten my favourite girl!"

Maryam swatted him with a tea towel. "I thought *I* was your favourite girl." She kissed both his cheeks then ripped off the baseball cap.

"My favourite *woman*. Hands down."

Maryam grinned, and her olive skin, already flushed from all the cooking, glowed. "Be careful or my husband will have your neck. Cheeky boy."

"You know me, Mrs. D, I appreciate the beautiful things in life."

"And still have a silver tongue," came the deep rumbling voice from the back stairs.

"I have a weakness for your wife, I'm afraid, sir." Jack grinned, turning to Sera's dad, Tony, who grabbed him in a bear hug.

"Don't we all, son. I had to fight the other boys off when we first met." He threw a wink at Maryam and Sera's heart softened. She could see how her mother had been overwhelmed by her father's smooth good looks. Even though his hair was greying at the temples, and the lines began to mark his face, age only seemed to make him even more handsome.

Sera had grown up luckier than most to see her parents madly in love with one another. After nearly forty years together, their love showed no signs of abating. A rare and very precious gift.

"Tony, not another story. We've heard it all before."

"I don't think I have." Jack played along.

Tony's hazel eyes danced. "Fancy a glass of wine? Chardonnay or Tempranillo?" He held up the bottles he brought with him from the basement, drawing Jack further into the house.

Sera watched the two men walk together, one fair, the other dark, talking as if it had only been a month since they had seen each other last and not over a decade. As if Jack hadn't left and broken Sera's heart.

Maryam sidled up next to her, eyes filled with sympathy.

"You alright?"

Sera spared her a brief glance and fought against wriggling under that knowing stare.

"Yes." She needed a few hours to recover from the shock of it, but she would be fine. This didn't mean anything.

"Don't get testy with me, Seraphina. A woman never forgets her first love, eh?"

She sputtered. "Mum, that was a long time ago. We were just babies."

"Babies!" She waved a hand, gold jewellery flashing. "You were what? Nineteen? I was pregnant with Omar by that age."

"Yes, but that was a completely different time. Things have changed since then."

Maryam tugged her arm towards the kitchen. "But the heart, Seraphina, it stays the same."

"Easy, Mum. Jack and I are ancient history."

Her mother's concern grated on Sera's serenity. She watched as everyone gathered around the dining table and refused to give any thought to her mother's goading.

So what if Jack was back in town? It didn't change a damn thing. But she it couldn't hurt to keep her guard up. Just in case.

Jack sipped at his glass of Tempranillo and eased back in his chair. He was on his second helping of Mrs. D's food and was pretty sure he'd smash out a third before dessert, because in this household, there was always dessert.

The jumpy sensation that had seized his nervous system since he left L.A. was humming under the surface, demanding attention.

Fucking hell.

He should have been relaxed with a glass of red in his hand. He should have been distracted by the golden-skinned goddess sitting opposite him.

But now that the adrenaline had worn off, all Jack could think about was the look on the producer's face once he found out what he had done.

His co-stars.

The crew.

He studied the deep burgundy colour in his wineglass,

trying to contain his thoughts. Jack was determined to put on the best performance of his fucking life to get through tonight. He wouldn't take away from Owen and Ally's celebration dinner.

No way. Fuck. That.

Jack placed his glass back on the table with a little too much force. Sera's eyes jumped to his. Questions, so many questions burned in those golden-brown depths.

Easy, Jack. You can do this. He flicked the band around his wrist for good measure.

Sera was always perceptive, preferring to sit back and watch than chatter away. She grew up in a boisterous family with loud, noisy brothers that would often take over the conversation. At least, that was what he remembered.

Who was he kidding? When it came to Seraphina De Lotto, he remembered everything.

At this moment, he wasn't certain that was a good thing.

Jack's eyes narrowed. One thing he appreciated about Sera, even back then, was her ability to demolish a plate of food and match him for seconds. Right now, her plate was full. He wanted to know what she was thinking but she had perfected an unreadable expression over the years. He should know. It was the very mirror of his own.

"So where is the rest of the De Lotto clan? I'm sure they wouldn't miss a feast like this?" Jack directed the question at Sera. It was Maryam who answered.

"Omar and his wife have had a baby girl, Kate. The boys have gone to Queensland for a visit before heading back to England which is their new home now. Tony and I only just got back from Queensland, and I already miss the baby so much." Maryam grew misty-eyed.

"We were there for two *months*. I had to force her onto the plane." Tony laughed, squeezing his wife's hand. "We video call them nearly every day."

"And I can't wait until they move back to Melbourne," Maryam sighed. "So, what have you planned for your visit, Jack? I take it you'll be here until the wedding?"

Jack straightened, then forced his shoulders to lower. The tension cloaked his body making his movements stiff. "I'm not sure actually, Mrs. D. There are a few things going on still in L.A."

His agent's words circled around his brain. Taylor was pissed. And rightly so.

"Nosey paparazzo at the hotel when he arrived," Ally supplied.

"What?" Maryam sat forward.

"It was nothing. Look, thanks for dinner, but I need to head off soon, find a place to crash. If I do stay longer, I'll most likely look at an apartment rental, but for now a hotel in the area—one that is discreet if you know of any—would be ideal." Hell, he'd be recognised wherever he went. Especially if that paparazzo leaked the private conversation he had with his agent. Nowhere would be safe.

Jack swallowed. The delicious food he'd inhaled threatened to resurface. "It'll be a far cry from The Maison but it's only temporary."

"The food festival..." Ally clicked her fingers. "That's why everything was booked up at your usual hotel."

"Just my luck."

"Jack, the wedding isn't until December, so that'll give you plenty of time to tie up loose ends if you need to, perhaps even stay for a few weeks before jet setting off again?" Ally offered.

"Or settle in for an extended holiday?" Tony raised his dark eyebrows.

"Yes! Stay, Uncle Jack. *Please*." Charlotte bounced in her chair. "We can do sleepovers and bake and go camping and—"

"Easy, Charlie." Owen grinned.

"But Mum and Dad are away this weekend," Charlie prattled on. "I'm sleeping over here coz grandpa and grandma are on holiday. You can stay here, too and we can do a big sleepover!"

"I don't think that—"

His mind swirled and he fought to steady his breathing. There was too much noise. Too many people. He just needed a bit of space. Time to—

"Of course you can stay." Tony waved his hand high. "We've all these spare rooms upstairs."

"Honestly, it's no bother." Maryam smiled.

"You can crash at our place, mate." Owen was fishing out his keys. "Ally and I are going up to Sydney tomorrow morning for a few days. Maddie and Sera have booked us a spa treatment for our engagement. If we had known you were coming, we'd have rearranged the short trip."

"I'd normally say yes, Owen, but now that I think about it, I don't want the paps anywhere near your home." He remembered the circus at his last visit, when Owen had been going through his custody battle. He didn't want the media hounding him with their wedding coming up. Or with the shit-show that would likely erupt once that bastard published his private conversation. Christ. "Look, you're busy with wedding prep and need your privacy."

"Such a star you are, Jack." Maddie winked. "A far cry from our college theatre days."

"You played a rocking Ophelia from memory."

"Then you have a very good memory."

"Like an elephant." Jack tapped his head then turned to Maryam and Tony. "I'm happy to crash at a local hotel if you know of any?"

"No. It's sorted. Charlotte wants her uncle here, and we have plenty of rooms." Maryam shot him a no-nonsense look she had perfected, no doubt, since her sons were toddling around, climbing cupboards. "You'll stay for however long you need and that's final. Nobody knows you're here, so you won't be hounded. Sera will be staying as well. You can take the weekend to catch up."

Jack glanced at Sera, bracing against the familiar guilt that wound around his gut. The guilt that always accompanied him when he thought about their break-up. He didn't think she would be happy to see his face again, let alone have him stay at her parents' house. "If it's alright with you?"

Sera's smile gave nothing away. "Why wouldn't it be, Jack?" But her tone suggested something else entirely.

"You two can get reacquainted." Maryam's smile was encouraging. "It's been such a long time since you've been home. We'd love to have you here."

Not every De Lotto seemed overly pleased by his presence. But maybe it was a chance to break through that wall that Sera kept in place. To make amends for what happened.

"Then I'd love to." He plastered a smile on his face even though his heart was heavy.

Through the fog and swirling emotions, Jack felt their kindness. It was genuine, without agenda.

He picked up his glass of wine and took comfort in the people around him. Jack knew all too well that the sensation would be short-lived.

CHAPTER THREE

*I*t was early on Saturday morning when Sera rolled out of bed. She had woken up agitated after a restless night, and instead of trying to fall back asleep, she decided a workout was the perfect antidote to clear her foggy brain.

The chilly air pervaded her small bedroom, and from her quick glimpse outside, it looked like it was going to be a cool start.

Sera added an extra layer beneath her long-sleeved tank top and stretched her legs on the circular purple carpet her cousin had given her for her fifteenth birthday. Most of her keepsakes were in her cupboard or storage. As much as she loved spending time with her parents, she was used to living on her own, and liked her small apartment. The water damage in her building meant there was a lot of items she would have to replace. The burst pipe had caused problems for not only her apartment but for most of her neighbours on that floor as well.

For now, she'd have to make do with her old bedroom and hope the repairs were quick.

Sera cupped the sole of her foot, enjoying the resistance in her hamstrings, leaning further into the stretch. She was always harping on her physical education students to include a proper warm up and cool down in their training, a habit she had drilled into herself from a young age.Her father's soccer-mad coaching days had instilled a love of the game and of fitness in all the De Lotto children. Perhaps in her the most, seeing as though she made sport and fitness a part of her career. Fitness, food and teaching kids—her three favourite things.

Sera slipped on a fresh pair of ankle socks and her trainers. A restless dissatisfaction fidgeted back and forth in her body, urging her muscles to move. She *was* happy. She had a very comfortable, blessed life, especially in comparison to those doing it tough.

So why was she so agitated? Beyond the sleep-deprivation, was an annoyance she couldn't shake.

His face drifted before her like some apparition.

Bloody Jack.

She didn't want to admit it but seeing his gorgeous face in the flesh had brought back a flood of memories and sensations. How long could one legitimately hold onto a grudge? A broken heart?

What happened with Jack was ancient history. The warm, gooey feelings muddling up her brain said otherwise.

Sera had been heartbroken when he had left all those years ago. For a long time, she had nursed the hurt, convincing herself that if Jack truly had loved her, he wouldn't have left. She had put on a brave face but had been confused by his decision to leave without at least trying to make it work.

She wanted that commitment. Even though it started as a summer romance, those few months they shared had left her wanting more. She was prepared to make it work. But he hadn't been ready to do the same, and knowing that, understanding that perhaps Jack didn't love her as much as she did, broke her.

Sera had come to accept that they were on different paths in life, and that whilst her relationship with him had been wonderful, it wasn't meant to be.

If Jack hadn't turned up on her parents' doorstep last night with that easy grin and L.A. charm, she would be going about her life content as ever. It wouldn't be long before he'd return to Hollywood, and she'd return to her apartment.

End. Of. Story.

Satisfied with her pep talk, she picked up her headphones and tip-toed across the landing, careful to keep off the creaky boards.

"Oof!"

Sera stumbled over a shoe at the base of the staircase and landed on solid flesh. Said shoe was encased in a foot...one that had no place being at the bottom of the stairs.

Like calm waters in a still lake, she felt the disturbance immediately: reverberations travelled down her stomach, past her hips, to the very tips of her cold toes.

Sera breathed in that familiar scent, a slight citrus zing that clung to his skin. One that would always conjure endless memories of warmth and sunshine, of stretching summer nights and balmy days. Of bittersweet longing and...Jack. The man whose hands were firmly clutching the curve of her butt.

An arrow of desire—one that always hovered nocked and ready for aim—landed dead centre between her thighs.

She looked down at a pair of amused blue eyes, his expression that of a man who knew *exactly* what he held in his hands.

Sera's annoyance blanketed her desire. Her body had no right to feel anything when it came to Jack. The churning in her belly was hunger, pure and simple. Plain ol' fashioned hu—

"If this is how you welcome all your house guests, I might have to extend my stay."

Jack's grin was slow. It stretched all the way across his mouth and ran over every inch of her skin, warming her in the process. But it failed to reach his eyes.

The disconnect made her wary. What had happened over the years to make him so...

No. Absolutely not. Nuh uh. No way. There was a reason why curiosity killed the damn cat, Sera. Wake up.

"Your hands are still on my ass, Jack."

He let go, holding his palms out in surrender. "Was just catching your fall there, sweetheart."

Sera launched off his chest. The slap of cold air left goose-bumps trailing down her arms. He grunted when her well-placed elbow caught him under the ribs.

"Sneaky move, De Lotto. I forgot you've spent most of your childhood surrounded by brothers." He rubbed at the tender spot, rising.

"Put your hands on my ass again and I'll show you moves you've never seen before, *sweetheart.*"

Jack stood in front of her. "Tempting."

"Didn't lose that one track mind, I see."

"I don't seem to recall you having any complaints."

"As much as I enjoy standing around in the dark, cold corridor exchanging *double entendres* with you, there's a running track that has my name on it."

Jack motioned to his own workout gear. "Great minds think alike. Mind if I join you? For old times' sake?"

Sera turned on her headphones to drown out the whispers of the past. "Sure thing, Hollywood. But you best keep up."

Sera wasn't the least bit surprised when he did. Matching her stride, Jack didn't seem phased by her pace or by her choice of track.

The gravel path lay beyond the local park and followed the Yarra River in all its brown glory. Take the track north and they would be in the CBD, an option that many cyclists took to commute into work instead of public transport. If they went south, they would be in the heart of suburbia.

Even though it was cold, Sera felt her tired muscles begin to fire up. By the time they hit their first mile, she was well and truly warm.

She let Jack talk, filling her in on all the amusing tales of the rich and famous. Despite the early hour and the years separating them, Sera was surprised to find their conversation was easy. Familiar. But then again, Jack could make a cactus feel welcome.

Even though he was making an effort to break the ice, Sera didn't want to get too comfortable. There was history there, and if she wasn't careful, she'd lose herself in it.

They ran the distance back in silence. But one question kept niggling at the back of her mind despite all her good sense.

They were cooling down in her parents' backyard when she asked.

"What brought you out of bed so early? If I recall, you weren't usually one to be up before sunrise."

Jack's eyes warmed briefly before he looked away.

"I've learned over the years to get used to early wake-up calls whilst on set, not that I'm ever happy about it. When they pay you the big bucks, you'd be an asshole to complain."

"That doesn't answer my question."

Jack's mouth kicked up at the corners. "No wonder your students fear you."

"Who said that?"

"I have insider information...and to answer your question, I can fall asleep like a breastfed baby, but staying asleep is a problem." He glanced over. "And yes, Mother, I've seen every doctor known to man."

"What does help?"

"This isn't bad. Though I'm not about to become some 3 a.m. gym junkie. Meditation, lifestyle changes..."

"Not the least bit cynical."

Jack flicked the rubber band at his wrist. "You study psych whilst I was gone, De Lotto?"

"Just calling it as I see it."

"Transparency isn't exactly a great trait to have as an actor. Nobody wants to be able to see through a performance."

"This isn't a set we're talking about here, Jack. It's real life."

His grin was fleeting and devoid of any of its usual charm.

"I'm weary."

Sera paused at the sliding door, her hand on the latch. "And a little lost by the sound of it."

Jack stepped forward, his expression troubled. Before she could comment, his face changed, replaced by a look she remembered from long ago. That of a hot, young actor who unlocked her desire, initiating her into a ritual she hadn't experienced before. At nineteen, Sera had been waiting for the right guy, and then she met Jack.

Her virgin heart and body hadn't stood a chance.

Jack had been a few years older and so very capable of showing her what she had been missing.

He inched closer, his gaze intimate, knowing.

In a move she was sure was rehearsed, he cradled the base of her head, stroking the column of her neck, making his intention clear.

"Sera." He tilted her face.

"Jack—"

"Maybe you could help me find myself."

Alarm bells rang in her head. "This isn't the answer."

"Then teach me." His mouth hovered close to hers as he spoke. She could feel his breath on her lips, enticing her to close the distance. "Help me, Sera."

It took every ounce of her willpower to tilt her head back and move away. Perhaps if she hadn't caught a glimpse of his sadness, she could have lost herself in the moment, in him.

But instinct told her Jack's hurt ran deep. And issues like that could have the power to overwhelm them both by its sheer force. Like a rip current in a seemingly calm ocean. Sera was all too aware of how she could drown in it if she wasn't careful.

Last night proved to her there was a lot more going on beneath the charming surface.

"Upstairs. To bed."

Jack's mouth moved a fraction. "Sounds like a killer idea."

Sera laughed, untangling herself from his grasp. "I meant alone. Shower and bed. Or at least breakfast. You're beat."

Jack's shoulders shifted in slow acceptance. "Cut me deep, De Lotto."

She opened the door now, stepping inside. "I won't be your Band Aid, Jack."

"Cruel woman. When did you grow a spine of steel?"

"Always had it, Jack. You've just not been around to see it put to use."

"That wasn't a complaint. I happen to find strong women ridiculously sexy. Or maybe my charm has worn off."

"I'll let you stew over the answer to that one on your own."

"Hey, don't believe everything you read in the gossip magazines."

"I don't waste my time on that."

"Then why do I get the feeling you're making assumptions about my type?"

It was her turn to shrug her shoulders. "Just a hunch."

They both stopped short of entering the living room. Sera's mother stood with her eyes bright, her small frame cocooned in a sunny orange bathrobe.

"Successful run?"

Jack strolled past. "You've no idea."

CHAPTER FOUR

*S*era was grateful that Charlie had stayed with them over the weekend. It meant that Jack was preoccupied catching up with his niece which, from all the howls of laughter over the past few days, had seemed to be going well.

What with her mother teaching them both how to make Middle Eastern sweets in preparation for next week's food canteen at South Row, Sera had some time to think about what it all meant and how she felt about Jack being back in town.

Whilst she knew that Jack's flirting was just that, she had found it difficult not to think about the look in his eyes, especially as he was staying in a room down the hall from her own.

Her attraction to him had nothing to do with the fact that he was a Hollywood heartthrob. To her, he was just Jack. The same Jack who stole her heart...only to break it in two.

If she were lucky, she would find the type of relationship that her parents still had after all these decades. Not that Sera was holding out hope in that department. It wouldn't do to fixate on the overly romantic and highly improbable idea of being somebody's first and last. That was the stuff of dreams. Or movies.

She lived in real life, with real responsibilities.

Sera closed the trunk of her car, loaded with extra school supplies for her tutoring session with the South Row kids. The small group of teenagers that rocked up to the dilapidated library annex each week for help and tutoring were just a small sample size of the individuals who needed support in South Row.

When a kid had a birthday, she made sure to bring a cake and snacks to mark the occasion. The look on the kids' faces when she brought it in was priceless. Sundays to her were about giving back to the people who needed it most.

Yet every time a child blew out their candles, Sera felt the sharp pang in her chest for the little boy who should have been with them. The little boy whose life was cut fatally short.

Gut churning, she watched Jack and Charlie leave for a walk around the block. While she could hear the young girl prattle away, she noticed that Jack's shoulders were hunched, his body stiff. Dark sunglasses shielded his eyes, and she wondered what had happened for him to arrive so suddenly. Sera shook her head. Whatever he was going through was none of her business.

She returned to the kitchen just as her mother was placing the last of the cookies into the Tupperware containers.

The smell of dates, cinnamon, and butter wafted out of the oven.

"*Ma'amoul*? Am I taking this batch too?"

"They're for Charlie. Don't open the oven!"

"I wasn't going to." Because she was, Sera moved the tea towel hanging over the oven window and peeked at the trays of sweets. She had a weak spot for *ma'amoul*: spiced dates encased in crumbly pastry. She'd eat it any day of the week.

Sera turned and placed the Tupperware containers into the last crate. She looked at the cake her mother was decorating. It was spectacular. Something you'd see in a high-end bakery. But

Maryam insisted that these kids be treated and spoilt just as all kids should be. It was that generosity of spirit that she loved so very much.

"So tell me, *habibti*," her mother's voice was soft, but those eyes of hers were ever discerning. "Is there something between you and Jack?" Maryam slid the three-tiered white cake, decorated with sprinkles and glitter, into the cake box.

"Mum, I love you, but you're as unrelenting as a Bulldogs supporter in the Sydney Swans cheer squad."

"You and your football."

"You and your romance."

"*Binte*, what is this life without it, hmm?"

Sera helped her load the last crate, and twenty minutes later, with the *ma'amoul* cooling on the kitchen counter, they were out of the house.

"Do you ever get sick of cooking?"

"Do you get sick of eating?"

Sera flicked her mother a quick glance then stopped at the red light.

"Good point. What time am I picking you up?" Her mum and dad still only had one car, insisting two was just a waste of energy and money. They had raised four kids with economy in mind, teaching them to be grateful for what they had been given.

"Whenever you finish tutoring. I'll be with Anwar and his wife until tomorrow if they have their way."

Sera laughed. Anwar and Fatima were another refugee couple that her mum had known through her volunteer work. They were trying for kids but finding it difficult without being able to afford IVF.

The tireless way in which her mum did what was needed, not only for her family but the community, never ceased to fill her heart with gratitude. That spirit was born from many years of struggling as a refugee when she had arrived in Australia.

Displaced by her own country's trouble in the early 90s, Maryam had lost her father and brothers in a bomb attack and had claimed refugee status with her mother and two sisters without a lick of English, except her name.

Despite that, Maryam managed to get herself two jobs, attend English class and look after her sisters. It was at night school that she met Tony, and after a brief courtship, they married. Forty years...and still in love.

From a young age, Sera watched her parents support refugee families in everything from filling out forms to finding jobs. Seeing the power of such charity, Sera had known she wanted to give back in some way as well. Her work in South Row was important to the children as much as it was to her.

Maryam touched her arm. "When you have enough for your family, it's your duty to give back to the community, Sera. It will never be a chore, never be a suffering. Because those children going hungry, they're the ones hurting."

"I know it, Mum."

Sera pulled up outside a set of commission houses where Anwar and Fatima lived.

Even though it was cold out, various items of clothing hung from the small windows across the towering yellow structure. Sera wasn't sure if it contributed to the overall bleakness or opposed it.

Lifting the bag of food, she followed her mum inside.

"You still haven't answered my question." Maryam huffed as they climbed the stairs.

Sera had hoped she would drop it, but her mother was tenacious. "No, there's nothing happening with Jack. What was between us years ago is long gone, for a reason. I know you and Dad want me to settle down, but you've set the bar pretty high when it comes to relationships. I'm not going to settle with someone just because I feel pressured."

"That's the last thing we want for you, *habibti*."

"You and Dad have something special that I want to find for myself. I'm willing to wait for however long it takes to get it. And if I don't ever find it, I'm fine with that too."

Even if the thought did give her indigestion.

"There's waiting and then there's waiting."

"What does that even mean?"

"It means you haven't brought a boy home in a long time."

"You don't need to worry about my sex life, Mum. I date."

Her mother held on to the banister and 'tched'—a sound that signalled her mild annoyance, and dismissal, of the comment. All throughout her teens, Sera had delighted in shocking her mother. Perhaps it was Maryam's harrowing past that prompted Sera to try to gain a reaction by being bold.

It wasn't until recently that she realised nothing much shocked her mum. But it didn't stop the habit she had formed as a teen from dissipating either.

"You know I don't speak of that. I meant a long-term relationship, of something more than just bodies slapping against one another."

"Ew, Mum..."

"It's easy to be crude, Seraphina. And to take meaning and twist it."

"When the time and the guy is right, I'll bring him home. But for now, my life is full *and* fulfilling."

The last thing she wanted to do was talk about her love life with her mum. Or the ridiculous idea that she would just pick up a relationship with Jack as if he had never gone.

He had made his decision to move to America, and she had made hers to stay here. He was a big-shot actor who would be back in L.A. by the end of the week.

She would bet on it.

CHAPTER FIVE

*I*t didn't take long for the shit to hit the fan. Jack had been expecting the call, not that it lessened the sting as the venom seeped through the speakers of his phone, eroding the protective barriers he had erected.

It had been four days since he left L.A., yet it felt like a life-time. It should have disturbed him how easily he slipped back into life in Melbourne. Christ, less than a week and he was losing himself.

"Please tell me you're still not in some bum-fuck hick town. If you had half a brain, you'd be back home, J.D."

"You know that I'm in one of the biggest cities in Australia, right?"

"You might as well be with Croc Dundee for all that's worth. And if you don't sort through this fuck up, J.D., you may as well be chasing reptiles in the swamps, coz your career will be O.V.E.R."

"They mostly live in the tropics, Tom Tom."

He heard the sharp intake of air and could picture his skinny-framed, nicotine-addicted agent dragging on his millionth cigarette. "Don't fuck with me, Skippy. Why aren't you back here like I told you?"

Jack bit back a goading retort. "I guess I did leave you in the lurch."

"In the lurch?" Taylor sputtered. "You fucked me over and not in a good way. What the hell am I supposed to tell the studio, J.D.? Their major star is a major dick who ran home to the boondocks?"

"I didn't run, I caught a plane. And there's no boondocks."

The sharp rapping of the phone on a metallic surface made him grimace.

Reel it in, Jack.

"Look, I'm sorry. I just needed to get out. I can't—"

"Do you know what strings I had to pull to stop that son of a bitch from opening his trap? You're doing an exclusive interview with *The Star* magazine while you're there. He's agreed not to spill the beans on our conversation in exchange for a three-page spread, but let me repeat, get your fucking ass into therapy or whatever you need to do to get back on set so we can bury this."

Jack groaned. He shouldn't have told Taylor about his panic attack on set, his reservations about finishing the film. The man had tunnel vision; great for securing scripts, not so much for mental health. Nothing got in the way of work when it came to Taylor Thomas.

Christ, what a fucking mess.

"J.D., listen. Whatever it is, you need to sort it out and get the next jet out of there and back on set. Because if you don't, it's both our asses on the line. When are you coming home? I expected you back already."

I am home.

Jack shoved at the baseball cap on his head. Where had that come from? Melbourne hadn't been his home for all his adult life. For good reason. Taylor was right; what the hell was he doing here?

"I don't know."

"You don't—" Another inhalation. "Fuck! J.D., I'm giving you three days to sort this shit out. Three. Days. I didn't take a chance on you all those years ago to—hold on."

Jack heard a female voice just out of earshot. No doubt Taylor was fielding three other appointments whilst talking to him. The man never stopped. Or slept, for that matter.

Even though Jack enjoyed pissing him off, he was eternally grateful for all his agent had done for him.

That first year in L.A. had been the hardest. By the time he had met Taylor, he was struggling to make ends meet, like most other artists hoping to become a star.

It had taken Jack a few months to realise that the cheap-ish place he rented in the Warehouse District, whilst comfortable, was a nightmare for any budding actor. Rent wasn't cheap. But neither were his dreams. Not that he minded his one bedroom condo at the time. It wasn't exactly a swish complex in West Hollywood, but it had worked for him while he bussed tables and watched his savings disappear faster than the pennies in a slot machine. Eventually the commute to call-backs and rehearsals hadn't been worth it.

So he had packed up his shit and moved to NoHo. Which meant more auditions, connections to other struggling actors, and access to the metro. When he wasn't scrimping, working, or auditioning, he was watching others in half-price plays and networking whenever he could.

Had Jack not landed his agent, and a very lucrative deal soon after, he would have been out on his ass, pitching a tent on the neighbouring Skid Row.

"You there, J.D.?"

"Uh huh."

"What *is* it, Mel? I told him he can wait forever; I'm not taking on new talent."

Jack smirked then remembered just how desperate he had been to nab an agent, an audition, hell, a meeting with someone who had even worked on a D-list movie. Anything to get his shot.

When he landed Taylor Thomas as his agent and scored his big break, it had been a balm on an open wound. Jack became an 'overnight sensation.' A term that used to piss him off because nobody in Tinseltown made it 'overnight.' Something was always sacrificed in the process: morals, relationships, mental health.

"J.D., Mel is up my ass. Listen, I don't care what you have to do but you fix this mess and you come home with a big serving of whoopee pie or I'll be whooping your ass. You got that, Skippy?"

A second later the line went dead.

Not the best conversation he'd had of late. He could, despite his desire to commit career suicide, concede Taylor's point.

Jack flicked the band on his wrist.

What the hell did he do now?

CHAPTER SIX

*S*era pulled up outside the large block of housing commission flats in South Row the following Sunday, ready to feed the masses.

No matter how many times she visited the area, she was still struck by the disparity. Sera and her mum would drive past the leafy, gated houses of Ascot to get to South Row, one of the poorest suburbs in the CBD.

Ascot was the kind of place Jack would live. Not that she was thinking about Jack at all. She had been so busy this week that she hadn't really been around him much, other than in passing.

When he decided to leave—any day now no doubt—it wouldn't change a thing. He might go back to his glitzy Hollywood life, while she would remain here, tutoring some of the poorest kids in Melbourne.

The homelessness in South Row was heart-wrenchingly high and the repercussions of the ever-increasing unemployment rate could be seen in every corner of the suburb. The dilapidated council building, with its dirty concrete facade was a marked contrast to the sparkling cream and brick homes of the elite.

Sera shook her head, helping her mother unload containers of steaming hot food.

At the end of the day, Sera was all too aware of the privilege she had going back home to a stable family and a steady income. And for every child or family they helped, thousands of others were still struggling.

She had learned the hard way, many years ago, that some people didn't get that chance. A memory flitted past, as cold and bitter as the fog in the air. Sera burrowed further into her scarf. She couldn't bear to think about poor Elijah Sheppard and just how badly she had failed him.

Sera relished the icy air that seemed to burn her lungs. She needed to snap out of it. That was a long time ago. A time when she was young and inexperienced. She hadn't been able to save him, but she could save the kids who were with her now. Losing Eli had nearly killed her spirit. She didn't have the strength to go through that again.

Sera pushed the trolley up the broken path, keeping one hand on the containers to prevent it from toppling over.

They always made a point of sharing their food with the kids and their families—together. They weren't a charitable service, nor would they become one. They were building foundations. Communities. Support. Something her parents instilled in her from a young age.

"Let's set up before the kids head over, we don't want to keep them waiting."

As the rain began to slowly drizzle down, they shifted the portable tables to the small undercover area adjacent to the rear of the building. Despite the council's efforts at keeping the space 'respectable,' the thick concrete pillars and walls were decorated with layers of graffiti.

She noted that some of the residents had begun to paint murals over the images. The kids were talented, but no matter how many times she asked for council support to foster more community projects, she had met resistance.

By the time they had set out the food, children of all ages trickled in. The deal was, if the kids turned up to the tutoring lesson every week, they'd get an extra dessert at Mrs. D's Food Canteen, a title they had made up. Having an incentive helped them stay on track. It also meant they weren't distracted by hunger pains.

"Khalid, hello! Come, have some vine leaves. Your favourite."

"*Shukran*, miss. You're the best cook!"

"You say that to all the mothers, eh?" Maryam's eyes warmed. "You're welcome. Now, make sure you take some home to your grandmother, you hear?"

"Yes, ma'am. She thought you made a killer lamb roast."

"I'll make it again."

Kahlid's brown eyes lit up, his smile, wide and generous always kept everyone in good spirits. The kid worked two jobs just to help his family survive, and he was only fifteen.

Just another reason why they would never stop supporting the tenants of South Row.

As Sera passed around plates and settled the kids with their meals, Maryam helped the parents. It was a better turn out today, no doubt given the poor weather.

"Hey, Ashley, where's Leila?"

Ashley wrinkled her nose, her piercing glinting in the grey light. "Dunno, miss. Haven't seen her for a month. She was at Devon's party but that was ages ago. We texted her to come to Maccas on Monday, but she didn't show. She keeps flaking."

Sera frowned. Leila was a tough cookie, but she had noticed that something was off lately. Call it superstition, but Sera always trusted her gut about these things. She had learned from her mistakes and knew not to dismiss an inkling when she had one. Right now, her protect-o-meter was going off the charts.

An hour later, their bellies full, Sera waved off her mother and walked with the kids to the dingy room in the local library. It was a small victory to have them show up for class when they could be anywhere but here.

Many were motivated to get jobs, which meant figuring out resumes and setting up bank accounts. She covered everything from real world skills to schoolwork. Not that their attendance or participation in their local school was stellar. The promise of a basketball game after class was good incentive for kids who didn't have any equipment with which to play.

Sera hoped that the little she could do would help. It at least kept them off the streets and gave them the support that many couldn't get at home.

By the end of the afternoon, Leila still hadn't shown up. Sera would have to follow it up for her own peace of mind. After what happened with Elijah, she wasn't going to take any chances.

She could only hope that the young girl was safe and out of danger until she could contact her.

Despite Sera's level head, she was beginning to fear the worst.

It was past time that she paid Leila a visit.

CHAPTER SEVEN

*I*f there was a woman Jack Davies would ever give up bachelorhood to marry, it'd be Mrs. De Lotto.

He sat at the kitchen counter watching her knead dough for the bread she was making.

"Is there anything you can't cook?"

Maryam's cheeks were flushed. "Give me a recipe and I will try."

"So that's a no. You can cook everything," Jack sighed. "Run away with me back to L.A.?"

"I thought you were running back here."

Jack wagged his finger. "Nice one. I forgot you were wily."

"Not wily. Perceptive. You have 'problem' written all over your pretty face."

Jack winced. Rumours had begun to spread even though Taylor did his best to make a deal with the pap from *The Star* magazine. People in L.A. were starting to talk, so it wouldn't be long before the hounds caught his scent.

Subsequently, he had avoided returning Taylor's calls. What good would it do anyone? Just the thought of going back to set made him want to throw up.

"What can I say? Trouble finds me."

"Sounds like a line from a movie." Sera walked in and opened the fridge.

"I'm sure it is."

She grabbed a can of Pepsi and guzzled it.

"Long day?" Jack asked.

"Longer night. I'll see you later."

"Hey, wait!" He jumped off the stool. "I feel like I haven't really had a chance to catch up with you since I arrived."

"I'm a busy girl, Jack."

"Too busy to give an old flame some time?"

Sera stared up at him, but her expression gave nothing away. It made him sweat a little. She was keeping him at arm's length, and he was itching to break down that barrier.

"I'm just getting changed and I have to go back to school for the Parent Information Night."

"After?"

She narrowed her eyes and answered after a protracted pause. "What did you have in mind?"

"A drink? Maybe a bite to eat?"

"I thought you were keeping a low profile."

"I am. But you, the lovely, anonymous Sera De Lotto, are not."

"Hmm."

"Don't sound so sceptical. I'll swing by the school and pick you up."

"I gotta go."

"Hey, I don't have your number."

"I'll be the one with this face waiting out front the school at half past nine. Probably in a dress. See you then, Hollywood."

Jack pulled up outside the school right on time in the unassuming rental car he'd had Owen book in his name.

The lights from the main reception were ablaze and Sera stood waiting at the curb looking effortlessly gorgeous. Her dress was a deep purple, and her curly hair was unbound and cascading down her shoulders. She had make-up on, elongating her brown eyes, extending her already thick lashes.

Time, the cruel bastard, had made her even more striking.

Jack unlocked the doors to let her in then shifted to face her in his seat. She was even more arresting up close.

"How did it go?"

"Alright. Standard stuff, lots of kids wandering about not sure what subjects they want to select. We run one on one consults with them to make sure they have some sort of direction. It's time consuming but worth it."

"And I bet you volunteer for that."

"I do."

Jack grinned, pulling away from the curb and into the inky night.

"So where are we going? And why couldn't I just follow you in my car?"

"Kebab shop just outside of the city."

"My mother would kill you if she knew."

"We won't tell her."

"She'll smell the shawarma the moment we step inside the house."

"We'll eat outside. I ordered a takeaway pack for us."

"I take it I'll be doing the picking up?"

"Not just a pretty face."

"Yeah, yeah."

It didn't take them long to get there at this time of night. And when Sera brought the boxes back into the car, Jack's stomach rumbled.

Sera held up two bottles of cider. "I figured we could use these too."

"Woman after my own heart."

Jack followed her instructions until they reached one of the parks just outside the city. It was deserted but he kept his baseball cap on low for good measure. Despite the cool night, they sat on the bonnet of the car, enjoying their food in silence.

Long-forgotten memories began to race over him, teasing his senses, luring him back to a time he had no business remembering.

"Want to sit inside?"

Sera crinkled her nose. "No, I was falling asleep with the heater on. I don't mind the cold. So what are you really doing here, Jack?" She munched on a hot chip, licking the chicken salt off her fingers. Jack had to swallow what was in his mouth or he would choke. The sound she made caught every nerve ending in his body and set it alight.

Sera raised her eyebrows, waiting for an answer.

Jack raised his kebab. "Want a bite of my meat?"

"Stop shit stirring. You know what I mean."

He did. But he had wanted to tease that exasperated look out of her, to heat her blood. She was amazing in full temper. They had dated just long enough for him to witness it a few times. To be turned on by it.

Easy, Jack.

He took a swig from his bottle. "I do. You also know that I use humour at any opportunity. The dirtier the better."

"It's been a while. For all I know, you could be a completely different person."

"I'm not. I mean, of course I am, nobody ever stays the same, otherwise you're not living life properly, are you? But the basics, that hasn't changed."

"Like I said, it's been a while."

Was he imagining it? The way a smile hovered over her lips,

the distant expression that flittered across her face as if she, too, were caught in the past...*their* past.

"It has. But sitting here with you, eating kebabs and shawarma, and talking in the freezing cold doesn't seem strange."

Sera's face softened. "Oddly enough, I agree."

Jack looked around the deserted park, they were the only people for miles. But life, his life, had taught him to be on guard. What had his therapist once told him? Find people who were worthy of his vulnerability and drop that shield when he did.

Sera was worthier than any of the women he had dated in the past ten years. He knew that instinctively. He could trust her.

"I hadn't quite finished filming when I left." Jack took a swig of his cider. It burned.

Sera's steady eyes studied him for a moment. "Don't they want you back then?"

"Either that or they'll be trying to finish me. Fleeing is a big no-no. Makes you seem flaky. Fuck, it *is* flaky. According to my agent, it's fucking career suicide."

"So why'd you do it?"

Jack grimaced. "If I knew that I wouldn't need a therapist."

"Don't we all. Don't ask." She raised a hand to ward off questions, but the pain swam in her eyes.

What had happened to the once innocent girl he had known? The clear-sighted teenager who was too good for him, even back then?

The woman beside him was no innocent. She looked haunted, hurt. Perhaps she could understand his pain more than he thought?

"I don't know what my next move is, Sera. I guess I just want some time to figure it out. And I know that the clock is against me, but I needed a change of pace. Something different, some time to clear my head."

To process what happened. Because it had scared the living hell out of him.

"But aren't you going to get into trouble?"

"Sweetheart, I *am* trouble."

"Can't argue with that."

"Which is why I need to get out of your parents' house as well. Especially once the paps hear of this."

"You know my parents; they love nothing more than hosting, especially fugitive Hollywood stars. They're insistent on having you around so who am I to argue with that?"

"Thanks. I appreciate the vote of confidence. But the thing is, I've been trying to figure out why you're avoiding me."

"Maybe you're just accustomed to women falling at your feet?"

"Harsh."

Sera studied the city skyline then focused on the bottle in her hands. "Maybe I've just changed, Jack. You said it yourself; nobody stays the same. You've been gone for ten years. More than. I'm not a teenager anymore, and you're not some young guy ready for a wild ride."

Jack clutched at his heart. "Ow. Way to wound a guy."

"A lot has happened in my life and a lot of time has passed. It's not something you can just fill in the span of a few hours. Or even a week."

"I get it. Why don't we make the most of getting to know each other while I'm here then?"

He should keep his mouth shut. Maintain the distance she placed between them. It would be doing her and her family a big favour. His life was a mess right now. He was a mess.

But there was something about Sera that made him want to forget all that...

"And how long will that be this time, Jack?"

He could see the hurt. She had buried it well, but Jack caught a glimpse of it in her eyes. A flash of annoyance. "Why are you mad at me?"

Sera jumped off the hood then whirled around to face him.

"How can you come back thinking we can just pick up where we left off? I'm not going to talk to you about my life because you're back in town. What? For a week? A month? Your place isn't here, Jack. So why should I be investing in someone, in something, that won't be around this time next year? Hell, this time next month?"

He tried not to let the words sting. But they had, and he suddenly felt like some naïve kid on his first day on set.

Why did he think that going out for kebabs would suddenly bridge the gap between them? That he would find Sera the same open, willing girl she had been all those years ago?

Christ, he was an idiot.

How self-involved could he get?

Jack slid down off the bonnet and stood in front of her. "Here, you're cold." Before she could protest, he slid off his jacket, leather, black, and the comfiest thing he owned. He placed it around her shoulders.

"Thanks."

"I guess I never saw it that way before, Sera. But I see it now." Jack turned, clearing their food off the bonnet into the takeaway bags.

When they were both in the car, Sera reached out, hand extended. The fire that had burned in her eyes moments before had reduced to a simmer. "Hi. I'm Seraphina De Lotto. Friends call me Sera. I love food, sport, and teaching kids."

Jack nodded, extending his hand to shake hers. "Pleased to meet you, Sera. I'm Jack. Lover, not fighter. Maddening egomaniac and a fan of mountains and the outdoors. Oh, and your mum, she's amazing."

Sera laughed. "Agreed."

Jack accepted the olive branch, even though the fear wound its way around his heart. He cranked up the radio, drowning out the voice that warned him to keep his distance. To stay away.

He glanced at Sera; her eyes were soft, her expression a little less guarded.

Jack's grip on the steering wheel loosened.

It was a good start.

CHAPTER EIGHT

There were definite perks to working with your two best friends. Unless one of them was getting married. Then it became a nightmare.

Any time Sera would see Ally in the main staff room, her bestie would add yet another item to their to-do list.

Being a bridesmaid was fast becoming a full-time job.

And now that Jack was in town, and the whole wedding party was on hand to help, Ally's stress levels had significantly increased.

So instead of spending their day off relaxing on the couch or playing football, Sera was on bridesmaid duty. Apparently bridal shops didn't get the public holiday memo.

Ally was going to be a December bride, and December in Australia meant hot summer days, and sticky nights. Not in a good way.

"Please don't tell me this weather is going to last until summer or I'll shoot you." Maddie's teeth chattered as they unloaded bags and boxes from Ally's car. It may have been the middle of September, but spring weather was nowhere to be seen.

"Jesus, Maddie, you're not wearing a coat." Sera eyed her friend from head to toe.

"It's supposed to be warmer than this! Plus, it didn't go with the outfit."

"Like the people selling us the ribbon cared."

"Look, sassy pants, do I tell you how to dress?"

Sera hefted another box. "That's because I dress appropriately for the weather."

"Uh huh. You're in shorts and a T-shirt half the time."

"That's my job."

Ally shooed Maddie away, reaching in for the last of the bags. "Stop complaining and let's get inside. It's freezing out here. Sera, did Jack mention anything about coming to the joint huck's party?"

Sera cursed the wind as it whipped her unbound hair across her face. "Err. No. Why would he?"

"You live together." Ally rooted in her purse for the keys. "I assumed the wedding would come up?"

"My spidey senses tell me that your wedding would be the last thing Jack and Sera would spend late nights talking about. And I still don't know why you want a combined hen's and buck's night...don't you care that your best friend will be deprived of male nudity?"

"You can go to a strip club any time you like, Madds."

"Not the same thing." Maddie pouted. "Plus, it's not like Jack will be around for long anyway, so why are you rearranging everything to include him?" Maddie, ever the shit-stirrer, didn't see the panic in Ally's eyes.

"What?" Ally looked at Sera, eyes wide. "Did he tell you when he's going back? I thought Owen spoke to him about the change of plan." Her voice was now taking on a shrill edge.

Sera climbed the steps, arms straining against the weight of the boxes. "No. Jack didn't mention any of that. Your wedding is three months away, so it's unlikely he'll be here for that long."

"Maybe he'll come back early? God, there's still so much to do!" Ally frowned when the key wouldn't turn in the lock. "Damnit, I told Owen this was jammed, but he didn't listen. Bloody thing won't open!" Ally growled, wriggling the key with more force than necessary.

Sera shot Maddie a pointed look. But as luck would have it, Ally turned at that very moment.

"What? *What*?"

Sera tried her very best to sound soothing. "Nothing, love. Do you want me to try the door?"

"Bridezilla called, Ally. They want their attitude back."

"Maddie!"

Ally dropped what she was carrying, angry tears spilling over. "Bridezilla?" she wailed.

"Fuck's sake." Maddie muttered, taking the keys from Ally's hands, while Sera ushered her inside.

"I don't mean to be a Bridezilla, but there's so much to do." Ally brushed back a tear. "We still have to send out invites, and bonbonnieres and organise the huck's party, and now Jack is in town and he's so unpredictable, and something's up with him and I—I—"

"It's okay." Sera manoeuvred Ally to the kitchen chair while Maddie hefted all the bags and boxes, cursing under her breath.

Sera filled the kettle, hoping Maddie's blunt approach didn't make matters worse. If she knew her friends, they were both hangry and tired. Not a great combination.

Ally blotted her face with a tissue, big green eyes panicked and mournful. "How is it okay? I'm a bridezilla. Me! I'm the most reasoned out of all of us." She rubbed at face, stealing deep breaths. "Have I been that bad?"

"Yes."

"No."

Sera glared at Maddie, before sitting beside the anxious bride-to-be. She rubbed at her friend's arm. "You've not been yourself lately, Al, but that's understandable. Trust me, all the things will get done. That's what besties are for. I know Jack being back adds a bit of chaos, but don't plan with him in mind. I know that sounds mean, but Jack is all over the shop and it's better that you just focus on the things you can control."

"But—"

"I know he's Owen's brother, but don't worry about whether he's here or not for the huck's. It's in December, that's far away enough for us to organise it with or without him. Who the hell knows what Jack will do, he's a bit of a loose cannon, right? So take a deep breath, have a cuppa and we can tackle this to-do list while we order some lunch."

Ally offered a wobbly smile. "Okay."

"Great."

"Not so fast, De Lotto." Maddie waved her cookie in front of her, ushering Sera back in her seat.

Sera rolled her eyes. "I think you've put your foot in your mouth enough for one day, Madds."

"Perks of having a big mouth." Maddie smiled sweetly. "You're holding out on us."

"What?"

Maddie flicked back her fiery red hair. "Don't play coy. You said that you and Jack had a summer fling all those years ago. But girl, the sparks were flying at Ally's engagement dinner. There's more to it and you're holding out. So spill."

Sera put her hands up. "I told you everything."

"Bullshit."

"Can you please not wave that choc-chip cookie in my face and let me get a cup of tea for our distressed bride?"

"Oh no, I want the goss." Ally's eyes were bright, but no longer brimming. That was a plus.

"Tea, then gossip." Sera stood, crossing to the kitchen counter. "We have wedding invites to sort."

They set up on Ally and Owen's kitchen table while

debating what to order for lunch. Sera booted up her laptop while Ally brought in the printer. Tea was poured, cookies were laid out and with the thermostat on high, it was a cosy atmosphere.

"I thought you sent out invites?" Maddie picked up the list of guests, eyes narrowing.

"We sent save the date cards a while ago, so now that we have everything set with the venue, we can send proper invitations."

"So I'm not needed, right?" Maddie looked hopeful.

"Wrong. When Owen gets back with the invitations, you're going to help thread the ribbons on the top of them."

Maddie grimaced. "I suppose I can do ribbons. What I can't do is wait any longer for the goss. De Lotto, stop stalling."

Sera tried not to squirm. "What d'ya wanna know?"

"What happened when you and Jack dated?"

Sera double checked another name and address on the list before answering. "You were both overseas at the time and I didn't want to make a big deal about it."

"And?"

Sera looked up at her friends' expectant faces. "And he broke my heart."

"Oh." Ally's hand fluttered to her chest. "Honey."

"I knew he was moving to America when we met."

"The night we finished our production of *Hamlet*. I didn't even remember seeing you together."

"That was because you had a row with your ex-boyfriend and was rip-roaring drunk." Sera recalled. "As was Jack and I for that matter...we only made out that night, but it kick-started our summer romance."

"We should hate him for breaking your heart, right?" Maddie clarified.

"Hate is wasted in this situation. It was so long ago. But in short, yes, he hurt me. He chose to leave, chose stardom over us. He didn't even try to make it work, everything was so black and white. He was leaving, I was staying. The End. It hurt, a lot. And made me think that I loved him in a way he couldn't reciprocate."

"Bastard." Maddie muttered.

It was Ally's turn to offer comfort. "I'm so sorry, Sera. I wish you had told us at the time."

She shrugged. "I never expected to see Jack again, let alone to have him crash at my parents' place ten years later. I didn't want to wallow or have your sympathies. I got enough of it from my folks at home, I just needed to start the year fresh. To forget."

"And now?" Ally leaned in. "How do you feel about him being back?"

Sera frowned, running her fingers over the keys of her laptop. What did she feel?

Nervous. A gut-churning awareness whenever he was around.

But also, perhaps a part of her was excited, too?

This wasn't a fairy tale, or some Hollywood romance. Even if Jack decided to stick around, he would eventually go back once the wedding was over. Their lives, once again, would be on different paths. She had no room to dream for anything more.

She shrugged. "We're hanging out, as friends. It's all I can give. All I can expect from him." She would be a fool to let her guard down, to think he had changed.

Ally bit her lip but nodded. "That's wise."

"It's bullshit." Maddie wound a ribbon around her finger. "I saw the chemistry between you two, and it was electric. It's only a matter of time before Jacky-boy puts on the Hollywood moves. If it's not what you want, then I'd recommend getting a chastity belt. Or I could give him a good kick in the balls."

Sera laughed. "Maddie, you're ridiculous. And wonderful. But life isn't like those romance novels you read."

"Where do you think authors get those ideas from? Real life. Just saying, De Lotto. Start wearing your granny knickers. Or maybe grow a moustache."

Sera rolled her eyes. "Thanks for the advice, but I'll be right."

She ignored her friend's pointed look and worked with Ally on the address list.

Eventually Maddie stopped grumbling and double checked the names and addresses before they printed them off. By the time they heard the front door open, they were done and ready for lunch.

"Invite delivery." Owen's deep voice rang through the house.

"In the kitchen!" Ally's face lit up, spotting her fiancé.

Sera smiled, enjoying the sight. Then straightened.

"I also found this stray on the way." Owen jerked his thumb at his brother.

"More like this idiot woke me up," Jack grumbled.

"In my defence, it was nearly midday."

"I didn't get to sleep until—" Jack shoved off his baseball cap. "You know what, it doesn't matter. M'lady, your invites." He bowed down to Ally. "Is that coffee?" He picked up Sera's cup and sniffed.

"Nope."

"Bummer. I'll put a pot on." But he leaned back against the table and looked down at her instead. He appeared relaxed, but she could see the swirling emotions behind his cool blue eyes. Why did he feel the need to put on an act?

"Hey, De Lotto."

Sera smiled. "Hey, yourself."

"Do you ever stop to take a break these days?"

Sera twisted her lips.

Maddie cut in. "Never. She's a bloody machine."

"It's a public holiday today. You're all off work, so shouldn't you be out at the pub?" He shifted, picking up a coaster, tapping it against his thigh.

"If you didn't notice, we've bridesmaid duties." Ally gestured with her hand to the table.

"After that?"

"She's free." Maddie sing-songed.

Sera shot Maddie what she hoped was her best withering look. "And how would you know?"

"I used my best friend powers to deduce that you were free. That, and you didn't mention any hot dates."

Jack grinned. "Perfect. I thought we could hang out."

"And by hang out you mean—"

"Hole up in your parents' house with a movie, cards, and takeaway?" The restlessness around him was a tangible cloud.

"My mother would kill you."

"Your folks need a night off from cooking."

Sera felt the pressure of her friend's foot under the table.

Friends. Just friends. "Sure."

"Great." Jack was about to pull up a chair when Owen tapped him on the shoulder. "What?"

"This was a pit stop."

"*What*?"

"We've more wedding stuff to do, best man."

"Jesus, Owen."

"You sound like Charlie. But it has to be done, I'm afraid."

"Can't a man get a coffee?"

"I'll make you a takeaway cup, bro, then it's back on the road."

"So much for that low profile."

"Speaking of low profile," Maddie chipped in. "How low is low?"

"Why do you ask?"

"Remember my senior drama class I was telling you about at Ally's engagement dinner?"

"You mean the unsubtle hint that you think they'd benefit from my instruction?"

"Bingo. You promised to make an appearance before you left."

"I did. And I will. Soon."

"I'll hold you to it."

And five minutes later, they were gone.

Sera turned to Maddie. "I hope you have insurance."

"For what?"

"To pay for the doctor's bill I'll be sending you. Why the hell did you crush my foot?"

"Because I know you, and you were about to reject Jack's offer without actually thinking about it."

"So what if I was? It was my offer, and I get to do whatever I want with it."

Maddie picked up the scissors and hacked at the ribbon.

"Hey, don't take it out on the material." Ally glared at her. "That's way too short a length."

Maddie placed the scissors on the table. "If he broke your heart and you never want to speak to him again, I will totally back you up. It's a dick move, and I'm not so keen on you getting caught up in all that. But from the looks of it, you seem to be drawn to him. If I didn't see it with my own eyes, I wouldn't have pushed."

"I'm not..."

Maddie's look spoke volumes. "Why deny hanging out with him? It doesn't mean you're hooking up again. If you've moved on from all that, then this might be a chance to get some insight into what happened all those years ago. Or, hell, De Lotto, to just enjoy his company. Have a little fun?"

"Are you interested in more than friendship?" Ally pulled out a chair, eyes bright.

"He made a choice a long time ago, as did I."

"But—" Ally protested.

"No buts. That doesn't mean that I won't hang out with him. If *I* want to, not just because he asks."

Maddie swirled the ribbon in the air. "That's my girl. Give him hell."

Ally cut in before Maddie could continue. "It won't make you less of a person, or a woman to be charmed by him. It's Jack. He's pretty dazzling. Don't deny yourself a bit of fun, Sera."

Maddie shifted closer. "I'm all for letting go and getting wild, but just keep that guard up."

Ally's voice was soft. "You can't cut off life's pleasures just because of what happened with Eli."

Sera's head snapped up. "I..."

"We know you still blame yourself," Maddie continued. "But you've starved yourself of any fun ever since. You can't keep punishing yourself for his death."

Sera allowed the emotion to well up inside her, feeling the pain, sitting with it, before responding. "I can't trust myself sometimes. What I think is true or right, turns out to be completely wrong."

"Don't." Ally shook her head. "It won't help to doubt yourself. You've been burned, but Eli, of all kids, wouldn't want you to cut yourself off from living."

"I'm not..."

But the denial was weak, lacking any strength of feeling or truth.

Living life at a reckless pace had been fine when she was nineteen without any responsibilities. Jack was the epitome of fast living. There had been an energy about him even back then that drew her in.

But she was no longer a young girl eager for a thrill. She had seen too much, experienced too much to just pretend like life was one big adventure.

Not when there were so many kids out there who needed her. So many she had yet to save.

That fun, spontaneous side of her seemed to have dissipated since Eli's death. She *had* changed.

"Everyone makes mistakes, honey." Ally's voice was soft, but firm. "Don't say no because of the past if it's something you actually want."

"I won't." She squeezed Ally's hand.

But her past with Jack was so far removed from her life now. She couldn't pretend that their lives would somehow merge.

"Jack equals fun," Maddie added. "And girl, of all people, you need to let loose and have some."

"Okay smarty pants, if you want me to go have some fun, you'll stop talking and help me get this stuff sorted for our bestie's wedding."

She was glad for the distraction. Now wasn't the time to think about Eli, or even her past with Jack.

Nothing could change the death of a young boy, or the blossoming relationship that had ended. The past carried with it memories that had no business in the present. It would only cloud her judgement.

She'd hang out with Jack while he was here, enjoy his company, keep it light. But she would remember this was not his home. He would go back to L.A. Back to his life.

And she sure as hell wasn't going to mend a broken heart a second time.

CHAPTER NINE

*L*ater that night, with containers of Chinese food spread out before them, Jack sat beside Sera on the sofa to catch up on old times. He had been restless all day. The looming mess that was his life was waiting behind every text message, lurking in every missed call.

He couldn't bear to even scroll through his social media accounts, afraid that some tell-all story had been published about his panic attack on set. Panic attack? Who was he kidding? It was a total breakdown.

He wasn't dealing with it. Couldn't deal with it.

But being with Sera chased everything away. Even if momentarily.

The day hadn't been a total fuck up. He did manage to successfully convince Sera's parents that they were never too old for a date out in the city, so that was a plus. He had arranged a car service to pick them up, making it a grand affair.

The twin expressions of surprise when he told them they had half an hour to get ready was well worth it.

"That was nice, what you did for my folks."

Jack wiped the peanut sauce from his chin. "I had an ulterior motive."

"That may have been a part of it, but I also know that you're a big ol' softie beneath that Hollywood cool."

Jack shrugged then speared a dumpling. "I'm not going to be claiming saint-like status any time soon. If you had seen me in my first few years of fame, you'd be running a mile. Money can be dangerous."

"You forget, I met you at the beginning of that wild phase. I was only nineteen...so innocent."

"I was older and wiser."

"Only by a few years, and wise was not how I remember you."

Jack was curious. "What do you remember?" Apart from someone who was terrified of responsibility.

"Fun. Laughter. You were always up for a good time. A little wild with it, but nothing too crazy. You introduced me to a lot of firsts." Sera pressed her lips together and Jack remembered that night all too well. A man never forgot the honour of being someone's first. It was what had sparked the beginning of their relationship. Their summer romance.

Jack grinned, another memory barrelling through his brain...the bit of fun they had in the lingerie department had been wild as well. The image of Sera in a lace get-up stirred something in him. But then again, one look at her was enough to get his blood pumping.

He shovelled more food and focused on the sofa cushions. It didn't take much to get aroused when it came to Sera De Lotto.

"I think you were a bad influence."

Sera made a sexy sound through a mouthful of food. Memories flashed through brain, a movie reel of all the things he had forgotten, all the experiences he had suppressed.

They had only dated for a few months, but it had been passionate and intense. Jack had shared things with Sera that not even Owen knew at the time. Being with her had unlocked something in him that he hadn't felt since his parents' sudden death as a kid. And it had scared the hell out of him.

Apart from his family, Sera was his last good thing about being in Melbourne. And he went and screwed that up too.

"So, you volunteer with disadvantaged kids these days?"

"Yeah, I teach them every week, mostly just tutoring them through their homework and basic life skills. Resume writing, applying for a bank card. Some have very poor literacy, and others are just behind. Then every month, Mum and I do a food canteen, as the kids call it. For some, it's the only decent meal they get that month."

"That's hard work."

"It's the right thing to do."

"Not everyone thinks that way, you know. Dog eat dog world and all."

"But there's kindness there too. It's not like these kids want to be poor or in gangs or turn to crime. Some of them are just products of broken homes and their parents' bitterness. Poverty is only made glamorous in films. It's stark and hopeless; like enamel on your teeth, it hardens your arteries."

"But they have you."

"I'm not enough, I'm afraid." Sera sipped at her jasmine green tea.

Jack shifted closer. "I've made you sad."

"No, not sad. I just never feel like I can do enough."

"Why don't you focus on the stuff you are doing?"

"You sound like Ally."

"I taught her everything I know." He winked. "So what do you want to do with them? I know you've got plans."

Sera laughed. "I do. I'm hoping to set up some council funding, maybe get the arts and sports council involved with keeping these kids busy and off the streets. Not sure it will work though. Money is hard to come by. In the meantime, I'm going to try to clothe and feed as many as possible."

"And?"

Sera grinned. "And I've spoken to the council about the state of the commission flats, so we're petitioning to have it upgraded. We're trying to get someone to build a community centre nearby so we can have a place to host the food canteen, the tutoring, maybe even a basketball court."

"I knew there was something big coming."

Where he had his sights set on Hollywood, she had wanted to make a change much closer to home. She had always wanted to give back, to do more with her time.

Sera put down her tea. "But that is a big pipe dream. It requires land to be bought and builders contracted. It's a long-term goal."

"And who will be funding it?"

Sera raised her hand.

"What? Out of your miserable paycheck?"

"Hey now, it's not that bad. Used to be a lot worse. And with the Head of P.E. job that I want to apply for next year, I'm hoping I'll get a big fat boost to my salary. That will help too."

Jack shook his head. "You're amazing, you know that? You and your whole family put me to shame."

"This is *not* a competition."

"Not when I'd lose spectacularly, it ain't."

Jack threw down his napkin in mock despair.

"Okay, so your turn. What's your plan now, Hollywood?"

"I need to do something. Don't ask me what, as I'm clueless on that front. But I know I can't keep hiding from my agent. He'll probably jump on a jet and hunt me down if I keep this up much longer. That, or he'll send a private investigator."

"That bad, huh?"

"Worse. I haven't been coping with the whole fame game for a while now. My mental health is shot to shit."

Why was he telling her this?

"Therapy?"

"Been there."

"Medication?"

"Abused that."

"Jesus, Jack."

But once he started talking, he couldn't seem to keep his mouth shut.

"Short of dosing myself up to the eyeballs all the time, there's not much else they can do. Trust me, I've tried L.A.'s answer to life's problems and have felt worse for it. When you've access to everything, you develop a God complex, and with the wrong crowd, you get nailed to a cross pretty quick."

"What do you want from your life?"

Jack rubbed his face. Oddly enough, talking to her about this stuff felt...good. "Thing is, I don't know anymore. I would have said acting and everything that comes with it, is the life I had been dreaming of. I know it was what I wanted more than anything back then." He looked up, catching the hurt on her face. He could see it now. Jack shifted, uncomfortable.

Dating Sera had been equally wonderful and terrifying. She had evoked something inside of him that he was incapable of giving. A future with Sera had meant stability when he was reckless. Responsibility that he hadn't been capable of shouldering.

Hell, he had been messed up long before he had met her. And if he didn't get his shit together, he would stay that way.

"The lifestyle, the parties, it's getting old. Christ, maybe I'm getting old."

"You're in your thirties Jack, not ninety."

"I'm sure my internal age is close to a century."

"Live hard, play hard?"

"Something like that. I'm not proud of a lot of things in my life, Sera, and for the first time in a while, coming here, doing what I wanted when I wanted, felt right...in a twisted way."

"But the timing was all wrong."

Jack took a sip of his water. "I've been a selfish bastard for a long time now. I don't know how to fix it. But sometimes, hell, sometimes I feel like I've no control over my life. Like I'm a damn puppet. Go here, say this, smile there. A lot of what I do, well, it feels like the choices aren't always mine."

"It all looks so glamorous from the outside."

"I thought so too once upon a time."

"But surely hiding out never helped anyone. You're caging yourself inside and you're the one paying for it."

Jack nodded. "I know it. I also know how ruthless the paps are. Lately it's like I'm bursting at the seams. You don't get how good it feels to be surrounded by your folks, to see what a normal life, a normal family looks like. I haven't had that in..."

Sera squeezed his hand. "You miss your parents. That's normal."

Jack rubbed at his chest. "It still hurst sometimes. How is that possible?"

"The pain never really goes away. It fades just enough for us to keep living."

He had gone to America, just like he promised his dad he would do. And every day had been a small torture, knowing that his father never fulfilled his dream of wanting to be a film-maker, that he never had a chance to see his youngest son make it as an actor.

He remembered all the times they made home movies with their crappy camcorder. All the hours they spent watching films, dissecting characters and scripts. But it had ended too soon.

One day he was a risk-taking teenager with the world at his feet, and the next, he was moving in with Owen, a teenage dad trying to make ends meet.

Nothing had been the same since. What hurt most, was that it was all his fault. His parents' death was something he would never get over. If it weren't for him, they might still be alive.

Just when Jack had finished his college degree, when he was counting down the days to leave Australia, he met Sera.

She had been there, when he was finding himself, when he was still lost and desperate to chase the next high. Sera had seen the raw pain and hadn't flinched. She hadn't tried to brush it aside but had let him sit with it.

Sera had been wise back then and seemed even more so now. Why? What had happened?

Something stirred inside him. It was an old, familiar feeling. She offered that calm, gave him that sense of assurance that he hadn't felt in a long while.

With her, he was strong and vulnerable at the same time.

With her, he could reveal his feelings without fear of judgement or recrimination.

Jack realised that he hadn't had a friend, a true friend to share his confidences with, in a long time. His brother was always there, but the distance had made it difficult over time. And his buddy, Liam, was often off filming or busy being a father to his new baby, which made it hard to talk.

His burdens were heavy, weighing him down for a long time now.

"I forgot how easy it was to talk to you."

"That's nostalgia speaking."

"When did you get so practical?"

Sera shrugged. "The hopeless romantic is buried there somewhere. Life has just honed my perception a little more, that's all."

Jack shifted. Had he done that? Was it his fault she was a little more guarded, a little less free? "And what's your perception of me then?"

Sera studied him. "You're still cocky. Self-assured, which

given the way you look isn't a surprise. But there's a caginess to you too. You're cautious, not as happy-go-lucky as you used to be."

He tried not to squirm at her assessment. "More."

"I think beneath all that cocky assurance, you care, maybe a little too much. Perhaps you're a bit wiser, and maybe a little more jaded."

"If that's possible. Any more jaded and I'd cut like broken glass." Jack brushed aside a curl off her cheek. "So with all this knowledge about who I am, what do you think? Do you like me, Sera? Have you ever thought about me?"

"Those are two different questions. I don't know you, not really."

"We knew each other pretty intimately one time."

A whisper of a smile graced her lips. "That was a long time ago."

"A familiar dance all the same. You haven't forgotten the moves surely?"

"Stop goading me. I know what you're doing."

"Sometimes people don't change all that much, Sera. Not what's inside." He shifted closer.

"And sometimes they need to."

"I disagree." He cupped her cheek. "I'm making my move."

"Maybe you're right, maybe people don't change at all."

"I'd like to think I've perfected a few things over time."

"I'll be the judge of that."

She leaned in, closing the gap.

Jack understood her silent signal, the whisper of her body hovering close, but still at a distance.

Her mouth beckoned.

He followed her lead, appreciating the whisper of her tongue against his, the soft moan that floated between them.

Past and present wound around his senses, tugging at his memories, binding him closer to her, to what they once shared. Then his mind went blank, and he sighed with the relief of it.

Jack increased the pressure, just a fraction, enjoying the slight brush of her breasts against his chest.

He ran his hand up her spine, burying his fingers in a mass of curls, releasing that heady scent of jasmine he had once known so well.

She surrounded him, but still he craved more.

When Sera pulled back, chest heaving, lips swollen, he resisted the urge to grab her again. Pure lust clawed at his resolve.

But it wasn't just any woman. It was Sera.

They had history. And because of it, because of her, he needed to show some respect.

Fuck. The old Jack would have had her panties shoved aside, making her scream his name by now.

Easy. He tried to breath in as the scintillating images flashed in his brain. *Down, boy.*

"Umm." Sera licked at her lips, disoriented and unbelievably beautiful. All he could do was stare.

Sera shoved back her hair. "I didn't think that would happen when I accepted your invitation to hang."

"I won't apologise because I've been wanting to do that since the moment I saw you."

"I won't either, as I wondered what it would feel like again."

He watched as she picked up the takeaway containers, taking them back to the kitchen. His ego demanded to know more.

His mind cautioned against it.

CHAPTER TEN

*J*ack.
   Jack.
   Jack.

Sera had fallen asleep last night thinking about their smouldering kiss.

She had woken up this morning, dreaming about it.

And now she was driving to one of the poorest areas in Melbourne, reliving the way his hand had bunched at her hair, tugging it in that delicious, long-forgotten habit of his...

She was on dangerous ground. Kissing Jack was not a wise move. Spending time with him as friends wasn't one either. Perhaps when it came to Jack it would never be just friends. She couldn't seem to forget about the past and the fact that once upon a time they couldn't keep their hands off each other.

Kissing Jack, starting something with him on a physical level was too risky. Sera wasn't sure she could keep her distance. She wasn't certain she could trust herself to not get hurt again.

She had no time to be reminiscing about the past when there were real problems that needed her attention.

Sera found a vacant parking spot along the road and braced

herself against the evening chill. She crossed the concrete courtyard of the high-rise council flats to Leila Alwadi's apartment block.

Sera looked around the worn building, memories of Eli, of her failings, sat heavy as the grey clouds above. She would focus on those whom she could help and keep her mind on the here and now.

And right now, she was worried about Leila.

Just a quick visit, then she would return home.

Images of Jack, eyes shadowed, a slow, sure grin hovering on that handsome face, assailed her.

She stomped up the seven flights of stairs to the dilapidated looking apartment door down the hall.

Focus, Sera.

She heard the faint sounds of the television and knocked loudly. She waited a few more minutes before calling out.

"You can hide all you like, Leila, but I won't be budging. So unless you want your parents to find me loitering in the corridor when they get home, I'd suggest you let me in."

It took a few more minutes before the door opened slightly. "What do you want?"

"Hello to you too, sunshine."

"I'm busy. You got a problem, miss?"

"Yeah, your attitude."

"You're not even my real teacher, so what's it to you? Mind your own business and stop coming around like you give a shit."

Sera knew that her hunch had been spot on. Leila was hiding something, and she wasn't a De Lotto if she didn't get to the bottom of it.

"Newsflash, kiddo, you matter to me." Sera stole a quick breath as the image of a young boy drifted before her. Leila was not Eli. This was not the same situation. She'd make sure she didn't make the same mistakes. "You've been missing not just from class, but your friends are saying you're avoiding them too. That concerns me."

"Whatever."

Certain that the door was going to slam in her face, Sera wedged her toe in the gap, needing answers. Her mind whirled with potential problems: drugs, assault, domestic violence. Leila was retreating for a reason, and Sera wouldn't leave without knowing the truth.

"Leila, look, I know that—"

Before she had a chance to continue, the young girl swayed and fell backwards. Sera lunged, trying to break her fall, but grasped at thin air instead.

"Shit!"

She positioned Leila on her side, trying to make her as comfortable as possible, while her mind whirled.

Sera spoke, keeping her voice steady, while she monitored Leila's breathing until she began to stir. Stroking back her dark, matted hair, she helped Leila sit up, resting her back on the cracked wall. A musty smell assailed her, a combination of sweat and three-day old deodorant.

"Let me get you some water."

Sera ran the tap and gasped at the slightly tinted colour that came out. She checked the kettle and poured out a glass from there instead, just to be on the safe side.

"How long has your water been like that for? Never mind. Here, sip this, slowly."

Sera studied Leila properly now; the dark circles under her eyes and slightly off-colour pallor worried her. Whilst she was normally a slim girl, she seemed to have lost even more weight lately.

Sera handed her a protein bar then ushered the young girl into the bedroom when she was ready to move.

Leila lay down on the narrow bed, and Sera glanced around at the cramped room. There were a few mattresses on the floor and extra bedding, but other than a narrow table, furniture was scarce. At sixteen, Leila was the eldest and therefore responsible for her six younger siblings.

Sera's heart squeezed.

"Feeling a bit better?"

One slim shoulder shrugged.

"Leila, you know I'm not one to judge—"

"Oh yes, the martyr woman, saving us poor souls."

Sera frowned, bothered by the comment. "We're talking about you right now. Are you in any danger?"

Leila rolled her eyes picking at her oversized jumper.

"Are you starving yourself?"

"Fuck's sake, miss. I don't need to starve myself. If you hadn't noticed, we're poor as fuck, so not eating is kind of the norm around here."

"Well, what is it? Did you have a fight with William?"

At the mention of her boyfriend's name, Leila sat up, cheeks colouring.

"What has he said?"

"What's going on?"

Leila's panic diminished slightly, but her concerned expression remained. She began fidgeting with her nose piercing and avoided eye contact.

"It's none of your business."

"Maybe I can help?"

"It's too late for anyone to help me."

"Leila—"

She yanked up her jumper, and Sera gasped at the tell-tale curve that could only mean one thing.

"You're pregnant!"

"Duh. *Now* will you leave me the hell alone?"

Sera didn't expect it. She wasn't shocked by much these days, but for some reason pregnancy didn't seem to be on her radar.

The young girl launched off the bed then swayed again. Sera caught her, gently lowering her to the edge of the mattress. A second later, the heaving started, and Sera grabbed the closest thing she could find, a used plastic bowl.

"Easy now."

"I can't keep anything down. I feel so fucking miserable."

"I take it Will doesn't know?"

"Don't tell him!"

"Relax, take a deep breath, I'm not telling him anything. That's something between the two of you and frankly, it's not my business. But your well-being *is* my concern. I know you probably don't want to hear it right now, but you have options."

"Options? What, like, get rid of it?"

Sera nodded. "That's one. You shouldn't feel like you're under any pressure to keep a baby at sixteen."

"I'll be seventeen when it's born."

"I'm just telling you your options, there's adoption as well."

"Why are you convincing me to give up this baby? It's my child."

"I'm not. I'm just telling you that having a baby when you're sixteen, sorry seventeen, is going to be tough."

"Yeah, well, I'll figure it out."

"I take it your parents don't know."

Fear leapt into the girl's eyes now. She swallowed a few times and shook her head. "My dad will chuck me out. Or worse."

"Are you afraid he'd hit you?"

"Probably Mum for 'letting' me get pregnant. But whatever."

"You've made up your mind then?"

"It's kind of too late for an abortion, and I want a kid. I...I broke up with Will when I found out. I haven't seen him yet. I just wanted to figure it all out before telling him. Will and me have been wanting to run away and live together but like, in a few years, when I finish school and work full time and shit. He's got his job at Pete's workshop and he's good with the cars. But this is, like, sudden, ya know?"

"I can imagine. So how far along are you?"

"I dunno. Not exactly. I took a pee test when I thought I might be, and it's been months since then. I think I'm nearly six months? It's not like I'm regular, which is why I didn't notice it at the start, and it was easy to hide it. But the past few months...I've popped."

She pressed the jumper against her slim body.

"It's your first baby, so sometimes you don't show as much as the uterus is doing this for the first time. What are you going to do? You can't hide the bump forever."

"Run away."

"Leila, you're sixteen and pregnant, there's a lot you need to consider now, not just for yourself but your baby too. Do you have a local doctor?"

"You mean that shit free one that gossips about you to the rest of the community? No. Not going to her."

"You need to get a check-up and talk to someone who is impartial. Your diet and lifestyle have to change too."

"I gave up the cigs a while ago."

"And the red bull."

"Get off my case already, woman!"

"If I don't tell you then a doctor will, and it's important you know all the facts."

Sera's mind was trying to process it all. Was it too late for multivitamins? She didn't know much about genetic testing. When did they do the diabetes test?

"You have to promise not to run away."

"I can't do that."

"Leila."

"You don't live my life; you have no right to burst in here and make decisions for me. Or my baby."

Sera forced herself to take a breath and step back. She was right. But that didn't stop the gut-churning fear from taking hold. "That's true. I don't. But you're six months pregnant, your boyfriend doesn't know, your parents don't know, and you want to run away. You've not gone to see any healthcare professionals to help you out. I'm the only other person who knows about this. As a teacher, I've a duty to your well-being, and I'm not willing to sit back while you put yourself in a dangerous situation."

"What do you care? It's my decision at the end of the day."

"I'm going to pretend like I didn't hear that. When are you telling William?"

"Soon. It didn't feel real at first. Then when the sickness started, I got scared. I want to do it my way. If he doesn't want the baby, then I'll have to figure it out on my own."

"You've been holding this information and the pressure of being pregnant on your own already. Let go of that burden a little."

Sera was torn between frustration and admiration for Leila's tenacity. Her brave determination was a trait she figured that Leila would have all her life, not necessarily just because of her youth.

"There are options that might mean you can stay in school and get some support. We can talk to Centrelink about—"

"No welfare. I'm doing this on my own, in my own way."

"Leila, you've got to learn to ask for help when you need it. These services are there to help you. Don't let pride get in the way."

"Like I said, I'll figure it out."

"You'll need to see a doctor. At least let me organise that for you." Sera raised her hand in defence. "I know you don't want me to interfere, but I think you need to at least visit someone independent."

"Fine. Whatever."

"I'll pick up some supplements for you, and in the meantime, you need to be eating even if it means you're throwing up."

"I have a mother."

"Until you tell her you're pregnant, then you'll just have to listen to me, kiddo."

"Why are you doing this anyway? Not all of us are like Eli." Leila stopped picking her nails to glare at her, a suspicious pout revealing her true age despite her bravado.

Sera let the hurt wash over her. That was a conversation for another time. "I know that. Just focus on getting rest and eating well. I'll come back tomorrow with the vitamins, and we'll go from there."

Sera let herself out, walking back to the car, shock slowing down her movements. She made the drive across town, back to her parents' place, with a heart heavier than it had been for a long time.

She found her mother on the sofa, knitting a new beanie for some of the charities that sent clothes to overseas orphans. It was days like these that she was glad she lived with her parents, even if it was only temporary. She needed comfort.

"What is it, *habibti*?"

"Oh, Mamma."

"That bad?"

She knelt in front of the sofa, then shifted to lay her head on her mother's lap. The hand that stroked her hair was rough, the ridges on her fingertips roadmaps of the life Maryam had led, filled with responsibility and hard work. No matter how old she was, Sera never tired of the feeling of her mother's hand through her hair.

"Sometimes, when I work with these poor kids, I feel so helpless. Like I'm not really making any difference. I feel like I'm in the way and nothing will change if I leave. Look at what happened to Elijah."

"Stop. You can't torment yourself about that poor boy. He had a mind of his own and used it for no good."

"But he was—"

"You cannot save them all, sweet girl. Especially those who do not want to be saved. You've a soft heart, Seraphina. That's a good trait, but it can also get easily bruised. You've got to take care not to let yourself become overwhelmed in the process."

"But—"

"I know it's hard, but you don't see all the good you are doing. Even when you think that it's hopeless, you're there, you're showing up, and for many of those kids, you're the only consistent adult in their life. The only one who they can trust. That counts."

"I don't feel that way. Not tonight..."

"Tell me."

"Leila Alwadi...Oh Mum, she's pregnant."

"Eh?" Her mother's fingers paused. "Is she keeping it?"

"That's the thing; I think she is."

"And this makes you scared, why?"

Sera sat up. "She's sixteen years old! She's not got any support behind her. The boyfriend doesn't even know, and God help her when her parents find out."

Not content to be still, Sera stood, stalking the rug, frustration and fear twisting together in her body, winding her up.

"If she's not afraid, then why are you?"

Sera's eyes nearly bugged out of her head. "I just told you." Hearing her own frustration, she lowered her shoulders. "Leila doesn't have anyone. If William doesn't want the baby, she said she'd run away. She won't survive out there pregnant and alone."

"She has you."

And just as suddenly the fire diminished inside her. Even if slightly.

"What if I'm not enough? What if—"

"You can only do your best. Imagine if you weren't there at all? Be glad you can help. Even if it's only one pregnant teenager. It will be two lives you'll be saving."

"Oh, Mamma."

She slumped on the floor in front of her again. Sera rested her head on Maryam's lap, touched by her words. Tears stung at her eyes now.

"Don't cry, sweet girl."

But she couldn't help it. "I needed your perspective. I couldn't see through the fog."

"Your emotions are good. It means you care. When you stop feeling, when that disconnect between mind and heart happens, well, that's when problems begin."

"I know, but it helps to hear you say it."

"So what will you do?"

"I'm taking her to the doctor and will be getting her multivitamins. Maybe I'll even bring some extra food to the house."

"You're a thoughtful woman, Seraphina. I couldn't be more proud."

"Mama." She buried her head, taking comfort from her touch.

"Am I interrupting something?"

Sera's head shot up.

"Jack." She brushed at her face. She didn't want him to see her upset.

"Come in. I was just heading upstairs." Maryam gathered her knitting and kissed her daughter's head, leaving them alone.

Jack adjusted his cap. "Everything okay?"

"Not really, but I'm hoping it will be. Mum gave me a pep talk. It helped. Can we walk? I'm still a little restless."

"I know of something that's a perfect cure for that." He winked and despite her worry, she felt a zing of awareness race up her spine.

"Head out of the gutter, Hollywood."

"Never. Alright, I'll get my shoes."

They walked through the cold back streets, huddled in their jackets while dusk settled around them.

Even though there was a chasm of time that separated them, a wealth of experiences and moments that they didn't share, there was something ridiculously familiar and comfortable about walking with him on a chilly spring evening. Odd, it wasn't the first time she had thought that about him.

He wasn't Jack Davies, Hollywood star and playboy. He was just Jack, the boy she knew before he was famous. The guy who made conversations easy and life just a little bit brighter.

She hoped that never changed.

Jack paced his small room later that night, restless for the millionth time.

His life was falling apart around him, and he wasn't sure what the hell to do about it.

Jack read the sickening article headlines for the millionth time on his phone. His agent had emailed it to him after writing a scathing, albeit pithy email.

'Star Spins Out of Control on Set.'

'Hollywood Hunk Loses Cool.'

'Jack Davies' Psychotic Break.'

Jack winced, then locked his phone. That last one hurt. It hit a little too close to home.

By tomorrow morning it would be circulating here too. He had no doubt that gossip columnists were frantically tapping on keys and hunting down the other stars on set for an exclusive.

So much for Taylor paying off that pap. The slimy fucker had published his conversation...the fact that he had confessed to a break down on set. That he was losing his fucking mind.

Maybe he had. Filming that scene had broken him. He hadn't slept for a good week leading up to it and when it was over, he had sat on set, unable to move a muscle, tears streaming down his face. For hours.

They'd called the paramedics, which is what eventually spurred him to action. He refused to be admitted, going home instead. It had taken him less than an hour to pack and book his flight to Melbourne.

Not that it had helped. The mess was still there, and he would clean it up, he just needed a little more fucking time.

He knew his co-stars were worried. He owed it to everyone to make it right. But up until this evening, Jack hadn't been able to think about what everyone else was feeling. He hadn't the capacity.

Running out was a dick move. Fuck. What the hell had he done? They deserved better than that. It wasn't their fault he lost it. They weren't to blame for the ghosts that had lurked in his mind.

Because the guilt threatened to smother him, Jack had emailed his co-stars, Alex and Jane, unable to say much more than sorry, that he was okay. Or would be.

He owed them all a hell of a lot more than that. Had they shut down production? Were they hoping he would return? The thought made him want to vomit. How could he face them after this?

Sick of the feeling, the constant churning in his gut, Jack knew he needed to act. Hiding out, running away never really suited him. It left him on edge and the last thing he wanted was to be in a position where he needed a cocktail of drugs to cope. That part of his life was over.

Which meant that there was more in store for him, harder conversations he needed to have with himself and with those who mattered.

But in the meantime, he had to face the music. Which meant

he needed to call Taylor back before he had a heart attack and finally face what the hell he was going to do with his life.

It was approaching the end of his second week here. And whilst Jack loved being with the De Lottos he couldn't just hide out in their home, pretending everything was fine. As appealing as that sounded, he had to stop living in denial and figure out his next move. To do the right thing for a damn change.

Jack wasn't sure if he would be making a huge mistake, but he did make a promise. Why not fulfil it in the only way he knew how?

With a grand fucking entrance.

Once he had made a few calls and figured out logistics, he climbed into bed.

Jack's mind wandered to the woman down the hall who had sought his company this evening, when up until now she had been keeping her distance. Even though last night's kiss had been scorching, he was glad that she wanted to talk. It meant more that she confided in him, that she trusted him enough to share what she was thinking.

Supporting a pregnant teenager wasn't going to be easy, but Sera was compelled to do it. It hadn't even occurred to her not to...

Even knowing she was too good for him Jack couldn't help but be impressed.

Sera was the same, and yet different. Better. Stronger, in so many ways. Hotter too, if that were even possible. She was real, and damn it to hell, that appealed to him after a life of pretend.

Jack didn't know what it all meant, or where it would lead him, but whenever he was with her, the weight on his chest didn't feel so heavy.

It was time to do something right.

By morning he'd no longer be able to hide.

He no longer wanted to.

CHAPTER ELEVEN

*S*era heard the screaming from outside the gymnasium and wondered what the fuss was about.

It couldn't be rehearsals for the school play, not unless the whole school was now performing. She was about to step out of her office and investigate when Maddie, face flushed, sailed in.

"Do you have a mirror?"

"Huh?"

Her friend rummaged through her drawers.

"Tell me you have one and a bit of make-up in this god forsaken pit?"

"The gym isn't a pit, and why the hell would I stash emergency make-up? If I'm reapplying anything, it's sunscreen."

"Oh God! You're *so* not helping right now!" Maddie slammed the drawer before grabbing Sera's hand and dragging her outside. "Comb, foundation, powder, lipstick, mascara, perfume. The essentials in case of emergency meetings with parents, an after-work date, or—" She waved her arm at the swell of students, jostling and shoving at each other.

Sera blinked a few times, taking in the sea of smart phones bobbing amongst the crowd. The noise was deafening.

"What in the hell..."

"A social media frenzy."

And then she saw it. A familiar golden-blond head, the flash of a leather jacket, and a slightly panicked look on his face.

"Is that—"

"Your Hollywood hunk."

When the hoard of students on their lunch break began to get violent, Sera flung herself into the crowd, trying to help the teachers on duty.

This must have been what the Beatles felt like on tour. She blocked a blow from an eager Year 10 student and shoved her way through the mass of human bodies.

"Hey!" Jack yelled. "Help?"

"What are you doing here, Jack? Have you lost your damn mind?" She roared, unable to see past the mass of students surrounding them.

She wanted to murder him. She would have if she didn't glimpse the sheer panic that had flashed across his face. Instead, she dragged him through the crowd, with Maddie's help, towards reception.

"Sorry, Sera. I thought I could...ya know..."

"What? Sneak in through the back? This isn't a film set, Jack. You're like the hottest thing in," Sera grunted as a kid stepped on her toe. "Hollywood."

Once they crowd dispersed, Sera gulped in air. Too many sweaty armpits.

"Why didn't you tell me you were coming?"

Jack adjusted the collar of his jacket. "I didn't want to make it a big deal. I promised Maddie I'd take a class with her senior drama kids. After the shit storm in the papers this morning, I thought I better make an appearance at the school before the paps started following me."

"Wait, what about the paps?" Maddie looked over her shoulder as Sera ushered them into reception.

"You haven't seen it?"

"No. What's going on, Jack?" Sera pulled him close.

"Shit, I'll explain later. But I didn't think I'd get mobbed."

Sera could tell he was panicking as he snapped the band around his wrist a few times. His eyes were filled with dread.

"You're here now." Maddie pointed out.

"Hell, I didn't think. I'm sorry. Ally sent me a copy of Maddie's timetable and said to call her when I wanted to come by, but I didn't want to make a big deal of it. I knew that shit had hit the fan in L.A., so I figured to get in before the story broke here."

"What story?" Sera muttered.

"What actually happened on set." Jack's eyes were guarded, his shoulders hunched.

They couldn't get into this now. Students were milling about in the hallway, phones out.

"Alright, off with you!" Sera hollered, shooing them away.

"Uh oh." Maddie sing-songed as their principal, Jacinta Cavarello strode down the hall.

They were screwed.

Jack rubbed the back of his neck and closed the office door behind him. He spotted Maddie and Sera waiting in the foyer outside of the principal's office.

The teachers had managed to clear away most of the students, but the floor to ceiling windows afforded any loitering kid a prime view.

Dick move, Jack.

Jesus, even when he tried to do something good, he still fucked up.

"It's been a while since I've been sent to the principal's office, but the burn still feels the same."

"What did she say?"

"Let's walk over to my office as it's the closest. We'll have a bit of privacy there." Maddie steered them down the corridor to the English and Drama offices in Blue Block.

"I can tell you my charm wasn't exactly winning her over. She caned me for not giving the school adequate warning. Something about permission for an incursion, needing a police check to work with kids...It was a long list."

"She's fierce," Sera conceded.

"Which is what makes her a kick ass prin." Maddie's eyes were filled with glee.

"And utterly terrifying to students." Jack rolled his shoulders. "I enjoyed every minute of it."

Sera's sound of disgust made him grin.

"You're impossible, you know that?"

"Did I hear someone say irresistible?"

He held the cocky grin, hoping the panic that still raced around his heart didn't show.

"C'mon Romeo, let me show you the drama room before Sera gives you an even bigger grilling. I've a group of senior students who are going to go crazy knowing you'll be here. Not to mention my after-school production kids. I would have organized it had I known you were coming."

"Like I said, kind of on a ticking clock here."

"Sounds ominous." Maddie turned to Sera. "I'll drop him off to you for period six as my English seniors have a test. The last thing I need is for them to be distracted by Mr. Hunky Hollywood, if that's okay?"

"Fine by me."

"He can stay with me for after school rehearsals and I'll drop him off to your folks when we're done."

"Hello? Hollywood hunk, standing right here."

"Trust me, handsome, we know." Maddie rolled her eyes.

"Do I get a say in this?" He adopted an offended expression, enjoying himself immensely. If he kept himself in the moment, he wouldn't have time to think about the mess he was about to face with the media. Jack crossed his arms, trying to keep his heart in his chest.

Maddie huffed then turned to face him. "Jack, oh Hollywood royalty, are you able and willing to visit my seniors and stay for after school rehearsals?"

He pretended to think about it, ignoring the rambling thoughts in his mind screaming for attention. "Ow. That's abuse." He rubbed his arm. "You can't just pinch me to get your way. Though some people are into—"

"Jack!" Sera and Maddie cried out in unison.

"Alright, alright. Yes, I am willing to stay for after school rehearsals. Thank you for asking."

Maddie scowled. "Bloody hell, you're hard work."

"My agent says that to me all the time," he muttered, adjusting his baseball cap. He didn't want to think of Taylor and what he was dealing with in L.A. But he would have to...running away was no longer an option.

"I was told you were the one to contact about the riot at lunch."

The man in the doorway of Maddie's office was commanding. His crisp suit and neat hair screamed, 'I'm in charge.'

"Hello to you too, Gabriel." Maddie's tone was frosty. "I'm not responsible for anything. But as usual, you're quick to form assumptions."

"Am I? Is that why there's a Hollywood actor in your office and a bevy of crying teenage boys and girls in mine? And yet, you're telling me you don't have anything to do with it."

"For once, I don't."

"Wonders never cease." Gabriel's tone was dry.

"He's with me." Sera raised her hand.

"Hi. I'm Jack Davies."

"I know who you are. But even Hollywood stars need to

follow school protocol." Gabriel's arms were crossed. "Hello, Sera."

"Hey, Gabe. Jack, this is our vice principal, Gabriel Steele—"

"A true enforcer of the rules," Maddie cut in. "Without his guidance, we'd all be lost."

"How to damn with faint praise," Gabriel replied.

"In about two seconds, he'll be reprimanding you for not picking up a visitor's badge when you signed in." Maddie toyed with the lid of her bottle, agitated and annoyed.

"Right. The principal didn't mention that."

"That's because she was too busy ripping you a new one." Maddie smiled sweetly at him.

"This isn't a joke. Your friend's arrival is going to be hard to explain to parents," Gabriel admonished.

"You're just shitty because *you* have to deal with the fall out. If I could help I would but—"

Gabriel's stony expression brightened. "Perfect. You can help me write a notice to place in the newsletter about being visited by Hollywood's finest. A spin on the situation."

Maddie's mouth opened. At Sera's stealthy nudge, she closed it again.

Gabriel didn't wait for an answer, leaving just as suddenly as he arrived.

Sera held her hands up. "Wow. Okay I should follow that up. But I think we all need to sit down and talk about whatever is going on, Jack. Family meeting and all."

The warmth spread across his chest. Her concern was a comfort, a balm to his festering wounds.

"Sounds good." Jack watched her leave then launched himself up on the side of Maddie's desk. "Soooo...how long have you guys been dating?"

Maddie spluttered the water she had sipped, cheeks flushed. "Excuse me?"

"You and Steely Grey?"

Maddie's eyes danced despite her annoyance. "I like that. Sorry to burst your make-believe bubble, but we're not dating."

"What, no secret office romance going on? Huh...could've fooled me."

"Oh shut up, Jack. It's your fault I'm in this mess. You're just one big troublemaker you know that?"

Jack absorbed the hurt, and the sting of remorse at having caused so many problems when he had only been trying to help.

"Trust me, Maddie, I've been called far worse."

After a hectic fifth period, because the whole school seemed to be on a high after Jack's guest appearance, Sera walked into the stadium in a mood that was less than chipper. She could have killed her senior students for being so distracted, but when she stepped into the gym for her last class of the day, she decided she just might murder her work colleagues first.

There was a horde of teachers huddled outside her office. No guesses as to why.

Maddie was waiting at her desk.

"Where's the superstar? Lost him already?" Sera asked, placing the stack of exercise books on the floor.

"I've gotta set up the room for my seniors so this is a quick drop off."

"How'd it go with your drama kids?"

"He's a cocky bastard, but he knows his stuff. Sickening really."

"Please, God, don't tell him that."

"Do I look stupid to you?"

"Hey." Sera shifted closer, lowering her voice. "Is it always so..." She gestured. "Intense between you and Gabriel?"

Maddie's frown deepened. "I've just had Jack in my ear

about whether Gabriel is my secret boyfriend, so I'd rather not talk about him, thanks."

"Okay, just asking."

"Gotta go." Maddie turned.

"Wait. Where *is* Jack?"

"Shooting hoops out there." Maddie gestured to the basketball courts.

Sera picked up her whistle and chronicle. "I'll walk out with you."

What was it about Gabriel that made Maddie so damn defensive? No doubt her bestie would rather teach mathematics than admit she was attracted to their enigmatic vice principal, but the heart wanted what it wanted. You didn't get to choose who you fell in love with sometimes.

Sera glanced across the gym, to where Jack stood, laughing at something a few students had said. No, the heart refused to listen sometimes. Which could be more trouble than what it was worth.

Shaking herself off, Sera dismissed the rest of the teachers who wanted to ogle the shiny Hollywood star and began the lesson.

Usually, her Year 8 students were rat bags in final period, but with Jack in tow, they were brimming with eagerness and malleability. She'd never seen such acquiescence. And when Jack picked up a ball and started shooting, Sera figured she would chuck the curriculum for one lesson and let him run the show. Much to the students' delight.

And his.

But while he appeared relaxed, whatever it was that had happened, plagued him. She witnessed it whenever he lowered his guard. It was the merest flicker, a shadow of remorse. And her heart ached.

She realised now that Jack never really relaxed when in

public. Even here, he was on alert, surveying the room every few minutes, on the lookout for hidden dangers.

Sera couldn't imagine living that way, and something in her softened.

By the end of the lesson, Jack was flushed and grinning. He looked less like the Hollywood star and more like the boy she had met and fallen for all those years ago.

Whether he could see it or not, Jack was a natural with the kids, which is probably why her students had a blast.

"Did you have fun?"

"Yeah, I did, actually. I'm beat. Don't know how you do this every day."

"It gets easier with practice." She opened the storeroom, and they packed away the basketballs and gear. Sera turned to Jack. "As much as the kids enjoyed themselves, you know you can't just rock up like this again, right?"

Jack grimaced, rubbing his jaw. "I know. It seemed like a good idea at the time."

Shadows lurked behind his eyes, and Sera knew that whatever was going on with the media was really affecting him.

"Next time you have what you think is a good idea, Jack, call a hotline instead, they'll talk you down off that ledge."

"I dunno." Jack threw her a scandalous look. "View from up here is mighty fine."

And just like that, she was laughing again.

Damn Jack Davies straight to hell.

"So, what spurred the call to action, brother?" Owen sipped at his beer, leaning back into his chair. His other hand was at the nape of Ally's neck, fingers casually playing with her hair. "Ally filled me in."

Did they know how enviable they were right now? That easy affection, the casual intimacy?

He was ashamed to admit his relationships were never more than surface level. He hadn't been capable of emotional intimacy. How fucking sad was that?

Once Jack would have shrugged it off, downplayed the absence in his life with a flippant shrug of his shoulders, but now he couldn't. He had gone too far, was in too deep. Or perhaps not deep enough. He was dissatisfied with his life and couldn't go back to living the way it was, not anymore.

"Let me read what has been circulating online and it might make some sense." Jack felt the food they had consumed settle on his stomach like lead.

His voice wobbled as he read the most scathing of articles. He didn't want to downplay this stuff any longer. Not to those who mattered.

Even though Charlie was watching television at full volume in the basement, Jack kept his voice low. Once finished, he looked around the table, heart racing. He wanted to throw up.

"Oh, Jack." Ally's eyes were brimming with tears.

He glanced at Sera who sat silent and still. He wanted to explain, to make them understand.

"Partly why I visited the school today was because once the paps find out where I am, I'm done for. I didn't want to have them anywhere near the school or those kids. Anywhere near you guys. So I thought, hey, why not get in before they find me, right?"

"You wanted to control the situation," Owen offered.

"Something like that. From here on in, I'm a sitting duck."

"What happened?" Sera searched for more across the table. Her brown eyes seemed to penetrate every shield, every barrier; it was frightening and freeing at the same time. "On set, I mean. I'd rather hear your version of it than from a gossip column."

"I didn't go psycho, yelling and screaming at everyone as

89

they said, but I wasn't in a good place. My mental health wasn't great. I took on the film knowing it would push my limits, and after that scene, it did. I wasn't...right." Jack swallowed, unable to say more. The pain he had bottled up for years had outweighed his common sense that day.

"You don't have to continue, Jack. If it's too much, we can talk about this another time," Sera proffered.

"I need to explain. I want to." Jack flicked the band at his wrist and began. "When I landed in Melbourne, there was a pap was lurking at the hotel. He overheard my conversation with my agent which wasn't pretty. I basically told Taylor what had happened on set. I also said a few other things, namely that I felt like I was losing my mind and didn't know how to handle it.

"Anyway, Taylor had offered an exclusive with *The Star* in exchange for the pap's silence, but that didn't seem to be enough. They've been sitting on the story for a few weeks now. I'm surprised they waited so long."

"That's a low blow."

"That's show business." Jack's attempt at levity came out as bitterness. The cracks were beginning to show. How much longer could he play pretend? He refused to break in front of the media. He refused to be fodder for some hungry gossip mag. A public meltdown just wasn't an option.

But this film had broken him. It brought up everything he had feared for so long. And the one thought that he couldn't shift with booze or medication or denial, shrouded everything he did: if he had been more responsible that night, maybe his parents would still be alive today.

Jack snapped the band on his wrist. But he hadn't been, and now he was living with the consequences.

"So what now?" Maddie asked, eyes serious.

"I'll be followed, you might be too. But I'll try my best to keep you all out of it. The last thing I intended was for my troubles to find you. Owen, I swear, if I'd thought of another option, I wouldn't have called you. But the run in at the hotel freaked me out. I didn't have anywhere else to go."

Owen's eyes were sharp. "Never apologise for that, Jack. We're family, and we're all old enough to deal with whatever comes our way."

"Well hopefully the shit will hit the fan before your big day. I know you value your privacy, so I want to do everything I can to keep the media out of it."

"You can't control it, Jack." Ally's warmth radiated across the table. "Just like you couldn't control what happened on set. We'll deal with it, together. As a family. You don't need to worry about us."

"But I do. All this shit, it's because of me. And I will make things right before your wedding. They've forced my hand, but it's time I man up and deal with it. Make some decisions."

"We'll be here for you when you do," Sera soothed.

"Thanks, I appreciate the support, but some things I need to handle on my own."

It was well past time that he did.

As the conversation turned to wedding prep, Jack considered his next step.

He'd have to have to call the director, the studio...pretty much everyone who was affected by his fuck up. He had acted carelessly, and it didn't sit well with him. Not anymore.

That was the problem. He had chased the highs of his career, of success by anyone's standards, and in doing so, he gave up something that was meaningful. Something that was true.

Jack had lived without responsibility for so long, that he didn't know how to handle the important stuff anymore. But knowing what was wrong and knowing what to do about it were two separate problems.

His chest seized. The edges of another panic attack caught hold, crushing him in its grip. He was suffocating.

Not here. Not now. He thought he was making progress. But like a speeding train, it wouldn't lose momentum. Not unless it was derailed.

Jesus, Jack. Wake up. There's no fucking danger. It's all in your head.

But still, the persistent beating of his heart hammered him in place, nailing him to his chair. He was trapped.

A part of him, one that was always disconnected in these moments, was hyper aware of everything around him: the clatter of cutlery, the low hum of voices. But inside, he was imploding.

Would someone open a fucking window already?

Jack shoved back from the table and made a bee line through the kitchen to the back door. Sliding the screen open, he scrambled off the porch to the garden beyond, carefully cultivated and tended by Mr. D.

Did he want a garden, complete with veggie patch and a porch swing? Were the paps lurking in the bushes? Did he want to settle in L.A. forever? What about kids? The rolling thoughts looped around his mind. He was dizzy with it.

"Jack?"

He whirled around, soothed by her voice. But the pressure in his chest was relentless, beating him down until his legs began to buckle. He fought to stand up tall.

"I don't know if I want a garden."

"Huh?"

Sera stepped closer, slowly, as if approaching a bomb. He supposed he was just as volatile. Was he that bloody unhinged? Maybe the media were right. Perhaps he was losing his grip on reality.

Pull it together, Jack.

"What kind of flowers do I like?"

"Umm..."

"Do I even know what the difference between a petunia and

a pansy is? Do I care? What about kids? I've always wanted them, but why?"

His chest heaved with effort. *Calm the fuck down, Davies.* He was on this ride and unable to stop. The train was derailing and fast.

"Okay, breathe it out."

He shoved one hand against his chest, the other at his temple, trying desperately to keep his brains in.

"I can't. I fucking *can't*." He wheezed.

"It's okay. Listen to my voice. Focus on that." Sera was at his side, sitting him down on the grass.

"I need to—I have to—" he spluttered. Jesus he couldn't breathe.

"Listen to my voice. Count with me. 1, 2, 3..." Sera guided him. "Long deep breaths, that's it. Keep going."

Jack was torn between colossal panic and her firm encouragement. He was going to split in two.

"That's it. Keep that up. From here." She placed a hand on his diaphragm, keeping him upright.

When his breathing levelled out, his body shook a little. "Still in it."

"That's okay. Keep breathing." Sera settled next to him, her voice steady, her smell comforting. "Did I tell you about what happened with Jimmy Crane in my class yesterday?"

Sera was animated, guiding him through a mad lesson she had with her juniors. At first it was just sounds, melodious vowels and harsh consonants, all jumbled. Then her lively tone seeped through, until the words started to make sense. The sentences became coherent strings of information, a lifeline to which he clung tight. And then he was laughing.

"He said what?"

"I know, right? Never in all my years of teaching had that happened. I laughed so hard I couldn't really discipline the kid."

And just like that, the pressure on his chest lifted. Jack was left with only the remnants of the attack, a jittery unease, very faint in his belly.

"Thanks...the laughter helped. You helped."

"It's okay." She rubbed his back. "I'm glad I could. But Jack, we need to talk about this. About everything."

"We will."

"Good. How long has this been going on?"

"Too long. Years. I need help, Sera. I can't do this anymore."

"When you're ready, I'm here to listen."

He grabbed her hand, squeezing it. "Thanks. You know what would make me feel better?"

"What?"

Jack tapped his cheek.

Sera rolled her eyes but complied, soft lips brushing against his cheek, her unbound hair teasing his jaw. When she lingered, Jack turned towards her, captivated by the desire in her eyes.

"You read my mind," he murmured, drawing her in.

The kiss was more than just a spark. It was a fire that engulfed them both.

Jack's mouth was firm against hers, catapulting them headlong into the whirling storm of desire.

He needed this. Dear God, he craved this consummation, the feeling of being utterly whole when he kissed her. It seemed like nothing mattered when he did. All that worry, all of the questions and fears that bottled up inside of him for years, spilled out now. Into the kiss. Into Sera. The one woman who seemed to reach past every defence he owned.

She wasn't demanding. She didn't do it for any ulterior motive, just to offer her support. That warmth, that open, accepting way about her was compelling.

Jack yanked her close, gathering her against his body, shielding them both from the night air and anything else that threatened to break through.

He didn't know what it was between them, but the utter certainty of his need for her rang through his brain clear and true.

He wanted her. Wanted this.

Everything else was chaos, but with Sera, he found peace. When he kissed her, hugging that feminine body against his own, he was whole. And with every passing day, he yearned for more. It was the only thing that made sense, the only thing that felt right.

Jack raked his hands down her spine, then back up again, enjoying the soft mass of curls. His fingers found the back of her neck, and he kneaded, revelling in the sweet moan that surrounded him.

He deepened the kiss, groaning when her tongue danced with his.

Unable to help himself, Jack grabbed her ass then he lifted her, grinning when those legs wrapped around his waist. And still it wasn't enough.

He rolled, taking them both down to the soft, dewy grass. And using teeth and tongue, Jack drove her wild, revelling in the way her back arched beneath his, eager for more. He nibbled at her jaw, licked and sucked on that sweet spot beneath her ear, and felt all control snap. He was hungry for those sounds, needing to hear her pleasure more than he did his own.

Jack was so consumed by the woman beneath him that he didn't register the voice that rang out across the yard. It wasn't until the deep tone hovered above them that he stopped.

"And here I thought you were in need of a little cheering up. Looks like you're pretty damn happy out here in the dark."

Jack blinked, taking a few seconds to register his brother's presence.

Sera tilted her head back further in the grass and Jack was momentarily distracted by the swell of her breasts. She had a killer rack.

"Hi, Owen."

"Sera, sorry to interrupt."

"I thought I'd come out and see if—" Ally stopped short. "Oh, well."

"Doesn't look like our action hero needed any saving after all," Owen replied, amused.

"Not when he's sucking face with our heroine like that," Maddie called.

Jack flashed a grin, then gazed at his heroine. "You'd make a killer leading lady."

Sera cupped his check in a gesture as brief as it was sweet. It wrapped around his heart and ground him to her.

"Alright folks, nothing to see here." Ally shooed them away even as Jack rose, helping Sera to stand beside him.

Despite the heaviness in his gut, Jack felt steadier, able to face whatever it was that came next.

Hand in hand, they walked back in to the join the others.

CHAPTER TWELVE

*I*t didn't take long for the major news outlets to grab the story of the mega Hollywood star spotted in Woodbury's eclectic high school. Local news had obtained student footage of Jack's visit and had brazenly run with it in the morning headlines the following day.

But it wasn't the news that occupied Sera's thoughts that morning. All she could think about was kissing Jack. Twice now. Not that she was counting.

Holy smokes.

Rolling around in the grass with Jack's hard body on hers had unlocked something elemental inside her: heart-thudding, spine-tingling, take-me-now-handsome, lust. That's what it was, pure and simple.

But that wasn't the problem. What irked Sera was the feelings beneath all that, the ones that seemed to hover around her heart whenever she thought about him.

Which was often.

Jack made her want things she really had no business wanting right now. Or ever, where he was concerned.

She sipped her orange juice and tried to focus on the morning news, but it was all white noise.

Jack would have to go back to his life in Hollywood soon enough. He would be here for the wedding, sure, but he had no incentive to stay in Melbourne. He would return to L.A., she would remain here. And whatever it was that was bubbling beneath the surface would fade away. She just had to wait it out.

She could totally do that. *She* was in control of her feelings, not the other way around.

With a determined nod of her head, Sera bit into a slice of toast.

"I always knew you'd be famous," her dad remarked, walking past with the morning paper in hand and a grin on his face.

"Har, har."

Sera watched footage of yesterday's crush and stifled a mortified groan. Her face was set in annoyance as she accompanied Maddie and Jack across the school yard. It wasn't the greatest of expressions to have on national news. There seemed to be even more sneaky footage of Jack and Maddie after school as well.

She could imagine Gabriel was pulling his hair out right about now.

Speculation around the reason for Jack's sudden visit filled up the news slot before the presenters moved on to another juicy bit of celebrity gossip.

Seeing Jack so vulnerable last night had put a new spin on everything. Sera didn't know how he managed to lead such a public life while trying to pretend he was okay. To have to keep his crushing anxiety a secret all those years couldn't be good on his mental health.

Which is why she would do anything she could to help him through it.

A reminder dinged on her phone. She sent a quick text to Leila to confirm her doctor's appointment in the afternoon and finished her breakfast.

Sera was teaching her seniors in the morning but would pick up Leila at midday to take her to the doctor and then to social services. The appointment had been booked with a social worker who was experienced in supporting teen mums through their pregnancies.

A baby. The last time she had been preoccupied with a pregnancy, she had just been a kid, and knew absolutely nothing about the world.

Sera paused with her hand over her phone, cringing at the memory.

At ten she had thought she was pregnant when Peter Abromovitch kissed her behind the log cabins on school camp. When she had confessed to her family that she couldn't do her chores because she had baby aches, her mother had sat her down and taught her the facts of life. In detail.

After the hour-long discussion, Sera had been glad that she wasn't actually pregnant, but hoped that one day she would be with someone who loved her the way her father did her mother. It also dawned on her that perhaps her eldest brother's advice should be scrutinised as carefully as she did the year-old Easter eggs found in the backyard.

"Penny for your thoughts?" Her mother sailed in, orange robe tied around her small frame, wide eyes sharp but merry.

"Just remembering the time I thought I was pregnant with Peter Abromovitch."

Tony laughed, a gunshot sound reverberating across the room. "That shaved a decade off my life but also made me laugh so hard I almost put my back out."

Her mother 'tsk'd him before rubbing Sera's shoulder. "Speaking of babies..."

"You've one grandchild already, and an adopted granddaughter in Charlie, so not a word about babies and next generations."

Her mother held up hands that were lined after years of manual labour.

"Not a word."

Sera rolled her eyes and was about to head back upstairs when the doorbell rang.

"I'll get it. I made scrambled eggs with mushroom and thyme if you're hungry."

"You can't distract me with food."

"I can try," she teased then padded to the front door. Sera shivered as a fresh gust of wind chilled her skin. Her clothes were still damp from this morning's workout.

"Where is he?" Maddie stood on the porch, eyes hot, temper set to fever pitch.

"Who?"

"I'm going to murder him!" She barrelled through the door, glowering.

"Oh, you mean Jack."

Maddie whirled around to face her. "No, I meant Santa Claus. Did you see the news?" she screeched.

"Yes, we were on it."

"Exactly my point!" Maddie threw her hands up, earrings jangling as she tossed back her hair. "Gabriel is going to kill me when he sees it. He already blames me for this bullshit." She gesticulated wildly and Sera nearly lost an eye.

"Getting angry doesn't solve anything. It's done now, Madds. You can't rewind time."

"That's *not* the point! And whose side are you on anyway, De Lotto?" Maddie marched upstairs, clomping with every step.

"This is early for you."

"I know! That's because someone rang me at un-God o'clock to tell me about the stupid news feature."

"Sooo there's a body we have to bury?"

"Not unless you want to kill the bride."

"Isn't that like seven years bad luck?" Sera teased.

"It was tempting."

"Well, you look pretty fresh, Maddie darling."

"I've a full face on. I won't be making *that* mistake again. And you needn't look so damn chipper. Just because you two rolled around last night does not absolve him from this mess." She flicked back her hair once they reached the landing. "Which room?"

Sera pointed, unable to stop the bubble of glee at what she was about to witness, even if she felt a quick pang of regret. She should not take pleasure out of this. What the hell, she was a sinner after all.

"Rise and shine!" Maddie hollered, yanking back the curtains and slamming on the lights in his room.

Jack sat up in bed. He rubbed at his face, blinking rapidly. The sheets fell from his body and Sera hoped he wasn't naked under those blankets as she wasn't entirely sure that Maddie wouldn't castrate him. Given what he could do in bed, that would be an awful pity. At least, from what she remembered.

"What the hell? Am I dreaming?"

"Watch it, smart alec."

Jack blinked again then jumped out of bed. "Shit, am I late? Did I miss it?" He frantically looked around the room.

Pity. Not naked after all. Not that the boxers left much to the imagination. The man was built in a lean, mean, fighting machine kind of way. Toned and muscled and...*hello*!

Sera swallowed. "No, you haven't missed anything. But I'll be leaving soon so if you want a lift, you should start getting ready."

"You know what you *did* miss, Jack, darling? The morning news and their big ass feature of me, *sans* make-up, broadcast for all of bloody Melbourne to see! I looked worse than I imagined. I can't wait to hear what my mother will say!"

Jack's lips quirked a fraction.

Oh boy. He was done for.

"Oh, you think that's funny, do you?"

Jack tried to press his lips together but failed.

Sera supposed it was nice knowing him. She said as much.

"Hey, you're supposed to be on my side!"

"Just because the two of you swapped saliva last night doesn't mean she's automatically Team Jerk!"

"Ooh, good one." Sera high-fived her friend.

"Oh, I see. Chicks before dicks, is it?"

Sera held up a hand. "Don't, for the love of God, make up some dick quip or you'll really not be able to walk out of this room properly."

"Feisty."

"Just warning you of Hurricane Madds."

"On top of the mortification of seeing myself that way on TV is the fact that Gabriel 'tight-ass' Steele is going to be up *my* ass yet again with all sorts of bullshit about my role in all this now it's on the news. All because of you!"

"I'm sorry, Maddie. I can chat to him if you—"

Maddie flicked a hand out, shooing away his suggestion. Her temper, whilst hot, burned fast. Once she got the venom out, it was rare that she held a grudge. Which made her dislike for Gabriel even more peculiar.

"No, I'll handle Steely Grey, but I'm bloody pissed. I'm on auditions, you know, for a few theatre groups, and this isn't a good look."

"I doubt anyone—"

Just then Maddie's social media lit up. "Think again." Maddie muttered to herself before whirling out of the room. "Sera!" She called out, voice trailing down the stairs.

"Best be getting that shower going if you want to make your appointment with the real estate agent."

"Can I tempt you to join me?" Jack ran his hands up her waist, luring her in.

"As lovely and wicked as that sounds, I'm in actual fear for your package." Sera gestured. "So for the safety of your balls, you best be sorting yourself out this morning while I calm Madds down."

Jack's eyes were full of mischief. "Pity. I've a few new moves I want to try out. And Sera." He waited until she turned. "That Gabriel has no idea what's coming."

Sera was about to ask him what he meant by that, then thought better of it. She found it interesting that Jack had picked up on the vibe too.

Very interesting indeed.

"What's he doing here?" Leila gestured to the back seat as Jack climbed in, cap low.

"It's been a day so let's not rock the boat any more than necessary," Sera pleaded.

Gabriel had given them an earful. By the time they arrived at work, he had fielded more than two dozen parent phone calls. He was a bear, which made Maddie an even bigger bear, which meant Sera now had a headache.

She wanted to go home and bury her head under the covers.

"Don't mind me, I'm just part of the furniture," Jack quipped.

"Yeah, sure." Leila rubbed her belly. "If I didn't know who you were already, your mint leather jacket would be a dead giveaway. Plus, you smell like money."

Jack sniffed at his lapel. "You can smell that stuff? What about success, coz I got that too."

"So why is he hanging around this bumfuck town? Just so you know, I'm not into threesomes or pregnancy kink."

"Leila!"

"Christ. You're a baby!"

Sera turned in time to catch the satisfied glint in Leila's eyes.

"Old enough to get myself knocked up, eh?"

"Yeah, well, if it were up to me, you'd still be in a booster seat."

"What the fuck—"

"You're just a kid, and regardless of whether you got pregnant or not hasn't got anything to do with me. I'm here by happy coincidence and if it makes you feel better, you can pretend that I don't exist for however long I'll be hanging around." Jack assured from the back seat.

"What would make me feel better is if you—"

Sera heard the tone and interjected. "Enough. Mind your manners. Both of you. Like I said, it's been a hell of a day, Leila, and we're all really tired."

"Speak for yourself. I've been doing nothing but lying down, so I'm ready to move. I saw the news, by the way. You looked good, miss."

"Thanks. But if it's all the same, I'd rather not be on the morning news. Ever."

She glimpsed Jack's grin in the rearview mirror. "Too late for that now. Plus, the kid is right, you really did look good."

"Ah huh. What did the real estate agent say?"

"They've just rented a few of their penthouses, but they think they'll have some more on the market in a week or two."

"That's promising."

And it meant that in the meantime, they could keep him close. To have people around him to help him process what had happened on set. The last thing Jack needed was to be holed up in some hotel or apartment all by himself.

For now, he was better off surrounded by friends and family.

It didn't take them long to get to the doctor's office at this hour of the day. Jack waited in the car, keeping a low profile, while they went in. Once they finished, with blood taken and prescriptions sorted, they drove to the youth services office. When they did, Leila was the first to jump out of the car, but before she could take another step, she crumpled.

"I'll grab your bag and then—"

In a flash, Jack was by her side. Sera was impressed by his speed, and before Leila had hit the pavement, he had her in his arms. One minute she had been standing, the next she had fainted. Scooping her up, Jack hurried up the path, waiting for Sera to open the glass panel door. They lay her down on the sofa of the waiting area, but even before they could step back, Leila was struggling to sit up.

"Stop, just stay back. I'll get you some water." Sera was ushered through by one of the receptionists.

When she came back, Leila was already protesting.

"I've low blood sugar. I'll be fine soon enough."

"You're six months pregnant and shouldn't be at the point of passing out. If anything, you need to be eating more often. Didn't you hear the doctor today?"

"Here." Jack reached into his jacket pocket and pulled out a packet of candy. "Chew on these. It helps."

Leila was hesitant at first, but then opened the packet. After a few minutes, she sat back and rubbed her belly.

"Feeling okay?"

"Better."

Sera encouraged her to drink. "I think I have some trail mix in my bag that you can eat. And then I'm taking you out for a three-course meal before we drop you home."

"Thanks. I won't argue with that. And Jack, these are alright."

"Plenty more where that came from, kid."

Sera looked at them both and had a moment grounded in reality. Not long ago she was living her life without any major hiccups or drama. Teaching at Woodbury High and her work with the South Row kids, coupled with helping Ally plan for the wedding, had kept her busy. Everything was smooth sailing, but not exactly remarkable.

Until now.

The past two weeks had been a whirlwind of activity. Jack's arrival, Leila's pregnancy...She was doing her best to keep up with it all.

Sera watched Jack open a second packet of candy and wordlessly hand it over to Leila. It seemed like she had blinked and all of a sudden her life was brimming, overflowing with colour and drama and, well, *life*.

Sera had always thought she had everything she ever wanted, that her life was fulfilling. But the past few weeks had made her realise there was a lot that was missing.

Sera wasn't quite sure what that meant, or what she would do about it.

CHAPTER THIRTEEN

*T*he drive to Leila's place the following morning was relatively quick. Sera's car was loaded with extra food she had cooked with her mum last night and her mind was clear.

Kind of.

The flashing cameras had blinded her as she backed out of the driveway. At one point, Sera thought she would be stuck in reverse. But when the hounds realised she was alone, they had slunk away, uninterested.

Jack's time was up.

She had sent him a quick text to forewarn him of the lurking paparazzi, ringing her mother on the landline for good measure.

She would deal with the wolves when she returned.

Given that Leila's parents were none the wiser about her pregnancy, Sera figured that a food drop would be a good enough excuse to stop by.

She had been relieved to hear that William, Leila's boyfriend, had been over the moon that he was going to be a young dad. He had insisted that they get back together, reassuring her that he wanted them to be a family. According to Leila, Will was going to pick up extra shifts so he could support them.

It never ceased to amaze her just how honourable some people could be. With that thought in mind, Sera knocked, juggling the heavy box of food in her hands. She didn't register the raised voices until after Leila's apartment door swung open.

"What the hell do you want?" A tall, heavy-set man opened the door, eyes angry. Sera jumped at his booming voice. She was certain all the neighbours could hear it.

Suddenly she felt foolish for coming alone.

"Who are you?" He bellowed.

"Leila?" Sera called out.

"I'm her father, what do you want?"

"Is Leila here? I'm her teacher, I'm dropping some food off."

The man's face was red hot. The veins in his neck were sticking out and saliva gathered at the corners of his mouth.

"We don't need your food." Leila's father spat.

"Miss D?"

Hearing Leila's voice, Sera rushed in, placing the box by the door.

"Leila?"

"Is this her?" he thundered.

"Bilal, please." A woman stood beside him, her eyes pleading, face lined with worry. She tried to restrain him but failed.

Sera crossed the small room to where Leila stood, trembling.

"I will not have this woman in our house! I will not have you, you *slut*!" He turned on his daughter.

"Bilal—"

"Shut up, Jena!"

"You, go pack your bags. You're no daughter to me. You understand?"

"I knew you didn't give a shit, but I don't care anymore. My boyfriend loves me which is more than you ever will."

"How dare you speak to me like that in my own house?"

"Some house! You're never here. I'm the one who has to do everything. Me and Mum, so don't think you're some big man who takes care of his family."

"This! This is what happens when you send her to public school. It's your fault!" he boomed, lunging at his wife.

"Don't fucking touch her!" Leila screeched, stepping in.

Sera launched herself between them just as Bilal struck out. She couldn't stop the first blow that glanced across her cheek, but she braced against the next one. It shocked her back into action.

"You need to get out of here, Leila." Sera helped her up off the floor.

"I have a bag. In my room." Leila cradled her stomach.

"Get to the stairwell. I'll follow."

She heard Jena's screams and scuttled across the room, only to pull up short at the small group of kids huddled inside the doorway. A little girl, no older than eleven, gathered the smaller children around her. Sera stalled. Taking a scrap of paper off the table, she scribbled her name and number for her.

"If you need me or Leila, call this number. We'll come."

Big brown eyes stared back at her and Sera's stomach churned. When the crash of the overturned chair reverberated through the apartment, she sprang to action. Grabbing the bag, she ran through the front door, heartsick and shaking.

As much as she wanted to whisk Leila to safety, she couldn't bear the thought of not doing anything for those trapped in that apartment. She knocked on the neighbour's door. It opened an inch. An older woman answered, eyes narrowed.

"I've already called the police, not that they do much, but I'm sick of him hollering at her so..."

"Thanks. I'll be calling them in a minute as well. There are little kids in there."

"I'll bring them over here and check up on her after."

"Thank you so much."

"About time she got away." She stepped out of her apartment now, nodding to Leila huddled at the top of the stairs. "Else she'd end up like us lot. She's smart that one, but mouthy."

"I'm giving you my number so you can reach us. In case the kids need to—"

"Best have a bit of space. Let the dust settle. I'll handle it." The woman shut the door, no doubt in an attempt to drown out Jena's screams and the ugly thudding sound of fist against flesh.

Sera's mouth was dry, her eye was beginning to ache from the glancing blow. She couldn't just walk away.

Torn, Sera ran down the corridor to Leila, taking her to the car. Once she had settled her inside, she ran back up the stairwell intent on rousing any neighbours she could. She spotted two guys, in their mid-twenties, about to enter their apartment a few floors below.

"Please," Sera pleaded. "You have to help us."

She didn't know if she was doing the right thing, but she couldn't think of anything else.

When Bilal opened the door, the two young men restrained him so that Sera could help Jena and the kids escape to their neighbour's apartment.

Before she left, Jena turned to her, face already bleeding and battered. Despite her bruises, her voice was calm.

"Take care of my girl and the baby. Please don't leave Leila alone right now."

"I promise. You have my word."

When Sera returned to the car, she called triple zero, adrenaline still coursing through her, leaving her jumpy and on edge.

She wasn't certain if she would need the police or the ambulance. She asked for both.

CHAPTER FOURTEEN

*S*he didn't know what the hell she was going to do. Because of the panic clawing at her throat, Sera focused on what was most pressing. Leila's wellbeing.

With that in mind, she drove straight to the doctor's office, grateful they were able to see Leila before they closed for the weekend. As it was a Saturday, her only other option would have been the hospital and given the wait times there, she thought it best for her to be seen immediately.

While Leila was being monitored, Sera stepped out, calling Maddie, then home. She needed some advice, and she didn't want to disturb Ally on her footy date with Owen.

She sent a message to Jack on the off chance he would have his phone close by. Realising it was almost lunchtime and given her parents' no phones at the table rule, it could be hours before she heard back.

Uncertain of what to do, and not wanting to take Leila to social services, Sera drove home. It was the only place she could think of where she could keep an eye on Leila, knowing she was safe and not on the streets, while coming up with a plan.

Over the years her parents often brought refugee families

home for a meal or a place to stay, so she was certain they would be able to help.

Sera stepped back inside the small consulting room and was grateful to hear that the baby had a steady heart rate and was not at all in distress. Leila on the other hand, was still visibly shaken.

While it was difficult for Leila to discuss her father's abuse, Sera noticed that once she did, the terrified expression in her eyes began to dissipate. She hated to think about how long she had endured such violence, without any hope for a better life.

Once Sera's face was examined to make sure there wasn't any serious damage to her eye or cheek, they were given the all-clear to leave.

Leila remained quiet and withdrawn on the ride home.

"Are you okay?"

"Now that the baby is fine, yeah. But I fucking hate my dad."

"I'm so sorry, Leila. You can stay at my folks' place until we get you back on your feet."

"I don't need charity."

"You need some support right now. It would make me comfortable knowing you're safe. I promised your mum I'd look out for you, so try to sit back and relax."

When Leila did, Sera realised she was probably more shaken up than she let on. An overwhelming surge of gratitude flowed through her. She was lucky she had not only supportive parents but a stable home. Even if she had fallen pregnant at a young age, she knew without a doubt her parents would have supported her.

Sera pulled up to the house then groaned. Paps. Lots of them.

"Head down," she instructed Leila, pressing the garage remote. She ignored the flashing lights and drove through, breathing a sigh of relief when the roller door closed behind them.

Jack was waiting.

"I guess I could count on you to check your phone." Sera stepped out of the car then circled to the trunk for her bag.

Despite all the chaos, Jack's quick grin did something to her insides.

"Got ya back, De Lotto. And sorry about the hounds out there."

"Not your fault." She slammed the trunk. "Well, not entirely."

"Ugh, it's him." Leila pulled a face as Sera helped her out of the car.

"Hello to you too, kid."

"Don't call me kid!"

"Okay, squirt."

Leila rolled her eyes.

Jack's smile froze in place. He stopped mid-step and the expression on his face made her stomach clench. His eyes were hot and hard, his voice, clipped.

"What the fuck...Who did this to you?"

"My dad," Leila replied first, hugging her bump.

Sera saw the confusion flit across his face. She shook her head and noticed it took a few more deep breaths and hand clenching for Jack to calm down.

"Are you both okay?"

"What do you think?"

"Stupid question, right." He turned to face Sera, fingers stroking the bruise along her cheek before disappearing. "You probably need ice on that."

"Let's go inside. Leila needs to sit down and get some food. We both do. Actually, could you take Leila to freshen up before lunch?"

Jack nodded, guiding her through to the house.

Sera took a moment to compose her nerves and glanced in the mirror in the hall. She sucked in a breath. Her eye and parts of her cheek were turning a lovely grape colour. She was only glad it happened now and not before the wedding.

The bastard had a meaty fist. And from the details Leila had passed on to the police, it seemed like he enjoyed using it if he wasn't obeyed. Which was a weekly occurrence.

Sera was relieved she was able to help her escape.

Lifting up her chin, she walked through to the kitchen and then to the dining room. The conversation at the table stopped short.

"Hey, Sera!" Charlie called out.

"Sorry, I didn't think I'd be out so long."

"We've just sat down for lunch." Tony answered, placing the bread on the table. "We were lucky to have Charlie join us." The smile froze in place when he glanced up at her. "Seraphina, what happened?"

"Honey, are you okay?" Her mother was by her side in an instant, her father not far behind.

"It looks worse than what it is."

She quickly relayed an abridged version of what happened, mindful that Charlie was listening.

Jack returned with Leila in tow, who glanced at her parents from lowered lashes, fidgeting with her oversized T-shirt.

For all her bravado, Leila looked nervous. She noticed that the curve in her belly was prominent now. A presence in the room. A little baby.

Her mother, ever the hostess, sprang into action.

"Mum, this is Leila."

"You must be hungry. Let me get you a plate."

"I could eat."

"And for two now, so you must keep up your strength."

Sera pulled up a chair squeezing her mother's arm. "Thank you."

"Get the poor girl settled. We can talk later," she murmured.

"She'll be staying. For the night at least. Probably more."

"I'll make up the spare bed. You just see she's comfortable."

She pecked her mother on the cheek and sat beside the young girl who seemed happy enough to be served.

Sera's heart was still heavy, but she hoped that this would be the start of something bright: a new life for Leila and her unborn baby.

Everyone was in a post food coma. The football was on the television and Leila was taking a nap on the sofa. The house was filled with noises, but unlike the scene she had stepped into earlier this morning, there was no tension. No violence.

At the urgent peal of the doorbell, Sera ushered Maddie in, surprised that the paps were still hovering at the gate. As usual, her friend was blunt and to the point.

"Please tell me you're kidding, De Lotto."

"Why would I be?"

"Because this is madness. And I'm not just referring to the crazy photographers out front."

They settled themselves on the beanbags in the lounge room, far enough away from where Jack and her father were seated with Charlie. They didn't want to be overheard.

"Coffee?"

"That's not why I'm here, so quit stalling and tell me what in the world are you doing bringing a pregnant teenager to your parents' house? That's what child services are for."

"Her parents kicked her out."

"That's not your concern."

"It is when they gave me this." She gestured to her face. "Maddie, I'm the only person she has."

"But you're crossing boundaries. Look, I'm the first one to

say screw the rules, but there are protocols about this stuff and I don't want you to get into a situation where you find yourself really attached to her and get heartbroken because you can't do anything about it."

Sera ignored Maddie's pointed look. She wouldn't think about that now. She couldn't bear it.

"But don't you see, I *can* do something. If I don't, she'll end up on the street, pregnant and alone."

"What about her boyfriend?"

"She's just gotten back together with him, and while he's hoping to support them, I can't just assume that they'll be living together. They're only teenagers."

"So for now, you're playing Miss Hannigan?"

"Yes. No. Wait, didn't she hate children?"

"She adopted orphans. Not dissimilar to your current situation." Maddie flicked her head to where Jack was nursing a drink across the room.

"Jack is hardly an orphan."

"He kinda is. Losing his parents at a young age. Living with Owen. Fleeing to the States...Orphans baby, you've got a thing for them. The need to save the needy. This isn't the first time I've told you this."

Sera frowned. "I just don't see it that way."

Maddie squeezed her eyes shut. "I don't mean to be hard on you. Sorry, I'm crabby and I'm being an asshole. You're doing a great thing, Sera. If it weren't for you and your mum, all those families, and those kids, would go without."

"I know it's not that simple, and I get what you're saying, Madds, but there's something about this kid."

"Just be careful. I don't want to see you get hurt again."

Sera hunched over, picking at the threads in the carpet rug. "Elijah was different."

Maddie rubbed at her back. "You say that about each of them. Ally is in coordination, chat to her about it. Get in touch with some student welfare counsellors so you're informed. Even though she doesn't go to Woodbury, it's probably easier for you to facilitate some mental health support and all the other things she'll need as a pregnant teen without her family."

"Since when did you become the responsible one?"

"Gotta grow up some time. Maybe. Speaking of which, what's it like having Jack here after that smokin' kiss?"

"Heated to say the least. But beyond that, and I know this is going to sound like bullshit, but it feels weirdly normal having Jack around. It's like we're in this little bubble. He's so removed from his life in L.A. which is probably a good thing given the state of his mental health."

"Which worries you."

Sera rolled her shoulders. "I guess I'm just waiting for the bubble to burst."

"And you're afraid that when the time comes, he'll just up and leave like the last time."

"Isn't that inevitable? He can't live in my parents' house forever. It's like housing a really interesting fugitive. Now the paps are lurking about, pretending that there would be any other outcome is just foolish."

"And hard." Maddie brushed a hand down Sera's arm, offering her support.

"It is. And isn't in some ways. I'm trying not to think ahead. But his life is in America, not here." She drew her legs close to her chest. "And in the effort of full disclosure, can I say it's nice to have a man like him look at me the way he does? Even though I know he'll leave again, I find myself enjoying spending time with him."

"There's history there. You gotta respect that. Beneath all that sizzling attraction, I can see you're still friends, which makes what you share run a little deeper. Which means you need to look out for yourself. Protect yourself."

"I will."

She would do well to remember that it was a temporary thing. She couldn't afford to let those feelings she once felt resurface. Jack would be gone after the wedding. They could continue to enjoy one another's company until then.

"I've hounded you enough for one afternoon. You look worn out, De Lotto. And I bet that cheek of yours could do with a rest. And some frozen peas."

Sera winced; the throbbing was working through the layers of painkillers.

"Better me than her."

"Better no one. Bastard."

Sera smiled and then regretted it. An hour later, she said goodbye to Maddie then wandered out the back for some fresh air. She needed a breather and welcomed the biting breeze on her skin.

She'd check on Leila before going to bed, but she was certain the girl just wanted to be left alone to rest. It had been an exhausting day for everyone.

Sera rubbed at her arms. What would it be like to have that unwavering support from a young age? She knew her parents had married young, but in her head, she always saw that as a product of their time. Not necessarily something people still did now. Yet here she was, helping a sixteen-year-old through her pregnancy and marvelling at the support she had from her nearly eighteen-year-old boyfriend.

'When you know, you know,' her mother had said. But having that much faith, that much unwavering belief in another person so young was mind boggling. Even if a little impressive.

A whisper of the past caught her attention. She had once been young and in love. She had, she admitted with a bitter-sweet tug at her heart, been ready to give it all up for Jack.

Had Jack not gone to America, would their relationship have taken the next step?

But he didn't choose her. Jack had left, to pursue his career, his own life.

It hurt knowing she hadn't been enough.

Realistically speaking, it shouldn't be difficult. Seeing someone again after a decade shouldn't shake her foundations. What did they know about one another? They were strangers. Two people who once shared something, but for most of their adult life—the good, formative parts which made up who they were—their values, world views, hell, sexual appetites, were all shaped independently of one another. And even though they shared something years ago, they lived in complete opposition to one another now.

Jack's life was the stuff of fantasies, whilst Sera was ridiculously pragmatic. Her life dealt with the very basics of what it was to exist by restrictions—of money, class, education. She was surrounded by students and teachers caught in their own realities, unable to escape them.

Jack would realise this too.

Maybe not just yet, but by the time Ally and Owen got married, Jack would have figured out what he wanted from life, and he would return to L.A. without a second glance. No, that wasn't fair. He might feel a twinge of something, but it wouldn't be big enough for him to shift, to change his life completely.

Sera shook off the thought. She wouldn't want him to anyway.

He'd figure out soon enough that life down under was a temporary Band Aid on an open wound. It would take time for him to heal. But once he did, he would be gone.

Empty dreams. That's all they were.

So she would keep it light and temporary. Like Maddie said, she'd just be on her guard in the meantime. She couldn't risk falling for him twice.

Feeling a little more grounded, Sera meandered up the path and back inside.

Jack caught her on the stairs.

Even though he made acting his career, in her mind, Jack was the most genuine and sincere person she had ever met. Yeah, he tried to cover it with sarcasm and charm, but she could somehow always see behind the façade. Just as she could spot his concern now.

"How are you?" His thumb flittered over her bruise at the corner of her eye. It blossomed all the way down her cheek.

"I won't be winning Miss Australia any time soon, but I'll be fine."

"I meant here." He tapped at her chest, a gentle questioning.

Oh yes, it was best she kept those feet firmly on the ground lest she be swept away by the fantasy of him.

Sera so desperately wanted Jack to be the asshole A-list actor without a conscience. That would be so much easier than the reality. But Jack was not an easy man. She was beginning to realise that it was all the complexities of his character that drew her in; he was compelling. Dangerously so.

"I'm a little shaken up but I'm feeling much better knowing she's safe. For now, that's good enough."

"If you need me, you know where to find me."

"Thanks, Jack."

Even though a part of her wanted to reach out, she turned and climbed the stairs alone. There was too much brewing inside her this evening. She wouldn't trust herself with it. Not yet.

CHAPTER FIFTEEN

*J*ack was well and truly screwed.

Since his appearance at Woodbury High, the paps had been following him, circling like sharks, waiting for the time to strike.

He tweaked the blinds and cursed. They were perched on the pavement outside and it wasn't even 9 a.m.

Images of him carrying Leila were plastered all over social media. It was taken three days ago, when he had accompanied Sera to the appointment at social services.

Leila had fainted and the paps had chosen just the right moment to snap up pictures. There were dozens more of Sera, too.

"Love Triangle Lures Hollywood Star Home."

Bastards had been sitting on those pictures waiting to build more ammunition, taking bits and pieces of the past few days to concoct some salacious story.

Christ, he couldn't make up this shit even if he tried. He read the fluff pieces, and whilst a part of him wanted to laugh at the absurdity of it, he also felt sick in his gut. Speculation that Jack had cut out of a big budget film not because of his 'psychotic breakdown' but because his underage lover was pregnant left him cold and clammy.

As if on cue, his phone cried out. He considered letting it go to voicemail but knew it would only piss off Taylor even more. He was tired of hiding.

"Is there something you want to tell me, J.D.?"

He noted the thinly veiled tension in his voice. He was beyond angry. Fucking gossip magazines.

"You sound extra pissed off today. I wonder why?"

"That's rich coming from someone who won't have an agent by the end of this phone call. You'll be a has-been if you don't tread carefully, J.D."

"Better if I was a 'never was,'" he muttered.

"What the fuck are you playing at knocking up an underage kid, for fuck's sake? Do you know the shit I've had to field, as has your publicist? J.D., you better get it—"

"It's not true."

Jack heard his manager take a few quick puffs. He could picture him dragging on his cig and squeezing the bridge of his nose in tandem.

"If it is, we can—"

"Stop. Take a deep breath. It isn't true. She's a welfare kid that a friend of mine is taking care of. She has a loving boyfriend and a life that has nothing to do with mine. The paps are in on this and are out for blood."

"So are the studio execs. Jack, why the fuck aren't you here?"

"I told you. I needed to sort out some things."

"Not half-way through filming! You've been gone for over two weeks!"

"I'm going to handle it."

"This is handling it? Sticking your head in the sand?"

"Yes."

"You're going to get sued, I'm going to get sued, and I will not go down on this sinking ship."

"You jump, I jump?"

"This is not a fucking joke!" Taylor shrieked.

Jack winced, jerking the phone away from his ear.

"I'm sorry, Taylor. I am. But I'm trying to work through some heavy stuff right now. I'm not okay."

"I told you two weeks ago I don't give a shit if you lost your marbles on set. Everybody goes through shit, J.D. What I want to hear is that you're going to finish this fucking film."

"I'm going to contact them after I speak to you, to buy us some time."

"Look, you're fucking lucky that they haven't pulled production. The crew have been pleading your case, and they're filming everything else they can, thinking you'll be back. If you're worried about losing face, don't. They just want you on set. We'll deal with the fallout of this later."

"I will. Just...I need some time."

"Fuck you, J.D. Get back here before I have your balls for breakfast."

"You'd like that, wouldn't you?"

The line went dead, and a second later, anxiety crept in. When all the bravado was gone, he found himself hollowed out. Empty.

Taylor had always been a hard-ass agent. But for the past few years his agent's patience was wearing thin. His manner was abrupt, his chain-smoking out of control.

Or maybe it was Jack's tolerance for it all that had diminished?

Like an inch of light through an opened door, the answer peeked through.

The sliver of clarity, the one clear thought that rang through his chaotic mind surprised him. The answer was becoming clearer with every passing day. At first it had been a whisper, easy to drown out, to ignore. But it came to him so often now, he knew it had to mean something.

The problem was, he was terrified of the repercussions.

Jack Davies, Hollywood A-lister and mega millionaire, was ready to throw in the towel. To quit. To never fucking go back to acting ever again.

Funny thing was, he should have felt worse for it, but he was oddly numb. Would this bring him peace?

Jack didn't have those answers. Living in this half-state was driving him insane. He was rooted to the ground, immobilised by his fears, but he craved action. A change.

Taylor was right. He needed to sort through this shit, or he'd be in an even worse position than when he left.

He just didn't know where the hell to start.

CHAPTER SIXTEEN

*J*ack was itching to get out of the house and surround himself by nature. When Sera arrived home after work, it hadn't taken much to convince her to come with him. The conversation with Taylor earlier that morning had left him rattled.

He tried to ignore the paps that hounded them, desperate for a picture and managed to lose them half-way through their journey. He thanked the road accident and his skillful driving for that one.

They drove for a while up the mountain in silence, letting the late-afternoon light warm them both.

When they took the first bend up, climbing through the winding foliage and dense forest, Jack breathed out. But it wasn't until they had picked a walking trail that they spoke in earnest.

"You told them, didn't you?" Jack looked at Sera, dark hair framed by a halo of sunlight. His heart twisted.

"Only the bare essentials."

"Your folks are trying to convince me to stay."

Sera nodded, as if it made sense. "Why not stay, Jack?"

He adjusted his baseball cap, taking a deep breath. The fresh mountain air, the muted sounds of nature, calmed him. "You saw the circus outside your front door. The crazy stunts they pull on the road. I can't hang around like a bad smell, I'd only be bringing trouble to you and your family."

Sera stepped over a fallen branch, careful in her movements. "A bit late for that, Jack. Paps know where we live, it's silly to just isolate yourself out of principle. Look, for what it's worth, I agree with them. Stay, for as long as you need. Being surrounded by friends and family is a good thing right now."

"Afraid I'll do something rash? Offer an exclusive to the hounds?"

"I'm concerned for you, yes. We all are, Jack."

Just like that she could cut through to the heart of him. He couldn't pretend. His instinctive method of shrugging it all off, down-playing what was important, wasn't working for him anymore. It was all wearing so very thin.

"I fucked up, Sera." He kicked at a rock but continued walking. He needed to move.

"Okay."

"You haven't read the latest gossip?"

"Not really. Not with everything going on, so why don't you tell me."

"They think I fathered Leila's baby!"

"What? That's ridiculous!"

"Taylor, my agent, called. He's having a heart attack and I'll probably be sued by the studio or some shit and I've never done this before in my life and I think—" Jack wheezed. "Not again."

"Okay, I'm right here. Breathe in and out. Focus on that."

Jack flicked the dark band at his wrist, taking in deep breaths.

He focused on the trees, on Sera's voice, on all the sensory things that grounded him. Eventually the pressure eased enough for him to be able to speak.

But he was jittery still. His body was on red alert as if some threat was lurking behind every bush and shrub. He was fucking sick of it.

"This." He gestured.

"This what?"

"This isn't getting better. Just the thought of my job sends me in a spin. Sera, the truth is...I can't believe I'm saying this aloud, but I'm not sure if I want to keep doing this anymore."

"What? Acting?"

"Yes. Acting and everything that comes with it. Endorsements and appearances and interviews...I'm tired of it. And I think I want out."

"Wow." Sera nodded, seeming to process everything. "That's pretty big."

"Yep."

"Maybe this is a good break away?"

"I can't afford a break away. Not monetarily afford, but contractually. I've been fucking around like there isn't a problem when there is, a big one. I need to go back, to make things right and finish this fucking film. And then...then I can take a break."

Sera nodded, bumping his shoulder. "Are you in the right frame of mind to go back, Jack?"

"No. But I'm an actor. I can pretend I'm happy, smother those feelings with a grin, a bit of banter."

Sera's pointed look suggested his little act hadn't fooled her in the slightest. But then again, she was always one to see through his bullshit.

"I think you need to get real, Jack. Acting your way through it isn't going to help. Give yourself a bit of grace."

"I have. Over two weeks of it."

Sera frowned, displeased with his response. "What would happen if you didn't go back?"

"I don't really know, but there'll be fines and lawyers and basically a shit storm of a headache which I'm trying to avoid right now."

"I think you know the answer then."

Jack sighed, the weight of it crushing his spirit. "I'm struggling to accept it."

"You need to go back, but you can't the way you are, so I think you need help before you do. We'll get you the help so you can."

"Sera, what if this keeps happening?" Nothing had worked so far. What if he was stuck like this forever?

She squeezed his arm and in her eyes was an assurance that gave him hope. "We'll work through this, Jack."

He clung to her strength, to her support. Maybe he could get through this. With her at his side. He sure as hell didn't think he could do it alone.

"At least getting therapy might help you manage the panic attacks, so it doesn't get so bad. And if it means getting you back to L.A. so you can finish filming, then we'll do it. Whatever comes afterwards is something you can figure out."

They reached one of the summits, a clearing that overlooked the deep valley of trees. The only sounds they could hear came from themselves and rustling trees around them.

"Sera." He turned to her now. Unable to stop himself, Jack drew her close. "Hell of a view."

Her eyes grew wary. "Is this really wise?"

"I know my head is all over the place. And it's the worst possible timing to be starting anything..."

"But?"

Jack ran his hands up her back, then cupped her face, drawing her closer.

"But I'm not a man to play by the rules."

"Is that in general or just right now?"

"Where you're concerned, always."

"The thing is, Jack. I've spent my whole life abiding by them."

"Can I tempt you to bend those rules? To let go?"

He could see the desire lurking behind her hazel eyes. He wanted to give her the chance to unlock that, to free herself of the rules and regulations she lived by.

"I can't keep my hands off you." He ran his thumb over her mouth. Her lips were soft, beckoning. "I can't stop thinking about you." He brushed his lips over hers. "But mostly, Sera, I want to be inside you."

Her soft gasp floated between them, a tantalising response.

What was it she wanted? What did she crave more than anything? Jack wanted to give it to her, and more.

He was beginning to realise that it wasn't just about him anymore.

"But I'm not the only one standing on this mountain. So tell me, how do you feel about starting something, with me?"

Sera blinked, seemingly startled by his suggestion. "Scared."

"Understandable."

"Aroused."

"Also, *very* understandable."

She laughed, swatting at him.

He didn't hear her laugh very often. It struck him then that it was a part of their relationship that he had enjoyed all those years ago.

He wanted to please her. Pleasure her. To figure out what made her happy. It scared and thrilled him in equal measure.

"What do you need, right now, from me?"

She took her time replying. "To be open. Honest. Don't hide behind that Hollywood cool anymore, Jack."

He nodded. "Understood. Anything else?"

"You can be sure I'll tell you where and how hard, when the

time comes." Her mouth, soft and red curled in wicked temptation.

The blood pumped through his body, and Jack never felt more alive.

The past and future seemed not to matter when he was with her. Who he was, the persona he had spent years cultivating, seemed to crumble. It was like Hollywood didn't exist; acting was a thing he did in another world. When he was with Sera, he was Jack. Just plain old Jack.

He wanted that more than ever.

"Are we really doing this?" Sera asked.

"You tell me, De Lotto. If you want this, if you want me, then you can have me. I don't know what's going on tomorrow and my life is a hell of a mess but—"

She pulled him in, driving out his fear.

He jerked back. "Wait. That means a yes, right? I don't want to assume and then—"

"Yes. I'm bending those rules, Jack. Now shut up and kiss me."

He grinned then yanked her body against his.

She was small and firm and everything he needed right now. She tasted of cinnamon, of fresh spring mornings and hope. Since he met her, she was his strength, his compass. She grounded him in a way nobody else did.

Fuck. Whether it was nostalgia, a mistake, or something else, he just wanted to ride it. To give himself to her as much as his fucked-up self could and see wherever the hell it took them.

He held on tight, thanking whatever company it was that made her workout gear. It clung to her like a second skin, and he was appreciative of every curve and line of her body.

He took the kiss deeper, taking her past the edges of sweet and into the pool of sinful desire.

If he went much further, they would find themselves rolling around on the top of the mountain.

Even though it was tempting, he didn't think it would be quite as comfortable to have sex with sticks up their asses. It wasn't the kind of kink he was into. He didn't think she would be either.

But beneath it all, Jack wanted to treat her right. To prove he wasn't just a Hollywood screw up.

With a final squeeze, Jack broke the kiss, taking a few moments to appreciate the thrumming in his blood, the heightened passion she had stirred.

He wanted to drive her a little crazy, to send them both hurtling through the depths of desire until they were lost in their own black hole of need.

"Let's do this properly, Sera."

"I thought that was a great start."

"Great?"

"A brilliant start."

"That's better."

"I suppose you've had lots of practice," she teased. "A leading man and all."

"You can be my leading lady."

"Can I, Jack?"

His heart tugged. Regret was a rolling rain cloud dampening his happiness.

"I'm not the same boy you once dated."

"But he's in there somewhere, Jack. And this time you need to listen to him."

"Sera, I can't promise anything but the here and now. I can't—"

"Don't. Let's not talk about tomorrows, or what this will mean. We've done this once before. I'm going into this with my eyes wide open this time."

Why did it hurt so much to hear her say it? Beneath her passion was a pragmatism that irked him.

Of course she wouldn't throw caution to the wind. She'd

done that a decade ago and he had failed her. It shouldn't offend him that she wouldn't do it again...

If Sera had her guard up, then it was because of him. Jack would deal with it as best he could, and hope it was enough for them both. "To new beginnings."

CHAPTER SEVENTEEN

"*I* said, I'm going to annihilate your ass." Jack chortled with glee.

Gaming with his teenage niece was exactly what he needed for a few hours to relax and forget his problems.

Teenager. Huh. When the hell did that happen?

"Ugh, you sound just like Jasper." Charlie frowned, frantically mashing on the buttons of her controller.

"Ooh, your *boyfriend*, Jasper?"

"Ew. No."

But Jack noticed her cheeks had turned pink.

"Charlie has a boyfriend," he teased.

"I do not!" she squealed.

Jack chuckled maniacally. He missed hanging out with her. Missed having the easy company of family. There was no hidden agenda, no ulterior motive. Charlie loved hanging out with him, not because he sent her awesome birthday presents every year (coz he did) or because he let her eat junk before dinner (coz he did that, too). But according to Charlie, he was fun to hang out with because he was Jack: a good listener and an awesome not-old guy, who didn't lecture her about stuff. She liked him, just because.

Jack held that admission from her close to his chest. He'd take that warm feeling with him to the grave.

They were playing video games and eating junk from the pantry before dinner.

Jack was in heaven.

The paps had been relentless, so Jack figured it was better to hole up indoors and eat candy and popcorn, while trying to beat up on each other in vintage Mortal Kombat, rather than panic.

He needed a breather after the tough calls he made to the director and a few of his fellow cast members. He would be swimming in shit when he returned but at least they actually wanted him back on set. That was good. Sort of.

"Jack Davies, I'm going to kill you!" Ally hollered from the kitchen.

"Uh oh. Mum's going to go ape shit."

"You can't have candy and popcorn before dinner, Jack. Those are the rules." Ally stood in front of them.

"Rules shmules."

Ally's glare could have turned him to stone. "Outside, gamer-boy. You can help Owen grill."

"But—"

"And you, homework." Ally turned on Charlie.

"Muuuum."

"It's a school night. Don't make me switch off that game."

"Geez, take it easy." Jack scowled then turned to Charlie. "I'll ruin you after dinner."

She bumped fists with him. "Deal."

He spared one last, mournful glance at the big screen TV, before heading out back. He found Owen cleaning the barbeque.

"Mate, I feel it's my duty to tell you that you're marrying a very scary woman."

"I heard that."

"Jesus!" Jack clutched his heart.

"Skewers for roasting." Ally handed Owen the tray.

"Consider me roasted," Jack grumbled. "You know, if you weren't so nice and pretty and make the best brownies known to man, I'd be convincing my brother to run for the hills."

"Is that so?"

"Yep, coz then I'd marry you." He grinned, crossing his arms.

Ally smirked. "Get grilling. Now, Romeo."

"Yes, ma'am." Jack saluted, then bumped his brother's shoulder. "She's a real firecracker."

"She'd roast you alive."

"No doubt about it."

"Speaking of women..."

"Here we go."

"You and Sera De Lotto?"

Jack's heart did a merry jig at the mention of her name. "What about it?"

"Just wanted to know how long you'd be hanging around for, Jack. You're not known for your prolonged vacations."

"Why are you grilling me about this?"

Owen held up his hands. "I'm not. I'm just asking. You and Sera have history."

"We do. Not that it's your business."

"Defensive, much?" Owen got the grill going, sipping at his bottle of cider.

"Alright, I'm listening." Jack knew that look. Standing beside his brother who appeared ready to burst was worse than listening to what he had to say.

"What? I'm not saying anything."

"But you're filling the silence with a lot of energy and it's pissing me off."

Owen gestured with his tongs. "I'll only say this once, little brother. Tread carefully. You and Sera may have had something going on in the past, but that was when you were a hell of a lot younger, with a ton less baggage. I know you've been avoiding talking to me about your actual problems, and I've respected that, but when it comes to starting something with Sera, I just want to make sure you've got your head on straight."

"She has a father and three older brothers for that talk."

"Ahh, but Tony doesn't know you like I do."

"What the hell? You're making me out to be some kind of monster."

"I'm just saying, you're not always around. That makes it hard to have a relationship."

"And if we break up, it'll screw up the friendship dynamic you've all got going on."

Owen shrugged. "That's not the point. You'll have Ally and Maddie to deal with."

The thought of those women on his case was enough to have him reaching for the other bottle of cider. He cracked it open and took a long, deep, cleansing drink. He was parched.

"I'm not trying to be a party pooper, but I know that sometimes acting in the 'now' isn't always the wisest choice."

Jack felt the sting, even though it was kindly meant. Leaving L.A. on the back of a mental breakdown hadn't turned out to be so very wise either.

But ever since his parents' death, he had lived fast and loose. Reckless. It had been better for all if he wasn't relied upon for the important stuff. Which had been all well and good. Until now.

Being with Sera made him want the thing that he feared most. The one thing he didn't deserve.

Owen nudged his shoulder. "You're both adults, so whatever you do, I'm here to help you. But I will say this, you left her once, Jack. What's to say you won't do it again?"

Jack felt the sharp blow, and instead of deflecting it, he let it land right where it hurt the most. His heart.

He had left Sera because he hadn't been able to handle it. To be the man she would need to make a relationship work.

Dependable. Reliable. Responsible.

And didn't that make him a piece of shit?

"Gotta say, that one hurt."

"I'm sorry, I had to say it. I want you to be happy but you've a lot of work to do to get there. I know that whatever you're going through is big, so that's why I'm saying it."

"It is, and part of me isn't even sure I know what to do about it. But Owen, Christ, my mental health is shot to shit. I couldn't hack it being there anymore. But Sera...she seems to get it. Oddly enough."

"Seeing a therapist yet?"

"Now you sound like Sera."

"Therapy works. Eventually. It's a long game, and with the right person, it's gold. I know I've been really against it in the past, but as you get older, things change." He spaced the patties out then looked at Jack, square in the eye. "Something tells me you're ready for that change."

"I am." Even though they were alone, Jack leaned in, lowering his voice to just above a whisper. "Owen...I don't want to do this anymore."

"What?"

"Any of it." It still felt like a dirty secret, like a betrayal to say it aloud. Like someone would overhear and try to shove him back in his place, in his cage.

Jack explained his conversation with Sera.

Owen stared at him, nodding, taking it in. "That's big. Christ, Jack, that's huge. You're the hottest actor on the scene right now. Just last year you told me all the scripts you were considering."

"That was then."

Back when he was still in denial about his life. His choices.

But he had chased his dreams in honour of his father's memory. He had proved to him that he was worth something. It was bittersweet that his father wasn't around to enjoy it.

"So you've a lot to think about."

"Yeah, I do."

"We're here. Whatever you need, just ask."

"Thanks, Owen." Jack clapped his brother on the back and tried to figure out what he would do next. He hated being trapped, feeling like he had no way out, no safe place.

Then Sera's face swam before him. And he clung to it. Clung to her faith in him, her desire to start something without knowing where it would lead.

How could he ask someone to have that kind of faith in him, when he didn't even have it in himself? Jack rubbed his face, trying to shift the guilt.

He was sick in the stomach and yet oddly excited by what the future had in store. Not that he could think too far ahead. Maybe one day the very thought of putting down roots wouldn't terrify him so much. But right now, all he wanted was a bit of peace. To rid himself of the pressure, the constant gut-churning dissatisfaction that followed him around everywhere.

No, he couldn't think too far ahead. Who knew what else was coming around the corner? Best to enjoy what he had now and hope like hell it turned out right in the end.

It was a surreal feeling having her picture taken wherever she went.

Sera became wary of every stranger, jumping if someone

veered in front of her, scared that it was another pesky reporter or sneaky paparazzo. When she was with Leila, she was even more protective, unwilling to take her out unless it was strictly necessary.

The last thing Leila needed was more stress after the incident with her parents. Not that they had spoken about it much since it happened. Leila was happy to stay with Sera and her parents for the time being until she came up with a plan. She begrudgingly accepted Jack was a part of the household too. Though they seemed to be getting along a bit better now.

Sera only wished that they weren't constantly on alert every time they left the house. Every step they took was fodder for more gossip magazines.

The headlines kept shifting according to their whims.

"Love Triangle Betrayal" with pictures of her and Jack out at the park was the latest headline. It had only been a week since her conversation with Jack on the mountain, but so much had changed.

Of course, all her senior students wanted to talk to her about her love-life and the Hollywood hunk she was dating.

Wherever she went, it was Jack this and Jack that. It was humorous and exhausting in equal measure.

Sera stretched out her back and resigned herself to getting more paint on her legs. She had promised Maddie she would help with the set designs after school. Which would be fine, if Maddie wasn't acting like a sergeant major to anyone who was in her way.

No doubt the presence of Gabriel was adding to the tension. He was huddled over some carboard signs, his pristine white shirt rolled up, and a hammer and nails in his hands. He looked both out of place and oddly at home.

Jack had offered to come along but given that the principal had spoken to her only this morning about all the press she was attracting, Sera thought it best that he stay out of sight.

The last thing they needed was more attention in the media.

Ally shifted closer. "If Maddie gets any angrier, I think she'll explode."

"Is that even possible?"

Ally shrugged. "When it comes to Gabriel, she has a short fuse."

"Don't even mention that name to her."

"Mention what name?"

Sera and Ally jumped.

"Uhh."

"Nobody."

Maddie narrowed her eyes. "If you're talking about that insufferable man crouched over there then yes, don't even mention his name." Maddie stomped off to deal with a carboard car crisis.

"Okay, so we need a girl's night for all that stress." Ally motioned with her paint brush.

"I'm totally up for that."

"What happened with Jacinta this morning? Was it bad?"

Sera dipped her brush in red paint. "A dressing down from our principal is never a pleasant thing. Not as bad as it could have been. But there was mention of taking time off if the paps began interfering in school life."

"Ouch. Been there."

"Yep. I spoke to her about Leila, because it's everywhere, and she wasn't happy that I was getting involved."

"But Leila isn't enrolled here, so technically she can't discipline you for that."

"True. But all the paps following me and lurking around the school...you know what she's like."

"A bear."

"In the best sense. The seniors are heading into exam prep, so she wants them to stay focused. She's got the kids' back."

"And who has yours?" Ally's green eyes were soft, but her question was a direct arrow through her heart.

"I've got a lot of support, you know that."

"I meant with all the press attention. It's not easy to suddenly be catapulted into fame. You're dating an A-list Hollywood actor, honey. I know he's just good ol' Jack to you, but to the rest of the world, he's a celebrity."

"I haven't really thought about it."

"Well do. You're juggling a lot, and the paps will use anything to sell pictures and stories."

"Did I tell you that Leila asked Jack if she could do an exclusive with them for money?"

Ally's mouth opened in shock. "What? The cheek."

"She did it to goad him."

"And I bet he ate it up. How is she?"

"It's been a crazy few weeks, Al. I think she's adjusting to being with my folks pretty well, considering. I'm trying to get some support from social services though."

"Go through the names I gave you and see if they can see you sooner. I don't mean to be a downer, but things with them are a nightmare at the moment. A lot of kids fell through the cracks over winter, and they're playing catch up."

"Don't tell me that." She had hoped that Ally's work as a coordinator would mean she'd be able to speed up the process. But as Leila wasn't enrolled in their school, everything was harder.

"I wish we could do more, but she's in a totally different zone, and as she's technically a middle school student, nearly a senior at the city school, and that means the urgency tends to decrease."

"Great."

"Like I said, she's expecting, so it might work in her favour."

"I just don't want her to be placed in some foster home when she can just stay with us."

"What's she wanting to do?"

"Get a job, never speak to her family again. The usual."

Ally dipped her brush in the pot. She was painting a large tree. She had green on her slacks and her blouse already, not that Ally was one to mind that sort of thing. She may have grown up wealthy, but Ally McVeigh was the most down to earth person she knew.

"Trust me, Sera, whilst I can understand the sentiment, running away never solved anything."

"William is trying to support her as much as he can but it's hard as he's not yet eighteen and is still living with his mother."

"Owen was about that age when Rebecca told him she was pregnant with Charlie. That shook his world. He said when his parents died it was even more pressure to do it alone. Now that Leila doesn't have a home, I can't imagine how she feels. She might hate her family, but never seeing them again is a big decision for a sixteen-year-old to make."

"The funny thing is, Leila just keeps going. Her resilience is amazing."

"She'd have had no soft place to land if it weren't for your support."

"Don't make me cry into this bucket of paint."

Ally swirled more on her brush. "Just saying it as it is. The work you do for the South Row kids is life-changing, Sera."

"That reminds me, I wanted to thank you for helping out this Sunday."

"Any time. Charlie and I enjoy baking and wanted to try out a few recipes. I think it'll be good to have Jack see what you do as well."

"Really?" Sera stood back to admire her painting. It was shoddy at best. "Why?"

"I think it'll give him a different perspective, that's all."

Sera cocked her head. "Well, I'm no Picasso."

"At least yours *looks* like a stop sign. My tree looks like someone was trying to massacre it."

Sera laughed and immediately regretted it. Her cheek was still a little stiff, but the bruises were beginning to fade.

"What are you giggling about?" Maddie barked. "Back to work!"

Sera rolled her eyes. "Yes, slave master!"

The sooner Maddie sorted out this thing with Gabriel, the better.

CHAPTER EIGHTEEN

*I*t took a lot to impress Jack Davies.

After travelling the world, being invited to exclusive parties and one-of-a-kind destinations, it wasn't very often that Jack found himself in awe.

But as he watched Sera teaching other people's children—on a Sunday no less—he was more than just impressed, he was proud.

And it wasn't just the time she spent teaching and listening to them, it was all the preparation in the lead up to their sessions every week. She kept a mental tab on all the students, knowing when to push and when to back off.

She was brilliant.

And Jack was man enough to admit, he was smitten.

It astonished him how many of the kids actually showed up to the small, dilapidated study room at the local library for a session with her.

How many of them were even attending regular school?

How many of them would have received a birthday cake and treats like Khalid did today? He'd have to tell Charlie her cookies were a hit.

When the session was over, and the kids were out at the basketball courts, Jack helped Sera pack up, loading her car.

He had tried his best to ignore the paps in the distance. But when they hovered closer, trying to talk to the kids, he stepped in, promising a photo opportunity when he was ready. Not that it really made much of a difference.

"So what happens to them when you're on summer break?" Jack watched the kids play basketball, enjoying the sliver of warm, afternoon sun. The warmer spring weather was just around the corner. And while he wanted to bask in it, it was just a reminder of how little time he had left. Mid-October already...It didn't bear thinking about.

"Many of them will stay put or get summer jobs if they can. Some get into more trouble. Christmas is hard for them, so we try to do an end of year event for the kids and their families."

"It was thoughtful giving the Khalid a cake today."

"They don't really get anything nice, so if I can at least help the kids who come to class, it's worth it. For some, their friends are their family. For others, they find connection through gangs."

Jack rubbed her shoulder. "That's not something on you. Not your responsibility."

"I disagree."

"You do more than anyone expects. The schools should be responsible for these kids."

"A lot of the time they don't want to deal with them. I'm trying to work with their schools to count the sessions they do here as part of their attendance record."

"What did they say?"

"Whatever those kids do outside of school hours isn't their business."

"What?"

"Yep. You've gotta understand, most of these teachers are

fed up with having to chase the kid to come to class, let alone to get any work done."

"So what, they fail?"

"If only it were that easy. The school can't technically keep the kid down if the parents don't consent."

"Let me guess, the parents don't consent."

"Bingo. A lot of these parents are immigrants or refugees, working long hours. They don't get a chance to help their kids with homework or get involved with the community. And to many it's embarrassing to have a child that's kept down a year level."

"What happens?"

"The kids get pushed through, especially if they just meet attendance requirements and then they graduate with literacy levels of a ten-year-old."

"Christ."

"It's frustrating. I feel sorry for the kids because they get left behind. The more embarrassed they are about their inability to read or write properly, the more they rebel and turn to their friends and social groups for validation. What's even harder is that the council are stalling about approval for the community space I was telling you about. It makes it so hard when they're not willing to give them a shot."

"So why do the kids turn up for you? That class was jammed."

"I feed them and give them a chance to get some exercise, I suppose."

Jack shook his head. "Nah, that's not it, Sera. Plenty of food services offer meals. But you, you give them something—"

"Yo, D!"

The boys bounced the basketball and called her over.

"I'm needed for the game."

"Go, I'll hang with the girls."

Sera laughed, crossing the court.

Jack watched them play and marvelled at everything Sera had achieved. If only she understood her worth. He wanted to show her, somehow, just how important she was...he just didn't know how.

"Enjoy your little trip to the land of poverty?" Leila was reclining on the couch, popcorn bowl balancing on her belly, when they returned. She looked tired beyond her years and ridiculously young at the same time.

Jack adjusted his cap. It had been an informative afternoon. Eye-opening. He had come away from it knowing that there was so much more to his life than just making movies. So much more growth he needed to do in order to get there. "Okay, kid, I'll bite."

"Be nice you two," Sera called out, before heading upstairs.

Jack crossed the lounge room and perched on the arm of the sofa opposite. "Care to explain?"

Leila chewed. "I bet you feel pretty proud going to the shittest part of town today, huh? Gawking at all the poor kids, thinking, thank fuck this isn't my life."

"That's not what I thought at all."

"Uh huh. You'll go back to Hollywood and forget about us real quick. But we'll still be here struggling to get our shit together. And so will Ms. D."

"Leila, why do you think people rock up to the classes that Sera runs?"

Leila looked at him like it was a no-brainer. "It's coz she gives a shit. At first, we were sceptical, coz we've had all sorts of shady offers of charity, pushing a hidden agenda, but she passed the vibe check."

"She was cool?"

Leila rolled her eyes. "Yes, old man. She was cool. She listened. She didn't just feed us and lecture about Jesus or tell us to stop having sex. She got to our level. Actually gave two fucks about what we were going through."

"So she understood the assignment?"

Leila's sigh of disgust was worth it.

"Please don't try to be like us."

"Wouldn't even if I could."

"Most importantly, Ms. D. came back. She didn't leave us, she didn't ghost us, she showed up, even if we didn't. She would come to the library and wait until the session was over, then go to the courts, shoot some hoops, and go home. Nobody turned up. It was just her, sitting there, waiting."

"How do you know that?"

"We saw her. Once, at the start, when we rocked up for the food but didn't hang around, we tested her the next week, and saw she stayed the whole time. Each week she came back. Nobody was there, but she waited."

Jack could see the respect in her eyes, he could hear it in her voice.

"Ms. D. did what a lot of other people didn't do. She gave us her time. So we respect her by giving it back. Without her, we'd be pretty fucked up by now. Lots of times some of the guys get caught carrying or get asked to join a crew, and it's coz of Ms. D that they choose a different way. She shows us that way. Gotten jobs for heaps of us, like, referee checks and shit. No way we'd get them jobs by ourselves."

"Would you ever tell her that?"

"Nah. She knows we think she's alright."

"Does she?"

Leila frowned. "It's not like we write her poetry or some shit. But we like her. She gets that. What have *you* ever done for others?"

Jack shook his head. "Nothing, really. The world I've lived in isn't real. I know it, but it's afforded me a lot that I'm grateful for, so that's something."

"Yeah, but what have you done with it?"

"I give to charity." Jack could hear the defensiveness in his voice.

Fuck that. He wouldn't be that guy. Not anymore.

"Charity." She said it with a derision he didn't know was possible in someone so young.

Then again, he didn't really understand her world, or her for that matter. He was just beginning to appreciate what life might have been like for these kids. And just how important Sera was to them. Important enough that she would never be able to just pick up and leave. To run off to some remote part of the world. She was needed here for so many reasons. She was grounded in her work.

"Yes, charity," he repeated.

"That means nothing if you don't go and actually get involved."

He took the criticism on the chin. "Not everyone can teach kids or get into communities for food drives."

"I'm not talking about that, super star. I mean going to see what life is like for those charity cases you donate to. Then make changes with those big wigs who go and see your films and attend your parties."

Jack opened his mouth, but nothing came out. There was nothing he could say to that.

When did he last do something that was truly good? Something that wasn't just a token gesture. Sure, he felt it was important to give back to the community, but when was the last time he actually interacted with the people behind those charities? When had he done something that he could connect with on a personal level?

And it hit him. The force of it was so strong he was surprised he didn't tumble backwards.

The thing that niggled at him, the feeling of dissatisfaction wasn't necessarily his job, though that was a large part of it, it was the sense that what he was doing didn't have any purpose anymore.

That none of it mattered in real life.

If he died tomorrow, the world wouldn't be worse off for it. People wouldn't be disadvantaged. Nobody would really care.

He shivered.

Jack didn't want to leave the world that way. He didn't want to be known just for his acting and good looks. He was lucky to have both, but not enriched by it. Not anymore.

Jack looked at Leila, not as a pregnant sixteen-year-old, but as the future generation with a voice. A decent one at that.

An idea began to form, a whisper of something good, something that excited him.

"Tell me, what would you do if you had that money? What does the community need?"

And she did.

Sera lay in bed that night, wide awake and restless. Even though the afternoon at South Row went well, she was uncomfortable. Something wasn't right.

Perhaps it was just the very busy weekend that left her wired. Her eye was still sore, her cheek still bruised, but she knew that wasn't it.

Before she turned in, she had checked on Leila, who had fallen asleep on the lounge room sofa. Her mother had put a few blankets over her to make sure she was comfortable.

Maybe it was this thing with Jack. They had begun something, and even though her body was ready to jump him any time she clapped eyes on the man, her mind was still a jumble of concerns.

Nearly a month had passed since he arrived. And every day, Sera braced herself for the moment he told her he was leaving.

With Maddie and Owen's wedding in December, there was a lot to get done in between.

Which meant it didn't leave much wiggle room for Jack in terms of going back to L.A. and wrapping up filming. Sera shoved back her hair. Not her problem.

Jack had been hot and cold this week. One moment he was focused on building a connection, and other days it was like he was holding back. Attentive. Distant. Genuine. Flippant.

She had played this game with Jack once before.

It was a reminder that whatever it was they were getting in to, was best approached with an element of caution. There was only a few months until the wedding, certainly not enough time for this thing between them to get too serious.

Sera crept out of bed and downstairs. Maybe she'd make a chamomile tea, find a book to read and relax for an hour, anything to distract her wandering mind.

Leila was still asleep, though her blankets had twisted all around her.

Sera tiptoed across the room, careful not to wake her. When she reached the kitchen, she decided tea wouldn't cut it. Opening the freezer, she slowly shifted the bag of peas until she found what she was after.

"You too?"

She squeaked, jumping at the low voice behind her. The tub of ice cream in her hands nearly hit the floor. But even at one in the morning, her reflexes were pretty honed.

"Jesus." Sera clutched the tub to her chest, shivering at the icy cold. "You scared the crap out of me."

"Sorry. I couldn't sleep either and was craving something naughty."

"I bet. Grab a spoon."

"I'll just use yours." Jack hauled himself up on the kitchen bench. "Nothing like a bit of late-night indulgence. Good pick," he muttered after scooping up the toffee chocolate smash. "Never too late for this stuff."

"My sentiments exactly." Sera leaned her hip against the counter and found herself enjoying the company, despite her jumpy state.

"So today was a success, with South Row." Jack licked his spoon before handing it over.

"It was...Jack what are we doing here?"

"Eating ice cream."

Sera huffed. "I mean, one minute you're saying you want to start something, and the next it feels like you're avoiding me. Tell me I'm not imagining it."

"Ah." Jack rubbed at his face. "Sorry...I had a chat with Owen last week, about us. He questioned my intentions. Got me thinking about everything...Sera, I don't want to hurt you."

"Then don't."

"Hurt people, hurt people. Christ, that sounds wanky. I'm trying to find a good therapist. The guy I saw a few days ago wasn't the right fit. All they see is stars in their eyes and it makes it hard to open up, to move past all my shit. I want to do right by you, Sera, not just because my big brother gives me a talking to, but because I care about you."

Sera's heart fluttered, actually fluttered in her chest, as if tiny little butterflies were dancing.

"I care for you too, Jack. Which is why I'm bringing this up. And Owen isn't the only one with reservations. Maddie has warned me to tread carefully."

Jack nodded. "We've friends and family offering us advice."

"We do."

"Maybe it's time we listened to each other instead." Jack took the tub from her hands and placed it beside him. He slid down from the counter, standing before her in his T-shirt and shorts. Her heart thudded.

"What piece of advice would you have for me then?" Sera's voice hovered between them, a whisper of an invitation.

"To let me in." Jack cupped her face. "And what advice would you give me, Sera?"

"To have faith. In us."

Jack nodded. "I can do that."

"What else can you do?" She was afraid to breathe, afraid it would shatter the spell she was under. Despite the chill in the air, she was warmed by him, by the heat emanating from his body.

His thumb ran tantalising lines across her lips. His eyes held her captive.

Sera shivered at the cold evening air filtering through her oversized T-shirt. Her nipples pebbled against the cotton material, maddening, arousing.

"Let me kiss you, Sera. You're gorgeous in the moonlight. Stunning. Let me properly start this something between us, to pleasure you."

Sera had her fair share of confidence but standing in the kitchen with bed hair and a bust-up eye didn't make her feel like a sex kitten. She said as much.

"You're wrong. You're edible. And I'm dying for another taste."

She leaned in. She had enough time to see his devilish grin before she was devoured. One hand settled on the small of her back; the other cupped her jaw. The minute his mouth touched hers, Sera was flying.

Never in her life had she been kissed the way Jack kissed her. Heat and desire, and a surprising tenderness, set her pulse scrambling. Her mind whirling.

Sera wrapped her arms around his neck and opened to him. The warmth of his chest, solid and strong against her breasts made her feel protected. Jack made her feel like she was floating high, soaring above them both. Yet she remained tethered to him, and so very aware of his heart racing against hers, the way his hand shifted to her hair, gripping the nape of her neck. She never wanted him to stop.

How had she fooled herself into believing she was over him? How had she thought she was beyond all this? When every man she ever knew didn't measure up. Not like Jack.

As if in some old-time movie, Sera could see it all in her mind: the soft, romantic image, the soaring sounds. She was a lover at heart, unable to stop herself feeling everything old and new. It didn't matter. None of it did when his tongue stroked and teased.

She moaned now, unable to stop herself, unable to stop him. He did this to her. He coaxed the softness inside her, tempting her to romance.

Jack smiled against her lips and wrapped his arms around her waist, holding her tenderly. She felt delicate and desired. Needed and whole.

The soft mewling sounds broke through her reverie. They didn't own a cat.

It was low and distant at first but then grew louder.

"Miss?"

Sera and Jack broke apart at the same time with a loud 'popping' sound.

She stared at Jack, dazed and uncertain.

"Help."

Sera flicked on the overhead lights as Leila stumbled into the kitchen. They all winced. Not just because of the bright beam that illuminated the inky darkness, but because of the sight before them.

Crouched over in a nightgown was Leila, sweaty and dishevelled. Blood had pooled down her leg, clinging to the material. Leila clutched her stomach, pain and distress pinching her features.

Sera shivered, fear smothering her ability to move, let alone think clearly.

"Miss, help. I think I'm losing the baby."

CHAPTER NINETEEN

he trip to the hospital was fraught with tension. Sera's heart kept squeezing in fear then beating erratically. As it was the dead of night, they made it there in good time, but waiting for Leila to come back from triage with the nurse was agony.

"I feel physically sick."

"Tell me about it." Jack drew her close, offering her comfort and warmth.

"I'm so afraid for her. What if she loses the baby? She'll be devastated."

"Let's not think so far into the future. These things sometimes happen, and it doesn't necessarily mean she's having a miscarriage."

Sera looked at him dubiously. "Really?"

Jack wiggled his phone in front of her. "Dr. Google."

"Ah."

It felt like forever by the time they had her out again, and even longer before the doctors saw her in the ward. Jack stayed in the waiting area while Sera sat with her during the consultation.

It was the second time that she had seen Leila genuinely afraid. All the bravado that had existed previously had dissipated. She looked once more like a child, a pregnant sixteen-year-old who was terrified of losing her baby.

They had gone through the details of how much blood was lost, and for how long, with the doctor and the attending midwife.

"Now the fun part, to hear your bubba."

"Do you know what you're having?" the midwife asked, setting up the fetal Doppler.

"No. We're keeping it a surprise."

"That's exciting."

"This is cold. Sorry, lovely."

The midwife placed the gel on her belly and a second of tense silence later, they heard it. The whooshing sounds gave way to a steady beat, evidence that the little baby was alive and well.

Sera's eyes stung. The tears threatened as the wondrous sound filled the room. A little baby, a small, perfect little human being was there with them.

Sera was elated. Turning to Leila, she saw the relief on her face.

"That all sounds above board. Bub's heart is strong and steady. No issues there."

Wiping off the gel, the midwife stepped back, and the doctor put on gloves.

"Now for the internal examination."

They adjusted the hospital bed then placed Leila's legs in stirrups.

"Miss?" Leila reached out to hold her hand, gripping it.

"It's okay." She looked at the doctor, an older woman with an easy, open face dotted with freckles. "Is there any other way to do this?"

"I'm afraid not. I'm sorry, Leila, but we have to do an

internal examination. But try to just relax, and if you're uncomfortable, let us know and we can stop for a while. It's similar to a pap smear. We just want to make sure your cervix is doing its job and that there isn't any other bleeding, given the amount of blood lost."

Leila frowned. "I haven't had a pap smear before."

The doctor paused as she wheeled over the large lamp. "Oh, well."

"Just think about something else and I'll be right here."

The doctor paused. "Tell me if you want me to stop. Are you okay for me to proceed?"

Leila nodded, her breathing unsteady.

Sera held her close. "That's it. Focus on me."

Not long after, the doctor shifted back, taking off her gloves and switching off the light.

"We can see where the bleeding was from, but your cervix is closed so there's no issue there. Everything seems intact and there isn't any fresh bleeding."

"Do you know what caused it?" Sera asked.

"I'd love to be able to give you an answer, but sometimes bleeding occurs. That doesn't mean you're having a miscarriage. In fact, everything suggests that the pregnancy is going well. But of course, any kind of bleeding is always a concern."

"Blood was coming out me vag, so what are you saying? That it didn't happen?"

"No, not at all. But just that whatever it was, your baby and you are safe."

"You're not in premature labour, so that's a really good sign." The midwife patted her arm, trying to soothe her.

"So what? Go home and have a good life?"

"No. We want to keep you here for observation. At least twenty-four hours, but probably longer, to ensure that the bleeding has stopped completely and that you can get some bed rest," the doctor replied.

"I've got a part-time job."

"You'll have to call in sick."

"I'll lose my work."

"We can sort that out," Sera interjected. "What's important is that you keep yourself and that baby well. Which from what the doctor has said means staying here."

"Are you sure that the baby is okay?"

The doctor smiled. "Yes. And we'll be monitoring you to make sure that you're okay. We won't be sending you home until we're certain that you're well. But that also means you'll need to slow down a little. You're now in your last trimester, so that means increasing food intake and decreasing strenuous activity. But that's a conversation you'll have with your discharging doctor."

"Right."

"I'll come back to take you up to the maternity ward once a bed becomes available." The midwife instructed. "In the meantime, is there anything I help you with?"

"Can I come up with her?"

"You can see she's settled in, but you'll need to leave after that. She's been up all night and will need her rest. You can talk to the desk about visiting hours and we can put you on the list."

Once the doctor and midwife left, Sera studied Leila's face.

"How are you feeling?"

"I'm okay. Happy that the bub isn't in danger but still worried. Sera..." Leila huffed out a breath and tried again. "I really want this baby. I don't care what happens with me and Will or even with my parents; I don't want to lose it."

"I won't say something stupid like, I know, because I don't, or that it will all work out, even though I'm certain it will. But I'm really happy knowing that you feel that way because that means this baby will grow up with a mum who loves him or her with all her heart. And that's the best thing for your baby."

"Funny how you can end up just some stupid cliché. Nearly losing my baby made me see I want it more than ever."

"It's a cliché for a reason. And totally normal if it resonates with you. It's time to focus on getting some rest and making some changes. It's been a big month, with lots going on, so you need to cut yourself some slack. You can stay with us for as long as you need to regain your strength."

"About that." Leila fidgeted with her blankets. "I want to move in with Will and his mum. It's not our own place but I'm okay with that for now. He spoke to her about it, and she's agreed. I want this baby to grow up with family. Even if it isn't mine."

Sera smiled. "That's wonderful news, Leila. I think it'll be great to have that support. But we can sort it out once you're discharged. Just remember you've always got a room at the De Lotto house if you ever need it."

"Thanks, Miss."

"Don't mention it."

When the midwife returned half an hour later to take her up to the maternity ward, Sera made sure she was settled.

"Thanks, again. You're alright you know?"

Sera suppressed her grin. "I'll take that."

As she left the ward, her mind was still clouded with worry, even if her heart was a little lighter. And when Jack's arms wrapped around her, she huddled in close, accepting the support.

Maybe things might just work out after all.

CHAPTER TWENTY

"So how did it go with Leila?" Maddie popped gum and zipped up the emerald-green bridesmaid dress.

"She's officially moved in with her boyfriend and his mum."

"That's great news!" Maddie looked relieved.

"It is. I dropped her off yesterday, with a reminder to take it easy. Doctor's orders and all. With the stress of what happened with her parents, then the paps following us around, it may have been a bit too much to handle in such a short time."

"How is she coping with her parents?" Ally asked.

"She's upset about her dad and not being able to see her siblings. But I think her stay at the hospital was good for her. Being around other mums has put it all into perspective. She wants to make her own family, to establish a life for this baby, and I have to credit her for stepping up. Not many sixteen-year-olds would do that."

"Almost seventeen," Maddie interjected.

Sera rolled her eyes. "She reminded me every day."

Maddie smoothed down the dress again, studying herself from every angle. "I'd say she isn't the average teenager. Most wouldn't want a kid at that stage."

"Well, Will is sticking by her so they're intent on making it work. And now his mum is involved, I'd say she'll have a chance at finishing school while juggling a baby." Sera stepped back and studied her own reflection. "I thought the dress we tried on first was perfect, but now I'm changing my mind."

"And the green really suits both your skin tones," Ally mused.

Sera was taken by the elegant floor-length satin gown. The straps sat just off the shoulder and scooped down into a plunging V-neckline that ended at their waist with a sweet bow to accent. If it weren't for the gauzy sheer material, it would have been scandalous, but as it was, the dress was stylish, elegant, and a very fitting bridesmaid dress for Ally's wedding.

"I love it, Al. It's a gorgeous design," Sera sighed, dreamily.

"And it makes my tits look fab, even if it does hide my killer legs."

"You look sexy as hell, so shut up, Big M." Sera swatted her but had to hand it to Ally. The dress did bring out their features, even if they were polar opposites. The woman had an eye for fashion.

"Excellent. We'll take them."

Maddie smoothed down the fabric at her waist. "I think I'll need to use every day of the next few months at the gym with you De Lotto. This winter weight has given me a pooch. And spring hasn't been kind either."

"You look hot. But I could always use a workout buddy."

"You mean, you and Jack Davies haven't been doing a bit of cardio of your own?" Maddie wriggled her eyebrows before doing one final twirl.

"We might have had Leila's emergency not happened."

Maddie paused with her hand on the side zipper, eyes bright.

"You sly fox. You're banging Mr. Holly*wood* all week and you haven't dished the details!"

"Shh!" Sera flapped her hands, glancing over her shoulder.

Even though the change area was fairly vacant, she wasn't sure who might be eavesdropping. It was bad enough the paps had followed them. She didn't want her sex life to be featured on the news as well.

"Let's hit a few more stores then go home for lunch and cocktails." Ally winked, gathering up the other dresses.

"It's talk like that which is why I love you. And also why I'll never be a size six."

"Who needs a six when there's profiteroles?" Ally squeezed Maddie's shoulders. "I know a great patisserie. And you look stunning in the dress. Consider them my shout."

"What?" Sera put on her scarf, flicking out her curls from under the purple wool. "You can't pay for these."

"And the jewellery, too."

"What jewellery?"

"The ones we'll be going shopping for."

"But—"

"It's my duty as the bride to shower my bridesmaids in gorgeous attire. Owen and I have a wonderful budget for this wedding, and I won't be arguing about it because that'll turn me into a bridezilla again."

Maddie eyed the price tag. "Jesus, Ally, that much for a dress? I'm all for spending big, but this is price gouging."

"You only get married once and I intend to do it properly. Plus, I expect a banging huck's party, so consider this a gift in good faith."

"Speaking of banging, let's get moving so we can pepper her with questions." Maddie tied the sash of her jacket. "I want all the goss."

After a morning of shopping, Sera was feeling ridiculously relaxed. It was exactly what she needed off the back of such a stressful week.

But things were starting to fall into place: Leila was settled, Jack was searching for a therapist, and now her building manager called to say she could move back into her place in a few weeks. Sera couldn't help but feel a little giddy. But maybe that was the alcohol talking.

Perhaps drinking on an empty stomach wasn't the wisest of choices. Her stomach rumbled, and she glanced at the clock above the kitchen table. They were finishing off the wedding favours and thank you cards, waiting for what felt like forever for their takeaway to arrive.

"Have to say, if we weren't friends already, you would've bought my friendship with these bad boys." Maddie shook the bottle of cider.

"You can thank that gorgeous winery tour that Jack bought us for our engagement present. Honestly, it was bloody amazing, and the micro-breweries we hit up were phenomenal. Owen is wanting to get a wine cellar happening because of that trip."

"Your big ass wine fridge you bought will keep you going until then."

Ally grinned. "Wasn't it amazing? Twelve months ago, I would never have thought I'd be sitting here sorting through bonbonnieres with you because I'm the one getting married."

"We all thought it would be Sera, right?"

"What?"

"Totally." Ally nodded. "Can I just say that dude before Kenneth was sooo not the guy for you. What was his name?"

"Pritchard? Pierre? P—"

"Richel Houley de Vondenberg. The third."

Maddie snorted. "Jesus, he was up himself."

"But titled." Ally picked up another piece of ribbon. "You had to give him that."

"He was a total dingus," Sera conceded. "And never a real contender."

"I can think of a whole bunch of 'd' words I would call him." Maddie stabbed a carrot stick with her fork, only to have it fly across the room. "Why the hell are we using cutlery to eat vegetables? Screw that, why the hell are we eating vegetables?"

"Carrots stain our fingers, which stain the gifts." Sera threaded another bow around the bag of sugared almonds.

"Full marks for Sera," Ally cheered.

"When's our real food getting here? I'm in need of carbs."

Ally checked her phone. "Order is on its way, whingey pants. Eat another carrot, it shouldn't be too long."

"And then I can get these pretty hands all stained and saucy, right?"

"You can curry your heart out."

"Good, coz I'm starting to feel a buzz from these bad boys."

"Me too." Sera grinned, touching her flushed cheeks. "These look great, Al." She lifted one of the handmade notes she had helped decorate. It had a picture of Ally and Owen with a thank you message, and a name of the charities people could donate money to in lieu of a gift.

"Thanks. I know the Cancer Council is dear to Owen's heart, so we wanted to include it on the list."

"These diamante thingys are fiddly as fuck though." Maddie shoved back her long red locks. Her tongue poked out as she concentrated on gluing them on in a heart-shaped pattern. I think the tweezers make it harder."

"Jesus, you complain a lot, Fitzgerald." Sera rolled her eyes.

"I'd like to think of it as using my voice in a constructive manner. Speaking of constructive, have you thought about when you're going to put those knickers we bought to good use?"

Sera swatted her with the ribbon. "Maddie!"

"That was the worst segue known to man," Ally tutted.

"Brutal, more like it."

"You know me, I'm straight as an arrow." Maddie's eyes were bright, on the scent for gossip.

"A blunt one," Sera murmured.

"Well, lookee here, seeing as though we're on the subject of Jack, let's discuss your sex life." Maddie sipped her cider, face eager for the juicy details. "I restrained myself from asking questions all morning, and now we're home, you need to spill."

"That's because there are ears and eyes everywhere. Being followed by paps makes you paranoid. But the short answer is, Jack and I are going to screw each other senseless, it's just a matter of when."

Between spluttering laughter and choking coughs, Maddie managed a wobbly cry of appreciation. "Brava!"

Sera thumped Maddie on her back, grinning. "Weren't expecting that one, were you?"

"My influence," she wheezed, "is rubbing off on you." Maddie coughed again. "So proud."

"You okay?" Ally asked once she settled down.

"Yep." Maddie blew her nose for good measure. "Now, seeing as though I nearly died, you have to tell me about Jack and this sex plan of yours. Is this a wise decision?"

Sera kept her voice low even though they were alone. "I don't know. I won't know until it happens. I can't help but keep my guard up a little. He'll be gone after Ally's wedding, so I just need to be cautious until then."

"Isn't that going to be hard?" Maddie pressed. "Keeping the feelings out of it. Sex, especially sex with an ex will be brimming with emotions."

"Which is what will make it fantastic." Ally winked. "They're both adults, with a lot going on, but if it feels right, don't overthink it."

"I'm not saying don't shag the pants off him, I'm just making sure our girl doesn't get hurt again."

"I'm going into this very much aware of what I'm doing."

"Great." Maddie wiggled her eyebrows. "Now tells us about this sex plan."

"I didn't say I had a plan, just that I know sex with Jack is inevitable. Just like it was back then. It's a tingling sensation I get," she whispered.

"Oooh, sex goss, tell me." Ally leaned in.

"What do you need goss for? You're engaged and happily shagging your dreamboat man. I'm the one in need of scintillating sex details. So what about the tingle thing?" Maddie's mis-matched eyes were aglow.

"The first time Jack kissed me, and I mean all those years ago, I knew we'd end up in bed because of the tingle I got, here." She reached around, tapping her lower back. "Just at the base of my spine."

"Keep going."

"His kisses, well...I couldn't get enough. The thought of having sex with Jack made me giddy, and for all that man's bravado, let me tell you, it's not unfounded. The sex was amazing. Granted, he was my first back then, but every guy after just—"

"Didn't measure up?"

Sera turned to Maddie, nodding. "Kind of. I didn't realise I was searching for that tingle again. That's not to say I've not had some great sex over the years, because I have, but he set the bar *really* high."

"Until he kissed you all these years later." Ally's eyes were misty.

Sera sighed, wondering what she was getting caught up in again. Ten years had passed. More than, and she was wondering whether she was making a mistake. Whether she could move on so easily this time.

"I felt the tingle. I thought that maybe I had been imagining it the first time, but when it happened again, I knew I would only be fooling myself to think we wouldn't be having sex."

"Hold on." Ally shook her head. "Rewind a little. Your first? Jack was your *first* first?"

"As in, keeper of V? Your cherry popper? The knight that stormed the castle?"

Sera laughed. "Far out, Maddie, buy a vibrator."

"I have one. Many ones."

"Then use them."

Maddie pretended to cry. "Alas, I have no small, travelling vibrators. Maybe that's what I need any time stupid Gabriel calls another stupid meeting. I can just plug in and switch off."

"Don't you mean turn on?" Sera smirked.

"Alright, you two, this is heading to Only Fans territory."

"Maybe it'll be my new side business." Maddie's eyes were bright. "I'd have to book shows with that kind of notoriety. I could even get a reality TV show named after me and retire from my day job."

Sera laughed. "Somehow I don't think it's the kind of off-Broadway show you had in mind."

"Off-*off*-Broadway." Maddie's laugh was wicked. "Sign me up."

"Hold on, how did we only just find out about this?" Ally sidled up next to her. "I thought your first was..." She scrunched up her face.

"A guy from college." Maddie finished.

"Ohhh." Ally said, understanding dawning on her face.

"It's not like we had met Owen back then, or knew he was Jack's brother. Jack was just the guy Maddie knew from theatre."

"I didn't realise at the time that 'theatre Jack' was the same as 'virgin-popping Jack,'" Maddie replied.

"I was deliberately vague. To be honest, I didn't want to

focus on it, because him leaving had hurt. A lot. I needed distance from it all."

Maddie toyed with a piece of ribbon. "So sex with Jack won't just be sex with Jack."

"Exactly. Like I said, he's going to go back to America, so while I want to have sex with him, I know it's going to be a lot more complicated than that."

"And it's Jack." Ally's eyes were filled with sympathy.

"I've said goodbye to him once before. We were young and I was caught up in exploring the world and having fun, so I could pretend like it didn't affect me as much. But now..."

"We get it."

"I'd like to say I don't," Maddie sighed, squeezing her arm, "but I do."

"I'm not so naïve as I was back then. And he's...Well, there's a lot going on there."

Ally nodded. "Even though he shrugs it off with some sarcastic quip, he's hurting inside. Owen said he feels Jack needs to process what happened with their parents. He carries a lot of guilt about their death, I think."

"I think Owen's right. He's shoved it all aside and now he can't seem to cope. He's looking for a therapist to help him."

"Why not my therapist?" Ally offered.

"Isn't that like shitting where you eat?" Maddie placed another diamante on the card and sat back to survey her work.

"Not at all. I think Diana's been fantastic helping me out with my parents, and I don't think I would be so carefree about the whole situation if I didn't have her to talk to. Plus, it might help having someone who is real, who won't treat him like someone special."

"I love the idea. I think at this point Jack just wants someone who is good at their job, someone who can actually help him to work through all this stuff. It runs deep."

Maddie agreed. "That kind of shit always does."

"I'll get her card for you." Ally stood, stretching out.

"He means a lot to you, hey?"

Sera looked across at Maddie, toying with the top of the cider bottle.

"He does. I want what's best for him."

Ally came back in with the card and Sera slipped it into her bag.

"I hope it helps."

"Thanks, Al. Only way is up, I suppose. And stop, before you open that dirty mouth of yours, Maddie, when Jack and I have sex is up to us. I don't know when, but soon, given that they want him back on set. I know what's between us isn't a long-term thing, but it's still Jack."

"What will you do?" Ally asked.

"Get him into therapy, arrange your huck's night, and have what I hope will be mind-blowing sex with my Hollywood hunk?"

"Yes!"

"Now that's a plan." At the peal of the bell, Maddie leapt up. "Food! Thank fuck, I thought I'd die a dried-up spinster waiting for lunch. A hungry one."

Sera's stomach churned. Was she actually nervous about the thought of sleeping with Jack? It was ridiculous, but a part of her was a jumble of emotions at the prospect of going there with him again.

Maybe her friends were right. What the hell was she waiting for?

CHAPTER TWENTY-ONE

*I*t didn't happen the way she had expected it to, but perhaps that was for the best. It wasn't like the first time, where Jack booked them into a hotel, using his saved-up money bartending to splash out at a sit-down restaurant with a proper wine menu and fancy waiters.

No, it was nothing at all like their first time together.

But it was glorious.

Fresh. New. And still somehow, beneath it all, there was a strange familiarity about it. About him.

She had given him Diana's card on the weekend and had the real pleasure of seeing Jack call up for an appointment right then and there.

She could only hope that it would help him, that it would be the first step towards healing, or at least give him a chance to find his way through all the hurt.

But when she woke up that Tuesday morning, sex was the last thing on her mind.

She'd had a restless night, filled with dark dreams and the face of a little boy she hadn't been able to save. The cloud had followed her around all day, turning into a storm by the time she had arrived home from work.

The lurking paps had taken her annoyance into a full-blown temper.

Sera slammed the door, muttering to herself. It had felt good stomping through the house, releasing some of the aggression that had been building all day now. She had been on the phone with Leila's mother after what had been a difficult day off the back of a restless night.

She had hoped Leila's mother would be open to a reconciliation, but she had said it was embarrassing to have a daughter with no values. More likely Jena was terrified of her husband finding out. Which pissed Sera off even more.

Even though Leila didn't want to admit it, she could see her distress in not being able to visit her family. In particular, her mother.

Now that Leila was well on her way to becoming a mother herself, the reality of the situation was starting to sink in. Moving in with Will had made her realise that she was going to be a teen mum without any support from her own family.

How could her parents be so bloody short-sighted?

Sera took the stairs two at a time. She was in desperate need of a workout to stretch out her wound up body and to try to find some peace in her mind.

Stripping off her clothes, she rummaged in her drawers for clean workout gear and slipped on running shorts and a tank. She wanted to sweat it all out until she couldn't really think properly.

Sera raced back downstairs, and nearly bowled her parents over in the kitchen.

"Hey, baby girl!" Tony's arm was around Maryam's waist.

"Oh, I know that face," her mother muttered.

"What face?" She barked.

Maryam simply raised her eyebrows.

"Sorry. Bad day."

"Want to share?"

Sera was about to off-load to her parents when she took in their appearance. "You're going out."

Maryam smiled, her eyes glowing. "Your father is taking me to the city."

"You look lovely."

"I thought I'd treat us both to dinner and a movie. Maybe a late-night stroll through the park with some ice cream."

Sera's anger softened at the edges. She never tired of seeing her parents in love and taking the time to foster that love in all the little ways that kept them going strong year after year.

But a part of her—the mean, petty part—bitterly wondered if she would ever have that level of stability in a relationship. To be able to depend on another person to build a future together.

"We can delay for a little while if you—"

"No. You two crazy kids go out and have fun. It's nothing that can't be solved by a good workout."

"Or a chat," Tony suggested.

Maryam adjusted her earrings. "Jack is outside burning off some energy too. Must be the night for it."

"Or a full moon. Awooo," her dad howled.

"On that note, I'm taking this wolf of mine out before she starts biting."

"Good luck."

Sera, out of curiosity, made her way into the backyard. She had intended to go for a run, but maybe she'd start with weights first.

She knew that what hurt the most about today was the phone call she received from Elijah Sheppard's mother. Claire Sheppard had called asking if she would be attending Eli's memorial gathering. Of course she would be there. Of course she remembered. It may have been five years since he had died, but Sera still lived through the nightmare of failing him more often than was healthy.

She visited his grave on the anniversary of his death every year, as did the other kids who knew him in South Row. And still, even after all these years, Claire Sheppard asked: "Why couldn't you save him?"

The guilt stabbed at her. Sera gritted her teeth against it. She had asked herself that so many times before.

It was a question Mrs. Sheppard raised every anniversary, and every year it never failed to take her back to that place. To a time when she thought she could save him.

When she wasn't savvy, or streetwise enough to know the truth from a lie.

Did she shirk her duty of care when she had taken responsibility of these kids even though they weren't her own? It had been enough to make her want to run away, to pack it all in and give up.

But Sera didn't. She stayed and fought even harder to make it right for them. To make it up to Elijah's memory.

So she would do whatever she could to ensure that Leila and her unborn baby were safe. If that meant battling with Leila's mother, then so be it.

She watched Jack hard at it in a Cross Fit session. He used a few weights from the shed and had nothing on except a pair of shorts and a determined glint in his eyes. It may have been cool out, but he looked hotter than the sun.

The sight of him was tempting and infuriating all in one.

Sera wanted to stew in her own anger. To ride it out one laboured breath at a time. It was bubbling away under her skin, ready to strike out.

Jack lifted another kettle bell, squatting even as he swung it high then dropped it to complete a push up and burpee combo. Repeating the routine, his muscles straining, he worked until he spotted her stretching just off the porch.

"Plenty of room if you want to join me."

"I'd steer clear if I were you. I'm in a mood."

"That makes two of us. You okay?"

Sera shrugged.

Something in her caught alight. What did he care, really? He was here on a temporary thing and then he'd be out of the country and out of her life.

Careful, Sera. Tread carefully.

The fact that it bothered her should have been warning enough. It sounded like she was beginning to give a damn and she couldn't go there again. She refused to have feelings for a man who was committed to noncommitment, to living his life large and loose.

What was she even doing thinking about him in any way other than a temporary thing?

"Doesn't mean shit, Jack."

She executed a few knee lifts to get the blood flowing.

"I'm asking, aren't I?"

She heard the frustration in his voice but ignored it.

Needing to feel the burn, Sera started with travelling squats then shifted to a few isometric moves that worked her abs and arms.

"You just look after number one like you always do, Jack. You have the money and the means to do that. Meanwhile, I've got real problems."

"What does that even mean?"

"Do us all a favour and go back to being a hero on screen, Hollywood. You wouldn't understand."

"Wouldn't understand?" Jack strode over now as she began her squats. "Or are you afraid that I would? How about you try me, huh? But then that might throw out your neat little theory you have going on. I don't know what has happened since we spoke, but you've got it all wrong."

"I'm angry. My head is messed up after talking to Leila's mum, so you should probably just back off, Jack."

She lifted a heavy weight and rejoiced at the burning sensation as she continued her squats with tricep dips thrown in for good, punishing measure.

The build-up in her muscles, that precipice of pleasure-pain afforded her a satisfaction she had craved ever since Leila's mother refused to reconcile with her daughter, ever since Claire Sheppard called, reminding her of the boy she couldn't save. The family she had broken.

The guilt and anger fed off each other, diminishing her resilience. It drove her insane.

"I'm not looking for a fight with you, Jack."

"Could've fooled me."

"You're the actor, Jack, so go act. Leave me the hell alone."

That's what would happen in the end, isn't it? So why prolong the inevitable.

"What's going on? You've been in a mood since your dress fitting."

"You know what, Jack? I'm glad you're leaving back to America. I don't have time for some privileged movie star moaning about how bad his entitled life has been."

Her heart was breaking that he was going, even before anything had begun. She pushed through, pumping out another set, willing her heart to do the same. Because of it, she wanted to lash out, to hurt first.

"You know what I've realised, Jack? We both come from very different worlds."

"Well done, brainiac."

"You wouldn't understand what people like Leila have gone through, because she's a real person and not some cookie cutter Hollywood doll. She's dealing with a father who has disowned her and a mother who, for some *fucking reason* won't stand up for her child. Who does that? She'd rather let Leila raise this baby without her family than to go against her husband. It makes me so angry.

"But I'm also upset because Jena is terrified of her husband. So I'm this frustrated ball of anger-sadness and it is driving me insane. But there's no point talking to you about any of this because you'll be gone soon. You'll just up and leave—"

"Like the last time."

Her breath caught. And where there was extreme anger, there were tears.

"Damn it."

Sera turned, marching off with bleary eyes and a bruised heart.

"Sera, wait!"

Jack was behind her in a few strides. He caught her hand and blocked her path.

"Leave me alone."

"No. Sera, listen."

"I'm sick of listening to you. The man who has everything but isn't satisfied with any of it."

"Jesus, you drive me a little crazy, you know that?"

"I don't know anything anymore. All I know is what I feel, and it's heavy, Jack. It's a weight on my heart and I walk around with it, trying to shift it with work and the kids at South Row, but I feel like I'm sinking. Like no matter what I do, I'm not making a damn difference, and it's killing me."

Claire Sheppard's plea rang through her mind. Why couldn't she save him?

Jack cupped her face, brushing away her tears, and her pain with it. Why did he feel like the answer? Why was she so drawn to him after such a short time?

She was a damn fool, and if she wasn't careful, she'd be a broken one. She'd been swimming against the current for so damn long, and some days when it came to relationships, she was adrift.

With Jack, it felt like she was letting go, always letting go first, in case she was hurt again. When right now, more than anything in the world, she wanted to hold on. To close her eyes against all reason and judgment and good sense and cling to him, to the hope of something more. They may have agreed to keep it light and non-committal, but she didn't know if she could do it.

Her heart yearned for him. For a future together.

"If you feel all that, then Sera, we both have a lot more in common than you think."

"But is it enough?"

"It'll have to be. You're one person doing so much. It matters to those kids, so don't ever question that."

"I can't help it when I want more for them."

"You're enough. What you give, what you do is enough."

"What about us?"

"I told you I'm not in a good place, but I'm working on it. Yeah, I've a life back in L.A., but I've also told you that I want something different."

"For a week? A month? You're on holiday in my life, Jack. But my vacation with you ended years ago. We're both in different places right now."

"I know I can't offer anything other than my body, my time, and maybe a chance to figure this out together, but I want to try. Why are you pushing me away? What's happened?"

She opened her mouth but couldn't say it. All the hurt and guilt that she was feeling, all her fear about where she was heading with Jack melded together with the failings of the past. She couldn't talk about that, not now.

"I'm letting everything get the better of me. I'm sorry I'm taking it out on you."

"If you can't feel comfortable to talk to me, then what's the point, right? We can work all this out together."

"Can we?"

He crossed his heart, raising his two fingers. "Jack's honour."

Sera laughed, letting some of the tension drain away. It was a choice, to hold on or let go. "That's not even a thing."

"I'm initiating you." He pulled her close. "Okay?"

"I will be. Eventually."

The kiss, meant to be sweet and full of promise, was a torrent of need; a hungry, clawing desire that sought entry, no matter the cost.

"Sera, Sera, Sera."

"Shut up and kiss me, Jack. I don't want to think."

"Today is your lucky day, De Lotto."

Jack lifted her up, grasping her butt. She wrapped her legs around him, his body warm and slick with sweat. God, he smelled good.

He may have been a movie star, but right now he was Jack, just Jack. No matter what happened, he always would be.

"Upstairs," she murmured. "Now."

"Yes, ma'am." He slapped her ass and she squealed, laughter easing any remaining fear.

He broke apart for a second. "Just to clarify, we're about to go upstairs and have wild sex, right?"

"You bet your Hollywood ass we are."

Through her anger she had found desire. It flashed bright and hot and true. Sera was ready and oh so willing to take it a step further. Hell, it would be a giant bloody leap, but it was that, or possibly miss out on experiencing something she hadn't felt in a long time.

Missing out on him.

She wouldn't make that mistake twice.

CHAPTER TWENTY-TWO

*J*ack was lost. In her body, her scent, her every sigh as he undressed her. Sera was as he remembered, and so much more.

Gone was the soft, teenage girl. He admired her lean and muscled body, even as he feasted. Stripping off her tank top, he nibbled at the flat line of her stomach, enjoying the way it clenched. The spot at her hip used to drive her insane. How he remembered that he didn't know, but it was there, flooding his senses, guiding the way.

Her sweet gasp told him he was right.

So he drove her crazy. First with his teeth, little nips just at the soft, smooth skin beneath her underwear. Then with his tongue, licking and swirling patterns, holding her up by that tight ass, ready to make her wild for as long as he could stand it. And by the state of his cock, it wouldn't be too long.

Teasing her was equal parts satisfaction and torture.

"Jack. I can't stand it...too...much...pleasure."

"Never too much."

Sera gripped his hair, tugging, torturing, until he shifted back. In one fluid motion, he ripped off her sports bra too, and his heart did stop for a second. Her breasts fit in the palm of his hands; her tight dark nipples pebbled under his touch.

Tiny goosebumps dotted her golden skin as he circled her nipples, rubbing the edge of his nail over the tip. He feasted on her neck, her ear, nibbling along her jaw.

"You have to stop torturing me."

"Think again, Sera. We've got all evening."

She kissed him, and those sweet, soft breasts pressed against his chest, unleashing something wild within. Fuck. He wanted to pound into her until he couldn't breathe. He would give himself to her, without reservation.

Sera was worth the heartache, the confusion, and every inch of the pain. Because it dawned on him that she was important. Deep inside, she mattered. She always had.

Those once-forgotten feelings hovered between them, drawing him in.

Past and present tumbled and swirled, a whirlpool of sensations keeping him grounded, to her. All Jack knew was that he wanted more.

"You're a goddess. A queen." Jack tugged down her shorts and underwear in one motion. "And you're just as beautiful as I remembered."

"Are you talking to my pussy?"

"You bet."

Her laughter, the carefree bubble, floated around them, delighting him. He loved that sound.

Jack flicked his tongue out, bolstered by her shuddering sighs. When Sera gripped his shoulders, nails digging into his skin, he knew he was on the right track.

"Jack." Her hips rocked, and his mouth worked over her clit. He circled her entrance, slowly. Then again.

Her panting grew louder and more fragmented. Willing himself to take his time, he used his tongue to taste her, to sample and savour when he wanted to greedily gulp.

And suddenly he was a young, confident twenty-something-year-old out to impress the sultry exotic girl he was dating: cocky, care-free, and eager to please.

Had he known then what he knew now, would he have left her? Would he have given up what he didn't realise was one of the best relationships he'd ever had, to pursue that dream?

How many times had he shrugged off the clawing need in those first few weeks to jump on a plane and back into Sera's arms? How many nights had he longed for a glimpse of her in person, to hold her and kiss her and just wake up beside her?

He couldn't live in the past, in the recriminations and questions. But he could learn from it, and not make the same bloody mistake twice.

Feeling a surge of protectiveness, Jack continued, indulging in the way she moaned now, straining for more.

"I wanted to take you nice and steady, but I'm as raging as a rampant bull. I want to make you come until you scream." He had the satisfaction of watching her eyes dilate.

"Screw steady. Make me scream, Jack."

He lapped at her now, firm and rhythmic, using one finger and then another to enter her.

"Oh!"

He didn't stop, knowing she was building up to her orgasm. Her body arched off the bed, and her thighs squeezed against his head.

She was close. And fuck, the soft cries as she began to lose control was the sexiest sound in the world.

"Jack."

He increased the pace, his own blood pumping as she writhed and groaned. She was warm and wet on his fingers and smelt like heaven.

"Jack, yes!" She stilled, then shuddered, gripping his hair as she came.

He waited until Sera let go before shifting. Jack placed a kiss on her hip, before hovering over her.

"Mmm."

"Mmm good?"

"Mmm let's do it again, and again..."

Jack didn't need to be told twice.

"I like how you think," Jack muttered.

"I don't plan to do much thinking." She shoved against his chest and he shifted back.

Kneeling on all fours, Sera looked over her shoulder.

"I'm waiting, Hollywood."

Jack yanked at her ponytail and slapped her ass.

"I've changed my mind," Jack muttered. "That pussy is too good to pass up." And before she could protest, he was crouching down behind her, his mouth fused to her clit once again.

It took only one long, hard lick for her to jerk forward. Jack grabbed her hips, drawing her back, and his tongue drilled into her.

He used his thumb to work over her clit in rhythmic strokes until her legs buckled and she came a second time.

Jack nipped at her ass, then slowly turned her over. "That good, huh?"

"I think the word 'good' isn't the word I had in mind," Sera mumbled, eyes heavy.

"100% on Rotten Tomatoes?"

Sera laughed.

"Do that again."

Jack pulled her up, so that she was on her knees. A vice seemed to squeeze around his lungs. His throat felt tight.

"Do what?"

"Laugh."

"Why?"

"Because you look beautiful when you do. And I get a kick out of hearing the sound."

Jack cupped her face, drawing her in. The kiss started out gentle, sweet. In a matter of seconds, sweet turned to smouldering and the kiss drove them both down on the bed.

"Protection?" Jack murmured.

Sera pulled out a packet from the nightstand.

In a few deft moves, Jack was covered. With her legs flush against his chest, he drove into her. And saw stars.

Jack gripped her thighs as pleasure coursed through him. "Sera." She was tight and wet and fucking glorious.

"I need to fuck you."

"Do it. Hard."

He withdrew, flipping her over on all fours.

And when he entered her this time there was a feral quality to their lovemaking. Sex on steroids.

His hands fisted in her hair, yanking and tugging.

"Yes," she groaned. "That's it."

Jack covered her now, chest to back, fucking her hard and deep. He placed his fingers in front of her mouth. "Spit."

She did, and he worked her clit, aroused by her moans.

"Yes. Jack, yes."

In a frenzy he pounded into her, blood pumping, muscles straining.

When her cries filled the room, Jack groaned, increasing the pace, chasing his desire, until he couldn't hold back anymore. Jack cursed, letting go. He bit down on Sera's neck, coming in long hard bursts, holding her tight, until his pleasure subsided.

Jack took them both down to the mattress, enjoying her warm, soft body lying next to his.

He watched her now, and something began to shift inside of him. On a surge of protectiveness, he pulled her close, craving her touch. Jack wasn't quite ready to let go.

CHAPTER TWENTY-THREE

*I*t was like she was a teenager again, creeping back from a party after curfew, knowing which floorboards would give her away. Except she was in her thirties, and the man she was sleeping with was only down the corridor. Still, the illicit thrill of it was there all the same.

So for the next few days, Sera would sneak into Jack's bedroom in the middle of the night, tiptoeing back to her own in the early morning, giddy and flushed.

She hadn't realised what she had been missing.

Sex was one thing, and Sera hadn't put nearly enough time into getting her needs met as of late, but sex with Jack...even better than she had remembered. It was glorious and heady and everything she could desire in a lover.

Except, whatever was between them was fleeting. A mistake. The cautionary thoughts that told her she was foolish and rash seeped through her happiness.

She shoved them aside as she woke up in bed beside Jack, the ache between her thighs a wonderful reminder of what they had spent the past few days doing.

"So, what say you and I have a morning shower workout?" Jack nibbled at her shoulder, drawing her in close.

"I say that sounds like a wonderfully distracting way to make it through round two. I am, after all, very sticky and very sweaty. You might need to be thorough, just here." She placed his hand over her swollen clit.

She was ready for another round, and by the feeling of the man beside her, he was up for it too.

Sera rolled over him but was caught. Jack's mouth was at her breast, his tongue doing wonderfully delicious, torturous things to her body.

"See, the problem is, Sera," he murmured, not stopping. "I think I'm ready to go now."

She tried to think of something to say, but her body was caught in a myriad of sensations. Her breasts were heavy, her clit throbbing, and that ache, that delicious persistent pulsing deep inside of her, was demanding his attention. She craved it more than she cared to admit.

She was utterly addicted.

Jack jutted against her bottom then slid along her pussy to her clit, arousing her further.

Sera looked down at his face. His eyes were still sleepy, his golden hair messy and out of place. He looked less like the Hollywood stud and more like her hot lover this way. Her Jack.

She was caught between her mind and body. Suspended above him, she was wanting more with every day.

And boy was he giving it.

"I don't see the problem at all," Sera sighed, guiding him into her. She shuddered. No matter how many times they had sex, that contact, the point where he entered her and slid deep inside, never failed to dazzle her.

She was hungry for more. For release. For the sweaty, slick friction that only his hard cock could give her.

Total bliss.

She eased up, teasing them both, then slammed her body down, riding him in that lazy way that made him dig his fingers in her hips, urging her to quicken the pace.

Sera reached behind her, pinching at his bottom.

"Uh uh. I'm the one setting the pace here, Hollywood. You just need to sit back and enjoy the ride."

"Oh, trust me. I *am* enjoying it. But I also want to come all over you. So if you don't start riding me like the dirty cowgirl I know you are, I'm gonna take over, sweetheart."

And so she toyed with him, punished him—and herself—with it. Up and down, slow and slick, she moved until her breathing came in staccato bursts. Until his body went rigid with restrained need.

And when she felt that rolling, tumbling desire gather momentum, she didn't stop. Her hips jerked, her fingers flew, and within seconds, Sera was riding him, back arched, breasts bouncing freely.

Jack's hands gripped her waist, his cock pounded now, catapulting her higher and further than she thought possible.

She was caught in the weightlessness and abandoning all thought, she flew through the sensations.

Sera's body broke, shattered, and she cried out, coming in luxurious waves. And when Jack groaned, lost in his own orgasm, she shivered. That sound. That sex sound he made as he came hadn't changed. She was so glad it didn't.

Sera slumped against him, a boneless rag doll, sated and spent.

It was the perfect start to the morning.

Twenty minutes later, they tiptoed to the bathroom together, giggling. Sera admired Jack's naked butt as he walked ahead imagining him in a pair of tight jeans.

Then the bathroom door swung open. In a cloud of steam, her parents emerged, twin towels wrapped around them, twin grins in place.

Jack slapped a hand at his bits, attempting to cover himself, and suddenly Sera was in a fit of giggles.

"Er. Morning, Jack. Sera."

Her dad looked at a spot above their heads, a blush beginning to form.

Sera tugged down the scandalously short top she had thrown on. She must have rotten luck to be caught by her parents.

But somehow Jack seemed to turn the most mortifying situation into something funny.

"And a good one too by the looks of it." He grinned. Even butt naked the man had balls. No bloody shame.

It was then that it dawned on her. "Mum!"

"What? A woman can't have fun with her husband in her own house?"

"Ugh."

"Sir." Jack nodded to her dad then grinned at her mum. "I'd uh, open the door, but ya know. Hands full."

"I'll do it!" Sera stepped forward, pulling Jack into the bathroom behind her. She slammed the door, locking it for good measure. One look at Jack and she dissolved into breathless laughter.

"Still going strong. It's impressive."

"That's not your parents out there!" Sera wiped at her eyes then froze. "I didn't mean it like that."

"I know." Jack pulled her close. "Not your fault, remember? And I like seeing your parents that way. Makes me hopeful for the rest of humanity."

"Well, we're just showering. Nothing more. I'm still grossed out." She pulled her top over her head and was caught up in Jack's arms. "Put me down!" she whispered.

"Not until I get you nice and clean."

She knew that look. "How can you be up for it when you know what was going on in here?" She gestured to the tub. "Where's the disinfectant?"

"When I've a naked goddess in my arms, anything is possible. Let me show you what I've got in mind."

And he did.

CHAPTER TWENTY-FOUR

"*I* take it that the frenzy out there is one of the reasons why you're in here?"

Jack had woken up that Friday morning with Sera beside him, calm and relaxed. Then he had stepped outside and all the fear and anxiety had returned. The paps had followed him to his appointment, salivating at what their next headline might be.

While he knew he needed to work through his issues, Jack wasn't keen on the pain that it would no doubt bring.

He squirmed a little in his chair. He was always wary of therapists. Ever since he had seen his first one when his parents died, and all the bad ones in between, he couldn't shake that unease, the sense that someone was peering inside his brain. Judging him.

The restless discomfort was still there, but there was something about this woman, perhaps because she wasn't a 'therapist to the stars' that put him at ease. He didn't know why, and it probably wouldn't have any bearing on how she treated him, but it was a comfort all the same.

"You probably know who I am." Jack slipped off his baseball cap, running his hands along the bill.

"I know of you. But I can't say I'm a huge action fan. More of a romantic suspense or Nordic crime buff to be honest."

"A psych who likes crime fiction. Should I be afraid?"

"Only if you're committing a crime."

"Only in the movies."

"That's a relief." Diana smiled. "But I want you to know that I won't let any of that other noise get in the way of our sessions. If you feel at any time you don't want to continue, then I won't judge. You're free to never come back without any fear of any of this going outside these four walls."

"Good to know."

"So tell me, and I know this will sound cliché, but how does all that—out there—make you feel?"

"I've put up with it for so long, I don't really know. It gets a bit disconcerting, not that I'm not used to it."

"So it's safe to say you've numbed yourself to it all?"

"I think I've absorbed it."

"My aim, Jack, isn't always to make you feel comfortable, but I hope that talking to me and implementing these strategies will give you a bit more balance and healing. That might mean making changes you didn't think you needed to initially. Resistance is natural and expected. You might even need to reassess the company you keep. To decide who you can trust and to have people around you that aren't 'yes' men and women. Those who won't sell you out for a few grand."

"Ah, c'mon, Diana, I'm worth more than that."

"And using humour to deflect has served you well I'm sure, but it has no purpose here. Even if it is amusing."

"Harsh but fair."

"Great. So, Jack, take me through what's going on. Let's see if you think I'm worth it."

The hour passed quicker than he expected, and Diana Vanders proved that she was more than worth it. She was direct and clear but compassionate and funny, if you liked your humour dry.

But those demons that haunted him had their talons embedded deep into his soul. He wanted to believe that talking to this therapist would actually help him move forward, but he wasn't so certain. She'd have to rip through all those layers, the many years of pain and hurt to cleanse him.

Jack was beginning to think he might need divine intervention to help him through it all.

For now, he would hold out hope he could be saved.

Sera took off her heels and walked across her parents' backyard, past the flowers and vegetable garden, to the swinging tyres hanging from the tree. She hung off it, resting her chin on top of the warm rubber, desperate for a moment of peace.

Closing her eyes, Sera tried to clear her mind, but every time she did, the image of a young, scrawny ten-year-old boy appeared.

She swung like that for a while, letting the tears come, succumbing to the painful memories.

It was the hardest day of the year. The anniversary of Elijah Sheppard's death. Sera wanted to go upstairs and bury herself under her bed covers and never come back out.

Why couldn't you save my boy?

Sera, still raw from the memorial service in Elijah's honour, had wanted nothing more than to forget. It may have been five years since he had died, but to Claire Sheppard it was yesterday. And Sera would have to live with the knowledge that she had failed him every day.

"Your mum said you were out here."

She opened her eyes, then closed them. Jack settled in beside her, hanging off the second tyre, waiting patiently.

"Shit day."

"I bet. Why didn't you mention you were going to a funeral? I'd have come with you."

Sera shrugged. "I needed to be alone. And it wasn't a funeral. The boy has been dead for five years."

"Okay."

Jack swung beside her. His presence calmed her, and she was grateful for his company, but her heart was heavy, the weight crushing.

"He was only a little boy." She swallowed against the lump in her throat. Suddenly she needed to talk it out. To somehow absolve herself of her sins. To make Jack understand.

"Take your time."

She looked at him now. His face open, eyes reassuring.

"I was so new, so idealistic back then. I had just started tutoring the kids in South Row, just began gaining their trust. I hadn't sussed out who could be trusted, not entirely at that stage.

"His name was Elijah Sheppard and God, he was smart. I remember doing a diagnostic test to see what their literacy levels were like and this boy, Jack, this boy was gifted. And only ten years old."

Sera brushed at her tears then launched out of the tyre. She sat down on the grass, and Jack followed, resting beside her beneath the tree.

"He had an older brother, Rick, who was in a gang and most of their income came from dealing drugs. I kept telling Eli that he didn't need that life, that he was better than that. But he loved his brother so much. Rick was someone whom he looked up to, given their father wasn't in the picture."

Jack took her hand. "And from the sounds of it, you loved Elijah just as much as he did his brother."

"I did. The kid wasn't just smart, he was funny and outgoing. Wild, yes, but he was living tough, and I could see past it." Sera cleared her voice. "Anyway, I was supposed to take him to do a tutoring session, just one on one, then we'd go for ice cream. He said he wanted to tell me something.

"So I went, and he was saying his brother would have a big opportunity for him, and it would give them all more money and what did I think about it? Well, I said if he trusted his brother, and it wasn't something illegal, then that was okay, but that he should run it by his mum first. I asked him what it was his brother was doing, and he said he'd be a delivery boy."

"Ah."

Sera nodded. "I didn't know what that meant at the time. God, Jack for all my parents' charity work, I had grown up pretty sheltered from all that. In my head, I thought paper deliveries."

"Do you think he knew what it was?"

"I would have said no, but I'm not so sure. I asked him to speak to his mum about it, and if the job didn't interfere with school and didn't get him into trouble, then to go for it. This kid barely had a decent meal, so I though what was the harm..." Sera pressed her lips together. She had been such a fool. "Two days later, he was shot in the head. The drug run, which is what he was a part of, went wrong. And it was all because of me. It was all my fault."

"Christ, Sera, you can't take that on."

"It's because of my advice he's dead." She let the tears come, falling into her regret, allowing it to consume her whole. Jack held her, offering her comfort and strength. His arms were strong, the beating of his heart a rhythmic comfort.

"I wish I had been there today. You don't have to hold this all in, to go through it alone."

"I thought I was handling it. Every year that this anniversary comes around, I think I'm a little closer to healing, but it's really affected me. His mum still blames me for Eli's death."

"What?" Jack drew back.

"Claire asked me why I couldn't save him."

"More like it was his drug-dealing brother's fault. What happened to him?"

"Jail. I don't know where he is now. It's been hard to stay in touch, as Claire doesn't give me much information. And it's hard because of the anger, the guilt."

"Sera, look at me." Jack held her shoulders, guiding her with his voice. "There is nothing more you could have done. Eli sounds like all kids, eager to do as they please, regardless of your advice. Even if you said no way, he'd still have gone through with it."

"You don't know that."

"Yeah, I do. Because it was his brother. And as much as you think you had influence over that kid, his brother had more."

Sera let the advice sink in. "I never thought about it like that before."

Despite having grown up with three older brothers, Sera never felt drawn to following them around, or even listening to their advice. They were annoying and overbearing. Her role model had always been her mum.

"I'm telling you now, from the perspective of a kid brother. You do anything they tell you even if it's the smallest suggestion or the biggest dare. Did I tell you about the Red Bull incident with Owen?"

Sera shook her head then listened as he regaled her with the story, which led to another one, and by the time he finished, the oppressive weight was no longer unbearable. No longer crushing.

"Thanks, I guess I needed someone to talk to after all."

"You're welcome. You're not alone in how you feel, Sera." Jack studied her, eyes serious, yet distant. She knew what he was about to say was important. And difficult. "I've been carrying a lot of guilt since my parents died. I know I glossed over it all when we first met but you're not alone in how you feel."

"What happened Jack? You said they were in an accident, but you've never really spoken about it."

Except that one night, when he had been drunk, saying it was all his fault. She hadn't understood it then, and still didn't now.

Jack flicked the band at his wrist. "They were out that night because of me, because I had done something stupid at the school with my mates. I should have met them there..." Jack's breathing turned shallow.

"We don't have to—"

"I do. Sera, you need to understand. They were out at the school because of the stupid prank me and my buddies had pulled. I said I would be there for the meeting with my coordinator to discuss it, but I flaked." Jack frowned. "I was busy losing my virginity the night they died."

Sera's heart wrenched in her chest. "Oh Jack...I'm so sorry."

His shoulder's jerked. "Not your fault. Nobody's fault."

"Not yours either, Jack."

"I always felt responsible. But back then I thought everything was a fucking joke. If I had shown up, like I said I would, if I had been dependable then they would never have been there when that car lost control."

"That's a lot of guilt to carry."

"It is. And it gets heavier every year. Which is why I know how you feel." Jack rubbed at his chest. "Even if it hurts to say it, it needs to be shared. I'm beginning to understand that now."

Sera's throat closed over. "I don't think I'll ever totally get over his death," she choked out.

"It isn't something that anyone would, not easily. But give yourself time to grieve without the guilt."

"I'm trying."

"Seeing as though you're listening to my worldly wisdom, can I add that I know you're stressing about Leila's pregnancy, but you don't need to. You've done everything in your power to help that girl out, and it's more than anyone could do."

"I just feel like I need to—"

"To make up for what happened to Eli. I get it now. But it's enough. You're enough. And just so you know, I think what you're doing with those kids in South Row is powerful, important work. Because of you, it's thriving, so don't forget that. Ever."

Sera sniffed, brushing away a tear. "Geez, those therapy sessions seem to be doing well."

"Diana is proving to be the right person for the job. I have you to thank for that."

"You can thank your soon to be sister-in-law for the recommendation."

"Another hundred roses for her then."

"I said thank her, not torture her."

"Speaking of torture. I had a call from Taylor."

Sera's stomach clenched. "To go back?"

"Yeah."

"When?"

"A few days."

Sera gasped, heart wrenching in fear. She accepted it, knowing this was an inevitable part of the process of letting go. Letting him go. "I suppose you've been here for a while now."

"It's a decade according to my agent."

Sera willed the tears away. Six weeks. She had been counting.

"Hey, I'm coming back."

"I know."

"I am best man after all."

Sera nudged him. "Har, har."

"Of course I'm coming back. Sera, I'll be gone a month, six weeks tops."

"So you'll be back in time for the huck's party?"

"Why in the hell would someone combine a hen's and buck's party, I've no idea. But yes, I'm aiming to be back for that."

"Thanks for keeping me in the loop."

"We'll work through this."

Sera nodded, but she couldn't think about that now. Not yet.

"Have I ever told you how great a chef I am?"

Sera smiled. "No."

"Let me show you then."

She stood, allowing him to lead her inside. She'd take all the moments she could, all the time they had together before he left.

Their days were numbered.

CHAPTER TWENTY-FIVE

*T*heir days were numbered. That's what Jack felt. An unsettling sense of urgency before he had to go back to his old life. A life he wasn't sure he wanted so much anymore. But his flight was booked, an open ticket, so he could decide when he needed to return. He hoped it would fly by.

Sera had shown him her apartment, talking to him of the painting she wanted to have completed before she moved back in. It was a stylish two-bedroom place in the heart of the suburbs that, even without furniture, still felt like a home.

Funny how his bachelor pad, even after ten years, didn't have the same affect.

Before he left, he squeezed in another appointment with Diana. He had a lot on his mind after sharing the details of his parents' death with Sera. It had unlocked something inside of him, and he realised he needed to talk it through.

Jack wished he had more time but would take what he could get.

"So you're going back to L.A.?"

"Yep."

"And how is that sitting with you?"

"Mixed feelings. Relief that I can start to face it all. Dread to do it. And I've started a relationship."

Diana's eyebrows raised a fraction. "How's it going?"

"Great. We have history. We dated when we were young and didn't think much of the future."

"And now?"

"I'm old and don't think much of the future."

Diana spared him a look. "Are you afraid to leave her?"

Jack snapped the band around his wrist. Was that what the whisper was around his heart? "No, not afraid, at least I don't think so. But we've got something good, and I know that I'll be gone long enough to disrupt that."

"A month, that's not very long."

"I beg to differ."

"So it's serious?"

"Sera has been there through a lot of the hard things. I met her maybe five years after my parents died and I wasn't in a good place, and seeing her now when I'm dealing with the..."

"Anxiety. It's not a dirty word."

"Yeah, that. She's been a rock."

Too good for him. He had always felt she was just too damn good for him. He hadn't been able to give her what she needed all those years ago...could he now?

"Can you tell me about their deaths?"

"It happened so fast; one day they were with us and the next, gone. I had just turned sixteen. I remember I was feeling like a big man as I'd lost my virginity to Stacy Watts, high school cheerleader and all-around sex goddess. At least I thought so at the time.

"She let me go all the way when her parents were out. I still remember the walk home, feeling like a big man, excited to be the first of my buddies to have done it."

"And?"

Jack swallowed against the same odd, imaginary ball in the

back of his throat. He reached for the glass of water on the table taking his time.

"God, that feeling never goes away." He blew out a quick breath.

"There's no rush."

"I can see myself walking up to the house and all the lights were on. I thought that maybe something had happened to the baby. My brother Owen and his late-wife Rebecca were crashing with us. They were both teen parents, so there was lots of drama around that. But Charlie was a happy baby and my parents loved being able to help out. Anyway, I'll never forget the look on Owen's face that night. The police officers were saying the words, but none of it was registering.

"All I could think was, I wish I could wash the smell of Stacy off my hands. Off my body. I went from feeling like my life was amazing to stepping into the biggest nightmare of all. I wanted to take it back. To erase everything. But I couldn't."

"That's a natural response, especially at that age. So what happened next?"

"The funeral was a blur. And Owen was dealing with sending me to school and selling the house to pay off the mortgage and the credit card debts. My parents were in over their heads with money, not that they ever made that known to us, but when we had to deal with all that shit, it became apparent that my brother Owen had to grow up fast. A new baby, working a few jobs, renting a place for us all, trying to study, and then take care of his kid brother, it was a lot."

"And a big change in your life. To lose your comfort and home in one fell swoop."

"Yeah, I got a bit wild. Felt sick about sex for a while and then, like a switch was flipped, couldn't get enough of it."

"And I'm assuming you never really let anyone get close enough to form meaningful relationships."

"Bingo."

Not that he knew he was doing it at the time. But being back was giving him greater insight into his past than he thought possible.

"Is this something you'd like to change?"

"I didn't think it was a problem a few months ago. But yeah, I don't want this life anymore."

"Promiscuous sex?"

"Any of it. The life I've created is a sham. It feels like it was based on everything that I convinced myself I wanted. I told myself I couldn't stay in this country, that I needed to make it big, to prove..." Jack cleared his throat. "To prove to my dad that I could. That he didn't..."

"What?"

Jack shook his head.

"I wanted to make him proud. My grandfather was a tough man, and he wouldn't let my dad even close to a theatre, let alone to act in one. But my dad was still in love with the cinema and the stage. We used to watch films together when I was a kid, I think I still have a few home movies we made. He loved detective films." Jack's laugh was short and bitter. He pressed his hand to his chest, trying to contain the pain. "I told him that one day I'd make it big. 'Just you wait, dad.' So I left Sera, my brother and niece, and told myself I wouldn't return until I made it. But then the panic attacks started."

"Tell me about that," she said, making a note.

"I didn't know what it was. I just always thought I had indigestion. Girls I knew were talking about begin gluten and lactose intolerant. So I bought into it. Eliminated all that shit." Jack shook his head.

"And?"

"Turns out I was just intolerant to them."

Diana laughed. "Sorry."

"Don't be." Jack grinned, comfortable in the role of storyteller. But he wasn't here to entertain. "I ignored it for a long time, until one night after an awards ceremony, I found myself hyperventilating whilst sitting in a toilet cubicle. Bawled my eyes out and had to flee with my glasses on like some wanker before the after-party."

"Why is that a bad thing? Crying?"

"I—" Jack paused. He didn't know. A lot of his behaviours, the things he did or said, weren't because he was being true to himself. But more with his obsession with an image, his own Playboy persona he had cultivated over the years to protect himself.

"I didn't cry at my parents' funeral. Not when they carried them out from the church. Not when they buried them in the ground. Or even when Owen broke down. I couldn't show any emotion around it. Like there was some dam that stopped everything coming out." Jack shivered, rubbing at his arm.

"Then?"

"And then the panic attacks started, and the night sweats and palpitations, and suddenly I'm fucking crying at the drop of a hat." He clicked his fingers then stood, needing to move. Jack paced in front of the window now, desperate to get it all out. "I go from being at the top of my game to then having a breakdown on set. My agent is up my ass, everybody is pissed. I have a contract, people depending on me and here I am caught up in other people's lives pretending it's my own.

"Pretending. Always faking it. That's the nature of my job, right?"

"It doesn't have to be."

Jack stopped pacing. "I feel like I've been in too deep for so long that I don't know how to get out. I shouldn't have taken on this film. I knew it would push me after working back-to-back on films for five years now."

"That's a long time to be working constantly."

"I've fed off it. My popularity, fame, wealth all benefited from it. Hell, this film is coming out in another year and I've two more that will be released in the next six months. Not to mention the scripts I was considering when I left. But, Jesus Christ, Diana." Jack leaned over the back of the armchair, looking directly into the dark-eyed woman who sat calm and unmoving. "My mental health is screwed. I'm done with it all. I'm tired of pushing and running and pretending. I'm tired of the person I've become, and I want out."

"What do you mean by out?"

"I'm not suicidal, if that's what you're asking."

"I'm just trying to understand."

"I'm not there. But if I live like this for much longer, I might be." He peeled off his cap, throwing it on the sofa. Jack shoved a hand through his hair, suddenly weary. "I don't know; everything is so messed up. Tell me this, doc: How do you run away from the person you've become? How do you do it when it's a life you've created with your own two hands? Trouble is, I can't seem to get away from myself."

"Good news is, Jack, you don't have to."

Jack's shoulders lowered. He tipped his head forward, letting it hang with relief.

"What does that mean?"

"It means you've created it. You can un-create it. Or at least make the changes that will mean a better life for yourself."

And in that change, he saw Sera. Building something with her that was true and real. Something new.

Not to mention this new project, this glimmer of an idea, of a hope for the future that he wanted to pursue. He just had to figure out the details first.

"I want out of acting. I need to get away from it all."

"It's hard for the brain to make decisions when it feels constantly under threat. The way you've been living for so long has kept you in this hyper-vigilant state where threats, both real and imaginary are holding you hostage. Your sleep, relationships, and now your work is being jeopardised by it. So instead of making drastic changes, I would suggest starting small. That way you're no so overwhelmed by leaving your career and finding something new."

"So what do I do?"

"In some ways you're still caught in the sixteen-year-old boy's body, rebelling against a world that hurt him. But also the thirty-four-year-old man who is running away from his pain. You need time to establish what you want now as someone who is evolving. But first you need to figure out who you are. Lean into those emotions, embrace that fear, then let it go."

"You make it sound easy."

"It isn't. You'll fall down more than you'll succeed at first. But it'll get easier. We'll go through some exercises to help you sit with those feelings, acknowledge them, then let them pass. Give yourself breathing room and space whenever you can. But you have to do this every day, whenever those feelings emerge. Are you ready to make some changes, Jack?"

He nodded and hoped like hell he could handle it.

"I hate goodbyes."

"Lucky for you, this isn't one then."

Sera rested her chin on his chest. They were curled up in her bed, on the last night they would be together before he left for L.A.

She didn't want him to leave. Not just because she would miss him, but because it would mean a shift in the routine they had going. And one step closer to him leaving for good.

He'll be back for the wedding. He'll be back for the wedding.

"Hey." Jack brushed back her curls and Sera closed her eyes, savouring the sensation.

Would it always be like this? Constantly saying goodbye. Stolen moments of time. Picking up the pieces. Alone.

Her eyes stung. She didn't want to think about it. Making a fuss over it wasn't going to help.

But those feelings for him, those pesky bloody feelings that circled around her heart had infiltrated her system, flooded all her reason and good sense.

"Don't cry."

"I'll miss you."

"I'm coming back."

"I'll miss you too isn't hard to say, Jack."

Another reason why this would be hard.

Jack shifted back against the headboard, lifting her onto his lap. He cupped her face, brushing back the stream of tears, offering her comfort which would only deepen her pain.

"I'll miss you, Sera. I'm not great with words, but I'll show you just how much."

She met his mouth, channelling her feelings into the kiss. Into him.

Sera blocked out all other thoughts, desperate to savour the moment while it lasted.

She was terrified that there wouldn't be another.

CHAPTER TWENTY-SIX

*J*ack had barely landed when he spotted the pain brigade, otherwise known as the paparazzi, swarming, ready to attack.

They hovered around him as he walked through the gates, circling like sharks. The flash of the bulbs still penetrated through the shades of his glasses, and all he could think about was getting back on a return flight to Australia.

That familiar sense of dread, the churning in his stomach, made him want to throw up the breakfast he'd had on the plane. Which would be a pity, given that the smoked salmon he had was delicious.

But even though he tried to control his thoughts, his body had another agenda. His heart squeezed and thumped, setting an impossible pace. He wanted to run, release all that energy buzzing beneath his skin, but he focused on keeping his steps measured, his gait slow, almost lazy.

If he ran, it would only make the situation worse.

"What's happened to your secret baby?"

"Is your girlfriend legal?"

"Are you being sued by the studio?"

"When will your new girlfriend arrive?"

The flurry of questions swirled around him, landing in a heap on his back. He fought to stay upright, to keep calm, but the short time he had spent in Melbourne had made him forget just how frenzied the paps were in L.A.

Stupid really.

It was like Diana had said. He was caught like a frog in a pot of water, gradually boiling alive, none the wiser until it was too late.

His abuser wasn't some woman, or even a close friend, but his career. It had become his tormentor for so long that he had lost any joy, any satisfaction.

What had started as something so full of promise, what had been a dazzling beginning, was now wearing thin. He had wanted to act since he was a kid, then he had wanted success to make his father proud. To prove he could. But beneath the Hollywood veneer, he was left battered and bruised.

But he had an obligation, to his agent, his co-stars, to this film to see it through, to get it done. He'd figure it all out after.

Jack ducked into the nearest toilets, slamming the door shut. His breathing was ragged, his heartbeat erratic. Taking off his glasses, he rubbed at his eyes, and it freaked him out to see his hands were shaking.

What the fuck, Jack. Pull it together.

He went through Diana's breathing and visualisation techniques, using it in a desperate attempt to just stop the attack. But nothing worked.

He knew he was fighting it, knew he needed to settle himself before he could actually calm down, but the voices in his head were loud and persistent.

Maybe it was a heart attack. Maybe he would never be able to breathe again. Maybe he'd be trapped by his career, unable to leave, and end up alone and addicted like so many other stars he had met along the way.

Jack heard the barrage of questions through the door and jerked away. Splashing water on his face, he looked into the mirror. He clenched the sides of the basin and forced himself to look again. There were lines around his eyes, bags beneath them and a haunted expression that just wouldn't quit.

No matter how many times he tried to school his features and act himself out of it, he was left with the same tormented expression.

Jack was never leaving this cubicle again.

And the ridiculousness of it all made him laugh. Gusts of belly-rolling laughter tumbled out, echoing in the sterile bathroom. He was going crazy. This was what the beginning of a breakdown must be like. Who the hell wanted this?

Diana said to feel all the emotions, good and bad. To let them seep through him and back out of his fingertips. But he was absorbing everything, unable to release any of that energy. It would consume him until he exploded.

He didn't care if they thought he was crazy. He could see the headlines now: "Hollywood Star Cracks It in Airport Toilet."

And just like a fissure in a dam, the pressure built until the floodgates opened and he was sobbing into his arms, sad and broken, without any pretence.

When it subsided, he washed his face once more and rang the only person he could think of that would help.

He called Sera.

"Just go." Ally encouraged. "If it's what you feel you need to do, stop questioning yourself."

Sera gnawed on her lip, torn between wanting to help, and needing to step back. To protect herself.

"What did he say on the phone?" Maddie sat beside them on the sofa in the basement.

She had called Maddie and Ally needing advice, uncertain of what to do. Sera was fearful that what she instinctively wanted to do was crazy, foolish even.

"I could barely make out what he was saying. He was sobbing, like...really broken." Sera swallowed, clearing her voice. She needed to be strong. "I'm worried about him."

"Did you manage to calm him down?" Ally asked.

"Eventually. I used the strategies I did while he was here, and that seemed to work. But I think he was locked in the toilets and the paps were hounding him. He sounded really lost. Afraid."

"And you're nearly jumping out of your skin with worry." Maddie noted, concern written across her face.

Sera closed her eyes for a second, trying to block out the images that had haunted her since last night. "I keep thinking about him all alone, trying to face this by himself, when he's still not in a good way...I'm wondering if I should go."

Maddie's mouth opened. "To L.A.?"

"I think it's a fantastic idea." Ally's eyes warmed. "And exactly what Jack would need."

"What about what you need?" Maddie frowned. "Are you going to be okay throwing yourself into the mix like that?"

Sera shrugged. "It's not about me."

Maddie wagged a finger. "Nuh uh. Not this martyr business again."

"What?" Sera exploded, facing her friend. "What martyr business?"

Maddie raised her hands. "Easy, De Lotto."

"No, tell me what you mean by that, because I'm starting to get real pissed off."

Maddie's mis-matched eyes flashed. "You can't sacrifice your feelings or just shove them aside for the greater good, pretending like you're immune to how it affects you."

"I don't do that."

"Look at all the orphans you adopt, Sera."

"I'm sick of you saying that! I'm sick of you hounding me for doing what I think is important."

"I'm not doing that. I'm point out that you have this thing where you try to save people. First Eli, then Leila, now Jack. Look, Jack is an adult. He made these decisions, and put himself in this situation, so now he has to handle it."

"And what's so wrong with wanting to help him?"

"Because you're in too deep!" Maddie yelled back. She rubbed at her face, breathing in and out to calm down.

"Madds," Ally warned.

"I'm sorry for yelling. But I'm worried that you're falling for Jack when you told me you were just biding your time until the wedding. That it was going to be light and fun and you'd enjoy yourself. Flying half-way across the world to be with him as he deals with all this shit, isn't what a lover would do. That's a girlfriend move right there, honey."

Sera's heart thumped. Even if Maddie had a valid point, it wasn't what she wanted to hear.

"I'm a grown adult. What I do isn't any of your business. I'm always going to do the right thing. That's just me. It doesn't make me a martyr."

"But it does make you open to hurt." Ally soothed, squeezing her arm.

"Whose side are you on?" Sera grumbled.

"We're not taking sides." Ally raised her arms up. "Your generous heart is one of the best qualities about you, Sera. If you want to go to Jack, go. You've got leave owing to you. Hell, even the principal suggested taking a bit of time out with all the mad press lately."

"And you'll be walking into even bigger circus in L.A.," Maddie stated. "I'm not saying this to dissuade you."

"It feels like you are."

"I'm just giving you the same advice I'd want someone to give to me."

Sera didn't want to think about her advice. She didn't want someone to tell her what she was secretly fearing to be true.

Because irrationally, through all the reasoned arguments that told her not to go, to protect herself, was the one thing she couldn't argue against: her heart.

She wanted to offer Jack support and strength, to give him whatever comfort he needed to help him through.

And just like that she had made her decision.

"I don't think Sera needs our advice. Seems like she's made up her mind already," Ally replied.

"I have." Sera nodded. "I'm going to L.A. Tonight."

CHAPTER TWENTY-SEVEN

*I*t had been a whirlwind from the moment she landed.

Jack hadn't been joking when he said the paps in America were ruthless. She had been jostled and bustled from the moment she held Jack's hand, to the ride up to his house in the hills.

Which was stunning. And yet, oddly enough, a little empty. Devoid of what she thought of as the creature comforts of home.

But it wasn't *her* home. It was that of Hollywood star, Jack Davies. And boy did it impress.

"I still can't believe you're here." Jack drew her in for a quick kiss then grabbed her hand.

"I still can't believe it either. Your house is a mansion."

"Pretty neat, huh? But so much better now you're here."

She stopped him mid-tour. Jack had been a ball of energy since she arrived. She knew it was nervous tension, as he had a meeting with Taylor that afternoon and had been snapping the band around his wrist from the moment he picked her up at the airport.

Jack had negotiated a few days to settle in before he was back on set. But Sera could tell the prospect of facing the crew again was eating him up. There was a restlessness in his movements, a caginess about his eyes; the change in him was a little startling.

"Are you okay? Your phone call had me worried."

Jack opened his mouth, a careless expression on his face.

She could tell he was going to brush it off, down-play the call, and his feelings. But after a minute, he simply shook his head.

"No, I'm not. It's hard for me to say that. To admit it."

"That's why you have me and Diana and everyone else you can call to work through this. You don't have to do it alone, Jack."

"I do. Eventually. But I'm relieved you're here. This first bit is going to be tough."

"It will be, but I'm now going anywhere. I couldn't bear hearing you so upset. I know it's only ten days, but I thought it might help you get back into the routine, to have some support."

"I'm not wanting to." Jack led her to the blinding white, pristine leather sofa. She was momentarily taken by the floor to ceiling windows and the lush gardens beyond it.

He was trapped in paradise.

"What does that mean?" Sera sat beside him.

"It means I'm seeing my life clearly for the first time in a while, and I don't like how empty it is."

"Oh, Jack."

"It's true. Being with you, being back in Melbourne, hell, therapy with Diana, it's all making me realise that what I've been working towards doesn't satisfy me anymore. Once this film is over, I want to start fresh."

"So what are you saying?"

"I'm still working it all out. Being back has made me realise that I don't want this life."

"So what does that mean?"

"I'm going to have to give the best performance of my career to get through the next month. Then I'll figure it out."

Sera's heart ached for him. Even though he was finding clarity, she wanted to take his pain away. To help ease that blinding fear that had him reaching out for comfort. For her.

"So what can I do to help?"

"You don't need to do anything. Just being here, with me, is what I need right now. It's going to be brutal seeing the crew, and I've called a meeting tomorrow with a few of the key players to basically grovel."

"That's going to be hard."

"It is. For a while. But I'm realising I need to face it and not run away. As much as it makes me want to throw up, it's something I want to do."

Sera marvelled at the changes she was seeing. It was a big deal for Jack to be able to return, to want to make things right when he could afford to do whatever he pleased.

It also scared her a little.

Even through the pride at his progress, Sera was also afraid for him. She didn't want to see Jack disheartened when resistance came. And it would.

He was wanting a different life and she wasn't sure the people around him would let him go so easily. Or that he truly understood what that meant to step back from it all.

A part of her suspected that once he had positive ways of dealing with his anxiety, then the work, and all that came with it, wouldn't be so unappealing. That he would be drawn back to this lifestyle.

And away from her. Again.

Sera ignored the lancing pain in her gut. It wasn't about her.

She would support Jack because he needed it, and because she wanted to offer that comfort.

It wouldn't do to dwell on the future.

"Look at you, the new and improved Jack Davies."

"Or maybe just the old one, polished up a bit on the inside."

Sera squeezed his hand, hoping that he would find the answers he needed.

She hoped she'd be able to handle it when he did.

Jack walked out of the lift, Sera's hand in his. Knowing she would be at reception while he had his meeting with his agent was a massive comfort. Where once he would have seen it as a sign of weakness, he now understood that needing support was necessary in order to heal.

"You got this," Sera murmured, sitting down.

"If you hear high-pitched screaming, it's just me having my ass chewed, then handed back to me."

"That's gross."

"That's Taylor Thomas."

Sera swatted him away, and Jack focused on the fact that in a few hours they would be back at his place, takeaway containers in hand while they enjoyed each other's company.

Tomorrow's meeting with the crew was going to be hard enough. Jack could only hope that they were forgiving. He didn't imagine his agent would be.

He offered a quick wave to the tired-looking intern at the front desk. Well past knock off time by anyone's clock, but Taylor liked to work his employees to the same punishing standard he set for himself. Jack wasn't surprised that there was a new person to replace the last one. None of them really hung around for very long.

He knocked on the door and waited a beat before entering.

No, sympathy was not Taylor Thomas's style. He was a busy man who didn't have time for his own talent, let alone the line of newbies who were vying for a chance to represented.

Jack was one of the very lucky ones. He had appreciated his good fortune a million times since he had landed on his feet. But being back also gave him a good dose of perspective.

His life in L.A. wasn't nourishing. In fact, it was probably going to kill him in the end.

"Please don't tell me you've come in with some new crisis, J.D., coz I've had enough of your drama."

"I can't be that bad. You're still speaking to me."

"Don't tempt me."

Taylor looked even more haggard in appearance: he was a wraith of a man, living off cigs and coffee, with an ulcer the size of Texas in his gut, and a lifestyle that made no room for relationships, only acquaintances. Jack refused to end up that way.

"Is the damage that bad?"

"Don't expect the welcome wagon if that's what you're after."

Jack's heart thumped. "I won't. I know I'll be paying for this—"

"Fuck up? Yes, you will. And dearly. Millions, Jack. Millions upon millions for the delay, which could possibly affect release schedules and everything else that fucking comes with producing a film."

Jack winced then snapped his wrist band, feeling the rising fear seizing his spine.

You got this, Jack.

"I screwed up. I know it."

"You not only screwed up, but you also went and fucked off. Talk about a nail in my coffin. Jesus, J.D. I've been trying to keep your career afloat, while you've been jacking off in the desert."

"I'm apologising for it, Taylor. I mean it. You know it wasn't like that. I've been working on my mental health."

"And finding yourself a girlfriend is working on your health?"

Jack shrugged his shoulders. What the hell could he say to that?

"I don't have any answers for you. I didn't think Sera and I would start something at the time."

"You better start thinking, especially with your meeting tomorrow. They're pissed and want answers."

"I'll tell them the truth."

"And kiss your career goodbye."

"So be it."

Taylor shook his head. "You won't be saying that when you become a D-list actor."

"About that...I have some news."

"Do I need to sit down?"

"I hope not. I will make it right with the studio, so don't worry about that."

"You're a lucky son of a bitch that the studio wanted you back and didn't sue. I'm surprised the fine you'll pay isn't heftier. If it were up to me, I'd add another zero."

Jack couldn't help but grin. Of course Taylor would.

"J.D., people talk. This is going to jeopardise the roles coming in. But we can do a bit more PR work, even play up the mental health aspect and get you on some talk shows. Women eat that stuff up. Modern man, in touch with his feelings..." he prattled on. Jack let the words wash over him. He was peculiarly detached from it all.

Jack watched Taylor smoke, pacing up and down the length of his office. Beneath them, Beverly Hills was alive with activity, lights twinkling across the strip lined with exclusive stores and expensive cars. Amongst it all was a steady stream of tourists captivated by the glamorous celebrities and envious of the glittering display of wealth.

None of it mattered. None of it appealed.

"I've come to say I'm not taking any more offers right now. In fact, I'm taking an extended break."

Taylor, an already startling shade of orange, turned a little green. "I do need to sit down." And as he did, Jack glimpsed how much the news affected him. The sagging weight of disappointment hung off his bony shoulders.

Jack looked away, remorse twisting around his gut.

"So this isn't just some mad fixation?"

"No. I need time out, Taylor."

"So you're just going to pack your bags and move to the back of nowhere?"

"Australia is hardly the back of nowhere."

Taylor sputtered, dragging in smoke instead of air. "Australia?" he gasped. "Fucking worse than I thought."

"I've been looking into a home in Melbourne, somewhere off the grid. There's important work that I want to do there, work that will matter in real life, not just on screen."

"For fuck's sake, J.D., this isn't some come to Jesus moment, is it? Leaving Hollywood for life as a missionary, eating berries and living at one with nature?"

"No, but it does involve helping kids. And right now, that's a hell of a lot more appealing than being here. I need space to think, Taylor, to work it all out. Being back should make me feel good, I shouldn't be dreading it."

"So that's it?"

Jack knew it wasn't that easy. Cutting ties completely didn't feel wholly right either. "I don't want to just go cold turkey, but I've been working back-to-back for a solid five years and I need a break. I'm burnt out, fucking blubbering in airport toilets coz I don't have my shit together. I'm not good to any studio, let alone myself. I don't want it to get worse than it is.

"Before you say anything, I know I've commitments in the

new year and I won't be pulling a runner again. But I'm not taking any new scripts. I've solid amounts of press work with the ton of films that are coming out with my face all over it for the next two to three fucking years."

Taylor looked out the glass windows then back at him. "I knew this day would come."

It was Jack's turn to sit down. "What?"

"A few years ago, you were at a premiere for *Rogue Mountain*, and I saw it in your eyes. I thought at the time I was imagining it, but a few months later, there it was again. And even though I kept telling myself it would pass; I didn't want to hear it. I've invested a lot in you, kid."

Jack let the discomfort in, absorbing the hurt before letting it go. He refused to hold on to other people's emotions; they weren't his own. But this was different. He didn't want to let the one person who gave him a chance down. Even though he knew it was inevitable.

"Why didn't you mention it?"

Taylor studied him then put out his cigarette. "I didn't want to shove ideas in your head or be right about what I saw. That makes me a selfish bastard, I know. But since the day I met you, I knew you had that star potential. Not everyone has it, though it's a lot easier in some ways to get seen without an agent than it used to be."

"Are you apologising?"

"Do I apologise?"

"People change."

"Not always. I need to stay the same so that people like *you* can change. And it has taken me a few months to accept you're heading in a different direction. I think it'll be good for your career...eventually."

"Still think I'll have one?"

"Yes. Not as fast paced, but maybe a little deeper."

"I'll take that."

"And I'll take her."

Jack frowned, until Taylor turned his laptop around.

"Sabrina Alowyn Sykes."

"Mouthful."

"Handful, too. She's been trying to get me to represent her for a long time. Thanks to you, I now have the time."

"Another rising star?"

"Like someone else I knew a long time ago, she's hungry for it."

He had been more than hungry; he had been desperate, but for all the wrong reasons. Jack's need for fame and fortune had come from a desire to honour his father's memory, and the dream they both shared. He had accomplished that, many times over, so it was time to take a step back. Re-evaluate.

"I think I've been over-indulging as of late. I'm needing a detox."

"Don't starve yourself, J.D. Hollywood won't remember forever."

"I think I'm okay with that."

"I believe you might be." Taylor slapped the desk, his tall, slim frame already a bundle of energy. He hadn't seen the man sit for that long in a decade. "Now go so I can make this woman's dreams come true."

"Ever tire of playing God?" Jack stood, a pang of something like sorrow lancing through his heart.

"On nights like these? Not one fucking bit."

Jack laughed, seeing himself out. "Good luck." He was at the door when his agent called him back.

"Hey, Jack."

He paused, hearing his given name sounded odd, even if right. To Taylor, he had always been J.D.

"Yeah?"

"Don't be a stranger."

He grinned. It was as good as he was going to get from Taylor Thomas. Jack took it as a win.

The following evening, Jack let himself in to his home, mind and body utterly fatigued. He had somehow deluded himself into thinking that the meeting with his agent would be harder than the one with his co-stars and crew.

Stupid, really.

But he had arrived at the studio open and ready to eat humble pie. And boy was he full.

It didn't matter that he was throwing money at them to cover the delay. It didn't matter that he would be accepting more promotional work to make up for lost time.

It was the utter disappointment and concern of his co-workers and crew that he couldn't make up for, and it had hollowed him out.

But he spoke to them about seeking help, his therapy sessions, and the fact that this film was a haunting reminder of his parents' death. He was candid and open about his struggles, and even though it meant he was vulnerable, Jack realised there was a freedom in that.

No more hiding out. No more pretending he was fine.

Naturally, the cast voiced their concerns about what had happened, and whether he would actually stick around this time. Some were brutal, others were understanding, but facing them, owning up to his mistakes was the right thing to do.

Jack had been so consumed by his own demons, that he had forgotten that there were people on set that gave a damn. They were a family of sorts, and he had let them down. The fact that they were genuinely worried about him had brought up a lot of emotions he had wanted to crush but didn't. Not this time.

Jack slipped off his jacket and shoved his baseball cap off his head. He stopped in the hall, overcome by the wonderous smells emanating from the kitchen. His house had never been a true home. Not in the cookies-fresh-out-of-the-oven sense.

It tugged on his heart to know that it hadn't been that way since his parents had died. It also surprised him to realise that he wanted it now. His own piece of the domestic pie.

It should have terrified him. Instead, Jack felt a warmth spread through his body, lightening his mood, giving him hope.

"Honey, I'm home." Jack walked into his state-of-the-art kitchen.

"Har, har."

Jack was about to make a smart-ass remark when he saw the various dishes of food lining the island bench.

Sera, barefoot, hair loose and trailing over her shoulders, turned. And something inside him clicked into place.

"Wow."

"I'll take that as an approval. I thought you might want some comfort food after today's meeting." She brushed back her hair, colour high on her cheeks.

"I'm ravenous."

He covered the distance between them, eager for a taste.

"Good. I think I was nervous and needed to burn off some energy so I—"

Jack kissed her, craving every bit of her warmth and energy. Every bit of her.

Sera stumbled back, but he was there to catch her. Lifting her now, he groaned when she wrapped her legs around his waist. Jack carried her to the kitchen table, deepening the kiss, unable to restraint the lust that clawed at him now.

"Jack," she gasped as he devoured the side of her neck.

"I need you," he muttered, caught by the scent.

"Now?"

"This second." He squeezed her breast, then swore at the

thin cotton dress. He tugged down the material, and the bra beneath it, feasting on her nipples.

"Here?"

"No better place."

"The food..."

He drew back, blood rushing through his body, his need straining against his jeans. "Is the stove on?"

"What?" Sera shoved back her hair. "No, but—"

"It can wait." Jack reached under her dress, ripping off her underwear. Then he stopped. "Wanna fuck?"

"I thought you'd never ask." Sera grinned.

He kissed her again, every nerve on edge as she unbuttoned his jeans, tugging them down, along with his briefs.

"Someone's ready."

"When it comes to you, I'm permanently hard."

Sera laughed, then squealed when he nudged her down, laying her flat on the table then spreading her legs. Jack kneeled, fusing his mouth to her pussy. He licked and sucked, swirling his tongue in the way that drove her wild.

When she began writhing against his mouth, he stopped. He had the satisfaction of hearing her groan before he pulled her upright, feasting on her soft mouth.

Sera tugged at his T-shirt, and in one desperate move, Jack ripped it off, over his head.

He wanted her, wild and free and gasping with pleasure.

Jack inserted one finger, then another, enjoying the way she rocked over his hand. And before either of them could beg, he thrust into her. Jack froze, groaning. She was tight and warm and everything he desired.

It was like coming home.

When he was with her, it always felt like home.

"Jack..." she rocked against him, and he nearly passed out. "Fuck me."

"Yes, ma'am."

He gripped the side of her dress, bunching it in his fist, as he set the pace. He was overwhelmed by lust and a feral need to pound into her.

Sera's eyes were glazed over, her wild hair unbound and trailing down her shoulders. With every thrust, her tits bounced, and Jack watched with primal satisfaction as his cock disappeared inside her.

Fuck, she was hot.

"Jack, I'm close," she cried out.

"I'm even closer," he muttered, driving into her.

Sera's moans grew louder, her breathing more fragmented. Everything about her took his desire into overdrive.

And just like that, she was gasping, shuddering, lost in her own orgasm.

It took every ounce of Jack's strength not to come. But he held back, gritting his teeth, prolonging the pleasure, until he pulled out, losing control.

Jack couldn't breathe from the force of it. If this was how he would meet his maker, he was oddly okay with it.

"Fuck, Sera, that was..."

"Yep." She shoved back her hair. "I agree. Looks like I'm going to need another shower."

"I'm happy to help."

"I bet you are." She grinned.

Jack swallowed, his mind slowly catching up. "Shit, Sera, I didn't use protection."

"I know. I'm on birth control, it's okay."

"I wasn't thinking."

"Neither was I."

"Okay then."

Sera grinned. "Okay. Sooo, fancy some pasta?"

"Maybe for dessert."

"Dessert?"

"We've still got the main course." Jack grinned, lifting Sera, and carrying her upstairs.

By the time they had made it back to the kitchen, the food was stone cold.

Sera should have been annoyed, but the look on Jack's face when he sampled her manicotti made up for it. That, and the fact that she had hot table sex followed by even hotter shower sex.

She was tingling in all the right places, and wonderfully relaxed.

Sera curled up beside Jack on the sofa, sipping her glass of wine, letting him talk about everything except what had happened. She understood he needed a breather, that he would get to it when he was ready.

It was only after the tiramisu that he began.

"I didn't think it would be so hard, but Sera, it was pretty brutal."

"Tell me." She placed her glass on the table.

"We sat around, a few of the key cast, the producer, director and some other crew members and I explained what happened. Then they had a chance to talk, and they basically ripped me a new one. I disappointed a lot of people in leaving. But more so, I really scared them."

"I'm so sorry, Jack."

He ran his hand over his face, the hurt flashing in his eyes. "I deserved it. I left, in pretty shitty circumstances so I understand their anger."

"What happened?"

Jack cleared his throat. He picked up her hand, running his finger along her palm, up to her wrist then back again.

"We had filmed a tough scene. The part where the hero—

that'd be me—realises he was responsible for his father's death."

"Oh, Jack."

"We finished filming, and everyone was doing their thing, and I just sat there. Couldn't move a muscle. I sat frozen in place, practically swimming in my tears. They called the paramedics, and they were talking about having me admitted. I was sitting there for a few hours. Stuck. Catatonic. In a really dark place."

Her heart twisted. "I'm so sorry you went through that, Jack."

"I was messed up, without a doubt. I just kept thinking about the moment I found out about my parents' death. It was on a loop in my brain. I finally snapped out of it, got my shit together and left, refusing treatment. I was petrified of being put in the hospital. Of being admitted and sent to some psych ward. But I couldn't stop thinking about my parents' death. I was alone and lost and I just needed space."

"So you flew to Melbourne."

"I couldn't stand being here one more minute. Alone. I hate hospitals, and didn't want to go to some rehab centre, so I packed my bags and ran."

"It makes sense that your co-workers were worried about you."

"Bingo. One minute I'm catatonic and the next thing they hear, I've left the country."

"And today?"

"They said their peace. I said mine. It was both uncomfortable and liberating telling them what I've been going through. My anxiety."

Sera had never heard him say it before. It was another sign of his progress. A good sign.

"So now what happens?"

"I'm paying for all the costs, for the delays. Which is fine.

The one thing I don't have to worry about is money. But it's all the press that I'll be doing around it that's going to be another hurdle. To be honest about my mental health in interviews won't be easy."

"But perhaps it might be cathartic. Not that it's anyone's business."

"When you live your life in the public eye, nothing is off limits. But I know it's another step in this journey I'm on. And when I'm ready, I'll do it. I'll face it."

Sera smiled, placing a gentle kiss on his cheek.

"What's that for?"

"For being you."

"What? A nutter?"

"Real. For being real. With me, with your work."

"I'm a changed man, Sera."

For how long?

The thought felt ungenerous given all Jack had revealed. But a part of Sera was afraid that the next month apart might make Jack see his life from a new perspective. He might wake up one day and want to keep making movies and all that came with it.

But it wasn't her burden to carry. It wasn't her decision to make.

She wasn't in control, and it frightened Sera more than she cared to admit. Because beneath everything, she had feelings for Jack. Ones that ran deep and true.

And despite her best attempts, she was finding it hard to keep those emotions in check.

When it came to Jack, she wasn't certain she ever could.

CHAPTER TWENTY-EIGHT

*S*era sat backstage, smoothing down the hem of her red dress for the millionth time that evening. When that didn't settle her nerves, she picked off a bit of fluff from her sheer stockings, adjusting the strap of her heels. She was a bundle of frayed wires, exposed and charged. It wasn't a sensation she cared for at all.

Watching Jack work over the past week had been an eye opener. The way he handled himself was nothing short of impressive. It made the chasm between the haunted star who had returned home a few months before, and the man beginning to manage his anxiety very wide indeed.

Nobody would know it looking at him.

Sera watched the screen as Jack sat with three other guests on the *Late Night with Joe* show. It was her last night with him before she was going home. Back to reality. She shook off those thoughts and focused on her Hollywood lover.

His leather jacket and worn jeans only added to the overall dazzle that was Jack Davies. He was calm and confident, exuding affability and ease even though this was his first media appearance since coming back. Sera had to remind herself that beneath his easy-going demeanour was a man who was still coming to terms with his mental health. A man who seemed to be making progress.

Then again, all that stuff would take time.

Would she be there for it? The question circled around her brain. Arriving in New York to the maelstrom of media and press attention that afternoon had been nothing like she had imagined. It was one thing to be caught out by the paps back home, but here, it was ridiculously invasive. The sheer number of them, like a pack of wolves baying for blood, was akin to an assault.

No wonder he had left.

Jack seemed to be used to it, even if he barked at his agent about the constant attention. According to Taylor, all press is good press. Now that Jack was back, he was booked solid.

No wonder everyone had prescription pill problems. Sera couldn't believe that Jack hadn't lost himself a long time ago.

She sipped at the Pepsi she had been nursing since taping began. It was all so very surreal, being in New York at one of the world's most popular shows, seeing her lover on screen.

Sera couldn't imagine Jack walking away from it all, even if he told her that's what he wanted. It was in him. In his blood to do this. The level of his success was proof that his life was here, in this world.

For all the pushing and shoving she did, convincing herself that they couldn't make it work, Sera was searching for the way through, trying to find that path. But every time she did, she was left floundering.

Because she didn't fit. Sera didn't belong here, and she never really would. She'd rather walk away than make him choose.

She tilted her head back, desperate to stop the tears that gathered. She couldn't cry over it here.

They were going for a late dinner after the taping. Some swanky place, just the two of them. Sera would focus on the time she could spend with Jack and worry about the rest later. Otherwise, she'd drive herself crazy.

When the door swung open, Sera jumped, then stood to help the tall, striking woman with the door.

"Sorry," she whispered, juggling bags and what looked like a fussy baby in a carrier.

The baby squawked and wriggled in the papoose then settled back down once his mother patted his bottom. Even with a fussy baby, she looked calm. Her dark hair was pulled back in a neat bun, her outfit stylish. She made it look effortless, though Sera knew it was anything but that.

"Hi, I'm Angel, Liam's wife." She gestured to the Thor look-a-like on screen. The man was bulky and built, with tattoos up his neck and on the parts of his forearm that wasn't covered in a shirt.

"I'm Sera."

Her smile lit up the room. "You're Jack's girl. The Aussie."

Angel's accent was strong but had a slight twang to it that hinted at it being from another part of the country. The South? The West? American geography wasn't her strong suit.

"Yes. I'm here for a...guest appearance of my own you could say. It's my last night before going home. I'm a teacher."

"Me too! I do grade school."

"I'm high school."

"Is that like our middle school?"

"I'm so confused." Sera laughed then pressed her hand to her mouth. "Sorry," she whispered, but the baby didn't fuss.

"Oh, he's fast asleep again." She waved off the concern. "So you teach bigger kids?"

"Yeah, thirteen-to eighteen-year-olds."

"That's fabulous. I teach elementary school. Littlees."

"Sounds like a lot to juggle."

"My life is chaos. And I was meant to come out tonight without this little moonbeam, but he's teething something fierce." She looked down at the blond-haired child, his mouth open, body limp. "He didn't want anyone but his mamma, so of course I had to bring my baby bear. And Liam is always excited to see his boy."

Sera pegged it. The South, her accent had a twang that was soft and soothing.

Angel turned to the table with the platters of food. "I'm getting something to eat. Lord knows I can't wait until taping is over. Breastfeeding makes me ravenous. Some days I eat more than Liam does, and that man puts away a lot."

She began filling up her plate then sat beside Sera.

"Do you mind if I ask you a personal question?"

Angel waved her hand in assent, munching around the wedge of cheese.

"How do you manage it? Not seeing your husband and caring for the baby on your own? Don't you miss him?"

"Hell yeah, honey. But you do manage it, just like everything else you do in life. You adjust because you have to, and because you love that person enough to balance both your needs. It's difficult, especially with them big blockbuster films which take up to three months to shoot, sometimes longer. But we visit on set when we can, and usually it's lots of video calls. On the plus side, he gets a lot of down time if he's not taking on a new film."

"So you travel with him?"

"I did in the beginning, but with little bub here, I try to keep a routine at home. We live here, but we have a house in Canada, as a lot of the bigger films seem to be shot there these days."

Sera digested the information. "Aren't you lonely?"

"Oh sugar, by the time I've had Liam home for three months straight, I'm ready to send that man to Antarctica!" She wiped at her mouth, her silver rings glinting against her dark skin.

"Is it hard doing it on your own?"

She wrinkled her nose. "It's different. Like learning a new

language, everything is foreign in the beginning. I remember when Liam and I first started dating, my Lord, them paps at our door. I couldn't bring him back home to visit my mama because she was so embarrassed about being filmed. But you get used to it. He's been doing this for so long he can pick and choose his films. If a project is in the jungle and he doesn't like the script, he won't take it."

"So he's slowed down?"

"Oh yeah. But babies change a man. He wants to provide for his family, but he wants to spend time with his son more. Liam's daddy worked all the time and he didn't want that for us. If that means losing out on some scripts, he's okay with that. And yeah, life is busy when he's promoting this or doing an interview for that, but it's our life."

"And you're okay with that?"

"It wasn't easy at first, no. But I love him. I wouldn't want to be doing this whole mad mess with anyone else. And having success isn't all bad. I get to have my mama come and stay with us when Liam is off filming. I get my house cleaned professionally and people to come and sort out all those things I hate doing myself. I know how lucky I am."

"And happy."

"So happy I want to try for another one."

Angel's warmth reminded Sera of her own mother. Of the way her parents had made their marriage work, even through the difficult times. Would she ever have that?

Angel's warm smile disappeared, and her eyes widened. "Lord, girl, are you pregnant?"

"What?" Sera sputtered, the question jolting her.

"All those questions about babies..." She gestured to Sera's stomach. "I thought you might be expecting."

"Oh, wow. No. Not pregnant."

"I was about to pop the champagne!" She laughed,

smoothing her son's hair back. "Looks like nap time is over." His piercing cry filled the room.

Sera was lost in the next hour, playing with the curious and gregarious eight-month-old, whilst talking about teaching with Angel.

Hearing about her life, her perspective, offered Sera an insight she hadn't allowed herself to see before.

A part of her remained hopeful that it would all turn out for the best. But Sera wasn't sure she entirely believed it.

Returning to her old routine just didn't make any sense. Sera had become so accustomed to having Jack around, that she had spent the first week back drifting from one task to another, lost.

Going back to work had shaken her out of the fog a little, but she was finding that everything seemed to remind her of Jack. He had infiltrated her life so thoroughly she couldn't quite remember what she had done before he had arrived.

After giving her apartment a nice new paint job, Sera was slowly moving her things back to her place. She was in no rush, spending more time at her parents' house because her own just felt so...blah.

She had spoken to Jack nearly every day upon her return. But as the weeks crawled by, the contact between them became infrequent, sporadic. Often, she was busy in class or missed his call and found herself scrambling to remember the time difference.

Sera had Ally's huck's night to plan, as well as her tutoring to keep her busy. But beneath it all, she missed him.

The paparazzi still followed her, but with Jack back in L.A. she found she was able to do normal things like shopping or going for a run, without them hounding her.

Sera could only hope that Jack would have clarity about his

life when he returned. If that meant he wanted to continue acting and stay in L.A., then so be it. She would have to learn to be okay with that. Sera caught the emotions before it overwhelmed her. Nope. No point in wallowing.

Maddie was right. She couldn't sort out his life for him, no matter how much she wanted to help.

"Want to go out for some ice cream?"

Her dad sat beside her on the couch. It was another wet but warm spring afternoon, and Sera had found herself moping about her parents' house after coming by for a late lunch. Her mind was drifting. To Jack. Always back to Jack.

"No, I'm okay with just sitting here for a while."

"Been a busy month."

"It has, with Ally's wedding prep and Leila's birthday and baby shower, it's been non-stop action."

"I can't believe she's eight months pregnant...time seems to be flying by. Your mother said she had a great time being pampered."

"Her eyes nearly fell out of her head, Dad."

"It was nice of you to think of making a high tea for her."

"She needed a bit of fancy. We all do from time to time."

"You're a good person, Seraphina. With a big heart."

She smiled. "Thanks, Dad."

"And can I just say, I'm glad that you and Maddie have made up. I don't like to see you girls fighting."

Sera jerked a shoulder. "I understand why she said it, and we talked it through, I think I just wasn't ready to hear it at the time."

"You? Stubborn? No..."

Sera smirked. "I get it, I get it. I'm working on it."

"Good. So, when's Jack coming back?"

"In a few weeks. Filming is nearly over, he's wrapping up his commitments and some interviews, then he'll back."

"For how long?"

235

Sera's stomach clenched. "I'm not sure."

They had until the wedding. She knew that. Reminded herself of it, so that she wouldn't be fooled into dreaming of a future that didn't exist. She had made that mistake once, long ago.

"Are you happy with him, Sera? Without all the worrying and the long distance, does he make you happy?"

Sera didn't need to search for answers. "Yeah, he does."

But that happiness was fleeting. Her heart ached with the knowledge that she would never have what her parents shared. Not with Jack.

"Then focus on that when the madness kicks up again. You'll be under the spotlight when he returns and that can be stressful on top of everything else you're juggling."

Her dad wasn't a verbose man, but he seemed to know just what to say to ease her troubles.

Sera wanted desperately to believe that they could make it work. To believe the lie.

She turned, pecking him on the cheek. "Thanks, Dad. I will. So, ice cream?"

"That's a great idea. Should have thought of it myself."

CHAPTER TWENTY-NINE

*J*ack's heart was pounding, but in a good way. He had been a bundle of nerves on the flight home, desperate to fast forward time so he could see Sera in the flesh. Video calls just weren't enough.

He couldn't wait to catch the look on her face when she answered the door. Sera had no clue he was coming back today, and according to Ally, she was having lunch with Leila at her parents' place. They were sorting through a bunch of baby clothes that Maryam had sourced from the local community so they would be home all afternoon.

He would have to thank Ally later for keeping it a secret.

In his absence, he had somehow forgotten how hot it was down under in December, and he looked forward to getting inside and cracking open a cold cider. After ringing the bell for a third time, Jack began to lose heart. Maybe she wasn't—

The door swung open and Jack stared at Sera in horror. There was blood all over her hands, and up her T-shirt.

"What the hell—"

"*Jack*? What are you...Doesn't matter. Thank God you're here! You've delivered a baby before, haven't you?"

"What the hell? No!"

"Not even on television?"

"I played a doctor once, but that's a far cry from delivering a baby."

"Better than me."

"But you've got the..." Jack gestured. "The bits."

Sera looked torn between wanting to laugh in his face or slap him. He wasn't going to take his chances.

"I don't have time for this. Come *on*."

Jack hurried to keep up with her as she jogged through to the lounge room.

"Am I dreaming? Am I still on the plane?" Jack trailed behind her now, rubbing his eyes.

"No, this is real and I need help. You're the only one here until the ambulance arrives. There's been some massive train accident and most services have been routed there. I can't move Leila to drive her to the hospital, so it looks like it's going to be you and me, Hollywood."

"Christ, had I known this would happen, I would have booked a later flight."

"Lose the jacket, and I'd take off that expensive looking watch if I were you." Sera crouched down on the floor, next to Leila.

"Jesus Christ."

"Why the *fuck* is *he* complaining?" Leila ground out, dark hair matted to her forehead, face flushed and in pain. "He's not the one-ahh-giving birth to a...giant!"

"It's okay. You're doing really well. Jack, can you get another popsicle from the freezer?"

"Done."

"And a wet towel!"

Jack used the reprieve to boost his confidence. He could totally do this. Piece of cake. Women gave birth to babies in barns for centuries. Leila was going to be just fine.

He swallowed back his fear and returned to the lounge.

Then he took one look at Leila's tortured face and he wanted to run. Far, far away. He was not cut out for this. Not meant to be responsible for important things.

This was literally his worst nightmare come to life. And there was not a fucking thing he could do about it. Jack's lungs seized and the tell-tale vice around his throat reminded him of everything about this situation that made him fearful.

What if he did something wrong? What if he made the situation worse?

But he wouldn't run away. He may have been a wreck, but he was a wreck who would stay and help out.

And pray like hell he didn't screw things up even more.

"I thought you were having lunch with your parents. Where are they?" He snapped the band around his wrist. *Chill, Jack. You can do this.*

"Huh? They left hours ago." Sera's voice was calm, but beneath it he could hear her urgency.

They were screwed.

"What can I do?" Jack asked.

"Has someone new arrived?" A gentle voice came through Sera's phone.

"Uhh, hi. I'm Jack."

"I'm Emily. The ambulance officer looking after Leila. It shouldn't be much longer for our paramedics to arrive."

Thank Christ.

"We think she's about six centimetres dilated. Contractions are consistent so that's positive," Sera added.

Jack didn't want to know how she knew that.

Why was there so much blood? Was that normal?

"It hurts!" Leila cried out, writhing in pain. "Something's wrong."

"You're doing a great job."

"Everything is fine, Leila," Emily's voice was calm over the phone. Her soft but firm manner even made Jack feel at ease. *This was fine. He could do this.*

"Where's Will?" Leila sobbed.

"He'll be here soon, honey. I promise," Sera soothed.

"You might want to try pressure points to counteract the pain," Emily instructed.

Leila twisted on the floor as another contraction seized her body. "I can't do this!"

"How about you change positions, Leila?" Emily directed, once it had passed.

Jack helped Leila move at what seemed like a snail's pace between contractions. Finding cushions, Jack propped her against the couch, while Sera laid down towels beneath her.

"I need to poo."

Jack looked at Sera, horrified. "You're shitting me."

"That's normal," Emily's muffled reply was warm, reassuring. "It's the pressure baby is putting against your bowels. If you need to go, just go, but it's a good sign."

"Ahhh." Leila swayed, and Jack followed Emily's advice about pressure points.

His knuckles were white but he didn't dare stop, not when it seemed to be doing the trick.

"Nobody said there would be pain in between contractions," Leila moaned. "It fucking hurts."

"Here, sip this." Sera handed Leila the bottle of electrolytes.

For the next hour, Jack alternated hands, pressing down on Leila's back at each contraction, offering her water and juice to help her through it. He was sweating and nervous and could only thank the universe that Emily was at least on the phone with them.

Jack's hand nearly turned numb before Leila's boyfriend showed up. After ushering him through to the lounge, Jack stepped aside so William could take over.

He noticed how Leila's body relaxed, slumping into her boyfriend's chest.

Another thirty minutes passed and still no ambulance.

Just as he was about to suggest calling a cab, or hell, the paparazzi, there was a flurry of activity.

"Something's happening!" Leila cried out.

Jack tried to avert his eyes, but he couldn't, not when Sera yanked him down to the floor beside her.

"Can you see anything, Sera?" Emily's voice was still calm.

Jack kept counting in his head, keeping his eyes averted as he lifted Leila's cotton dress so Sera could take a look.

"No, nothing."

"Something's there. It's...it's like a bowling ball."

Emily's tone warmed. "Leila, that's your baby making its descent. You must have dilated really quickly, but it's super important you are breathing through it. No pushing. Okay?"

"There's so much pressure," Leila sobbed.

"I know, just breath. Sera, I'm not sure if she's dilated enough, and I don't know if there's still any cervix in the way blocking baby's descent, so if you would keep reminding her to breathe that would be great. And tell me what you see."

"Holy shit," William muttered, holding Leila's hand.

"Oh! It's...there's a head," Sera gasped, and Jack glanced down, frozen by the sight of a dark cap in between Leila's legs.

"Fuck."

"Okay, Sera, you need to be ready now to deliver this baby. So make sure you have a towel to wrap bub in, and don't worry about anything else, I'll guide you."

"Got it." Sera breathed out, hands shaking.

"Leila, you need to listen to me now. You might feel a—"

"It's burning."

Emily's voice was firm. "Okay, good. I don't want you to push. Focus on panting, lower your shoulders, and relax your jaw. Your baby will be with us soon."

"I can see the head a bit more. It's a hairy one." Sera laughed, incredulous.

Leila lifted her head. "Can I touch it?"

"Go ahead," Emily encouraged.

Leila leaned forward and stroked her baby's head. Her laughter was one of awe and jubilation.

"Okay, so keep panting."

"It's easing back in," Sera cried out.

"That's normal," Emily said. "It takes a little bit of time."

Jack looked at Sera's face, her concentration unbroken, a flush blooming on her golden skin. She appeared undaunted and courageous, and at that moment, something inside of him gave way. It was a feeling he wasn't certain he could name.

"Okay, it's nearly out. Oh my God," Sera gasped. "The baby's head is there!"

"Fantastic."

"Wait. Jack, look at this."

"Sera," he warned.

"Look!"

It was the urgency in her voice that made him turn his head.

Jack caught a glimpse of a naked bottom before looking down to see a small, round head, that was utterly blue in the face.

His heart thudded, an odd tattoo that didn't seem to regulate no matter how many times he dragged in air.

"What the hell?"

"What's going on?" Leila and William were on red alert.

"I think the cord is stuck. The baby's face is blue." Sera's voice was strained.

"You need to try to reach inside and untangle it. Now." Emily directed.

Sera looked at him, eyes wide with terror.

"Jack, you need to help me."

He didn't know where it came from, but a cloud of courage

hovered around him. It wasn't about his fears anymore, but a young girl who could potentially lose her baby. And he was in a position to be able to do something about it.

Jack had never been responsible for something so important before. He was afraid he'd screw it up.

"What do we do?"

Emily guided them through it, quickly and efficiently.

The first thing he thought when he touched the cord was how rubbery and strong it felt.

Jack manoeuvred into position and with Sera's help managed to shift the cord from around the baby's throat in slow, steady moves.

Once the cord was removed, everything happened suddenly.

Before he could blink, the rest of the baby was born, sliding out from Leila's body and into his arms.

He floundered for a split second then held the baby close.

Sera cheered, "oh Leila, you did it!"

Leila and her William cried out, exclamations of surprise and joy.

"Check that bub is breathing," Emily advised.

Jack did, rubbing the baby as per Emily's instructions, willing it to life. Its face was no longer a dark blue, but slowly turning pink. Then it let out an almighty cry and his heart thumped in relief.

A dizzy, gratifying satisfaction flooded his body. He was shaking and yet felt stronger than a thousand men combined.

"Yes, it is. Thank fuck, it's alive."

Sera wrapped the baby, taking it from him to pass to Leila. She was crying soft happy tears as she cradled her baby against her chest.

"Thank you. Thank you so much."

"Congratulations, buddy." Jack thumped William on the back.

"Thanks, mate."

"What is it?" Emily asked.

All four of them looked at each other. It was like they were in a daze. None of them had checked.

Leila shifted the towel. "It's a girl!"

"She's beautiful, Leila." Sera wiped away a tear, and Jack had to clear his throat a few times. He couldn't quite believe what just happened.

Emily stayed with them until the paramedics arrived. By that stage, Leila had begun to feed her baby, curled up beside her boyfriend, lost in her own blissful world.

Carefully, they transferred her to the stretcher, and it wasn't long before the new parents were off to the hospital, with their healthy little girl in tow.

With promises they would visit them, and praise from the paramedics, Jack stood in the lounge trying to process everything. He had just delivered a baby with the most amazing, impressively calm woman by his side. And that was the moment he knew.

It dawned on him that all the emotions he kept locked away, all the ideas he had about himself, were something *he* controlled.

He was responsible for every negative thought, every bad habit, and he alone had the power to shift that. He faced one of his worst fears today, actually being responsible for someone else's well-being, and he didn't fail.

Jack was only glad that the paps hadn't caught on to his whereabouts yet. But they would, soon enough.

He looked at Sera as they tidied up the room. She had been so brave, so strong. He wanted to be the man worthy to have her. The mistakes he made didn't preclude him from deserving a happy life. From building a future, with her.

It was a breakthrough he wasn't certain would have come about on his own. At least, not for a very long time.

But here he was, having delivered a human into the world, having saved a baby's life. With the one woman who meant the world to him.

"Jack? You okay?" Sera rubbed his arm.

"I think I'm in shock."

"Welcome back."

"Not home?"

Sera glanced at him, smile tight. "Welcome back, Jack."

"Thanks..." He blew out a big, deep, breath. But he could see she was pulling back, a little guarded. Something for them to talk about. Later. Much later. "That was wild."

"Not quite the party you were expecting?"

Jack grinned. "Far from it." Because he wasn't so steady, he sat down.

He looked at Sera. Sweat had matted her hair in place, loose tendrils framed her forehead and neck, and her cheeks were still flushed. She was the most beautiful woman he had ever seen.

Her strength and resilience amazed him. That quiet assured thing she had going on was impressive.

"You alright?"

"I think I need a drink."

"I'll get a glass of water."

He followed her to the kitchen, sitting at the table, and that was when the thought manifested itself, as bright as day.

Sera was his home. That was exactly how he felt about her. He'd felt it for months now. She was everything that was warm and comforting and dependable. He ached for it so badly, had yearned for it over the years so much that he had looked for substitutes in the wrong places.

When he needed solace, he searched for one-night stands. When he yearned for calm, he was the life of the party. What Jack had craved had been here all this time.

He had given up a relationship with Sera long ago, afraid of the feelings she had stirred. Afraid he couldn't give her what she needed.

But all that had changed over the past few months. Jack wanted to be the man she deserved. He was man enough to face those fears, to realise that working through them made him far stronger than he led himself to believe.

"Thanks." He gulped down the cool liquid and watched her do the same.

What now? He didn't have any answers. The epiphany hadn't changed anything in a tangible sense. But it was time he fixed that.

Now that filming was over, he could focus on what he would do next. To settle the past, he'd seek out his future. And maybe, just maybe, build some new dreams. With Sera.

Perhaps it was time to rewind. Start at the beginning. His time away gave him a chance to think about what he wanted and being back had cemented those feelings.

"I think we need to get cleaned up before my folks get back this evening."

Jack looked down at his own shirt and grimaced. "Good idea."

"I'll chuck the towels in the wash, and your shirt too."

Jack narrowed his eyes. "Any excuse to see me naked."

"I'm so transparent." Sera rolled her eyes. "Strip."

"After you."

She took off her tank, and the simple red sports bra beneath was ridiculously appealing. The woman could be wearing a Freddie Krueger mask and he'd still be turned on.

"Now will you take off your shirt?"

Jack complied, tossing it to her. "I'll get the shower going. See you in minute?"

"Is that an invitation?"

"Always."

Sera narrowed her eyes, then nodded. "Okay then."

He climbed the stairs, suddenly nervous. What had she been thinking? There was reservation there, more so than usual. He wanted to sooth any fears she had, to give her what she needed.

Jack wanted to take his time, to make this special. He craved comfort and the softness of a woman's body.

Inspired, he searched through the bathroom cabinet until he found the box he was looking for. Some things didn't change. In them, was a set of tea lights.

Jack arranged them around the bathtub then filled the bath. Grabbing the matches on the shelf, he lit them and stepped back.

When he heard the door open behind him, the room was filled with steam, the candles glowing.

"Sorry I took so long I—" Sera stopped short.

It was worth it to see her face light up. The way her brown eyes softened, the hesitancy melting away.

His heart hammered.

After what felt like eons apart, after so many nights alone dreaming of her, he wanted nothing more than to hold on and never let go.

Instead, Jack forced his body to move. He shed the rest of their clothes then guided Sera into the tub. He lowered himself behind her and began rubbing her shoulders.

Sera's sweet sighs set his blood pumping. He was desperate for more contact, but he would settle for slow and steady. For now.

Taking the loofah, he washed her back first, then her breasts, enjoying the way she squirmed against him. He used his fingers to trace lazy patterns across her stomach then inched further down until he stroked her clit. She arched against him, the tips of her breasts peeking out from the water. Her nipples were hard, her gasps soft.

Taking his time, Jack circled and stroked, pinched and

rubbed, toying with her until she gripped his thighs in the water, until she writhed back against his cock.

When she called his name, Jack bit down on her neck and absorbed her pleasure, breathing it in, letting it consume him. She shuddered, riding his hand until she was spent.

"Mmm," Sera sighed, body relaxed.

He kissed her shoulder, exploring, until he couldn't control himself any longer.

Jack stood, reaching out for Sera's hand.

Cheeks flushed, she shook her head, kneeling in the tub. Then she took him hard and wet in her mouth. Eyes playful, she sucked his cock with abandon.

Jack watched, mesmerised.

Her dark curls ran down her shoulders; her bronzed body was taut and tantalising. Jack groaned and hoped like hell his legs didn't give way.

Gathering her hair in his hands, he played with the pace, only to have her swat him away. She gripped his ass and tortured him now, teasing out his orgasm, making him wait.

"Fuck, Sera, you give amazing head."

She murmured around him and then he felt it, that familiar rush, building at an impossible speed, and there wasn't a thing he could do to stop it.

Jack tried to pull back, but she gripped his ass tighter.

"I'm gonna come."

She didn't stop.

Jack let go, succumbing to the intensity of his orgasm, riding out the waves of pleasure until there was nothing left.

Sera stood before him, face flushed, a cat-like smug smile dancing across her face. He gathered her close and carried her to her bedroom, heart full.

There were no words for what he was feeling right now and he was okay with that. As long as he had Sera by his side, it didn't matter.

He had missed her in so many ways. The strength of it only reinforced by seeing her again.

Who knew it would be so powerful? That he would feel it so intensely?

And when Jack laid her down on the bed, he took his time. He stroked and teased, built them both up until he was blind to all else but her need.

And when he drove himself into her, it was a connection that surpassed the physical. It wrapped around him, warming his body, soothing his mind.

When he came, he called out her name, home at last.

"I feel like we need to talk about what just happened." Jack shifted to his side, facing Sera in bed.

Her frown was fleeting. "And here I thought you were pretty well educated, but I'll humour you. When your penis went into my—"

He tickled her and enjoyed the sound.

"I mean with Leila. The whole thing was surreal, and I think it's going to sit with me for a while. I'm processing it slowly because it was so sudden."

"You're telling me. She's so not the textbook birth, especially for a first baby."

"Isn't she early?"

"Only by three weeks, so they say anything can happen at that stage. And the baby seemed a decent size. The paramedic didn't seem too worried after checking on bub."

"And here I thought she'd have a Christmas baby."

"Can't stop babies being born."

"I wouldn't know how long it all takes, but that delivery seemed really fast. I'm sure she'd call me a dickhead for saying that as it probably felt an age to her. But Sera, we delivered a fucking human being into the world. What the actual fuck?"

"And here I thought you wanted to talk about that thing you did with your tongue."

Jack laughed, a warmth suffusing him. She made him feel like a man in the most basic sense. And as great as it was for his self-esteem, it was even better for his psyche. How many other women had complimented him on his prowess in bed? It had stroked his ego but hadn't penetrated much deeper than that.

Sera got to the core of him, made him feel important and protective and damn it, as giddy as hell just to be around her.

He couldn't remember the last time he wanted to impress someone as much, to shower her with everything that she had never given to herself.

"You were amazing to keep your cool on your own for so long."

"Thanks. She thought it was just Braxton Hicks but had been labouring all that time. I'm glad I suggested she come to my parents' house for lunch. I don't know what I would have done if you hadn't arrived."

"I was this close to shitting myself."

Sera looked up at him. "You were fantastic. You delivered a baby. You saved her little life. You can add that to the list on IMDB. Maybe apply now for General Hospital or one of those shows, Doc Davies."

"You're so old. *General Hospital*?"

"I don't watch many soap shows so I have no references. But now you have actual experience. A director would snatch you up in a second."

Jack didn't know why it bothered him to hear her talk about his next gig, but it did. A worm-like, squirming annoyance weaved its way through his blissed-out state. He wasn't sure why it bugged him, but it was something to gnaw on later. Something to talk through.

"I can't believe that I did it. *We* did it. I've tried to tell myself that I couldn't handle anything too serious in my life, that I just wasn't cut out for it, but today...damn it, Sera, I'm man enough to admit it shook me up when I saw that baby come out. It fucked me over when that cord was stuck."

"Me too. But we helped her. We saved that little baby's life. You heard the paramedics, that's something good and true that you did."

"And I'm still in shock."

"That's normal. I am too."

"You don't look it."

"This is just the post-sex-with-Jack bliss. I'll come down from my little cloud soon enough."

"Do you think it'd be okay if we went to the hospital to see her? And the baby, if they're okay with that? This evening?"

Sera's smile was warm. "Something tells me that I think they might be. We can give them a call later."

"Later?"

"Mhmm." Sera straddled him. "First, I have plans for you."

"Really?"

"Uh huh. I've had over a month of no sex and I'm a horny girl."

"I suppose I'd be doing you a favour then."

"A very big one by the looks of it."

"Hey, I aim to please."

CHAPTER THIRTY

*D*ecember was a flurry of activity. They were wrapping up exams with their students, finalising reports, and heading into a very warm Christmas.

But before all that, they had Ally's bridal shower, which meant enjoying a day of pampering, before the debauchery that would be the combined hen's and buck's party this evening. A huck's party to rival all parties.

Even though it was glorious to have Jack back in town, Sera's feelings about where they were headed were more jumbled than ever. She couldn't think about it for too long without feeling gloomy, but with the wedding drawing closer, she knew their time together was limited.

Sera shoved the intrusive thoughts away, letting her body relax in the plush massage chairs while they waited for their mani/pedis to begin.

They had started out with a spa treatment at one of Melbourne's most exclusive day spas. Before that, they had checked into their penthouse suit and Sera's eyes almost fell out of her head. Thanks to Jack's connections, they were all being treated like royalty. The only downside was the paps lurking every time they stepped outside.

"So, tell us everything about what banging a Hollywood star feels like. I'm sure that's all you've been doing since he's been back in town," Maddie murmured under her breath when a nail technician walked past.

"Let's just call him Jack while we're out and about."

"I bet you call him lots of dirty things." Maddie wiggled her eyebrows.

"And if you expect me to dish on all the little details, then you're wrong."

Maddie pouted. "You're no fun."

"He's going to be Ally's brother-in-law soon." Sera jerked her thumb at the bride-to-be, who sat serenely in the neighbouring chair. "And I'm sure she doesn't want to hear about that thing that he does with his tongue."

"I'll swap you the thing he does with his tongue for goss on what Owen does with his hands." Ally grinned.

"Ohhhh, we need more champagne!" Maddie jostled about in her oversized massage chair.

Not that they needed any more pampering. They had each been lathered head to toe in oils and exfoliants, and if their masseuse had been anything like her own, they would all be floating on a little cloud of relaxation for days.

Sera's bones felt like jelly, and she was grateful all she had to do was sit upright like a rag doll in the chair and have her manicure and pedicure. She wouldn't be able to walk for at least another hour. Maybe two.

Maddie sighed, "I dunno what it is about massages, but it makes me ready for action."

"Might be the fact that a stranger is touching you all over?" Ally grinned, sloshing her feet in the warm water.

"Who doesn't like to be touched? It makes you feel all loose and floaty." Maddie closed her eyes.

Sera couldn't help herself. "I'd say you were used to being that."

She squeaked when Maddie pinched her arm.

"Trust me to have two best friends who are incapable of offering scintillating sex conversation."

"That's because we're having it," Sera teased.

"And I've been very supportive of the fact that you girls are too busy shagging to give me a look in these days." Maddie pouted.

Immediately Sera's heart squeezed. "Madds." She put her arm on her fluffy robe.

Maddie's smile was sly. "I'm only saying it to make you both feel wildly guilty. Our dear Ally is getting married, and you're all cozied up with Jack. Does Owen have any hot cousins?"

Ally's face lit up. "Actually, I think he might have a hot friend."

"Ooh, yay me!"

"I'm not sure he's able to make it tonight, but he's coming to the wedding."

Sera frowned. "Is this the dude that's been overseas for like, forever?"

"Yes! Phillip, Owen's best friend."

"There you go, Madds, potential hot dude for you."

Maddie wrinkled her nose. "I think it would be mighty weird if I were to hook up with Owen's bestie. It'd be this odd little triangle."

"I think it would be nice," Sera offered.

"You think it's nice when twins marry twins," Maddie squawked.

"It is!"

"But all their babies would look alike. Weird."

Sera laughed. "Yeah, well, I'm shagging Owen's brother and

that hasn't made things odd." She frowned. "But then again, it's not like Jack and I are serious."

Ally leaned forward in her chair. "Not serious?"

"What Jack and I have is a temporary arrangement, nothing more. He'll go back to L.A. once the wedding is over and then who knows when I'll see him again."

"What's going on?" Ally pressed.

"Trouble in paradise, De Lotto?"

"No, just being realistic. Once all this is over, there's no real reason for Jack to hang around."

Maddie's eyes turned to saucers. "Uh, Earth to Sera, there's a big reason and I'm looking right at her."

Sera shrugged. She'd learned her lesson long ago, and she wouldn't let herself get hurt again.

Ally leaned in. "I thought you said he was wanting a change? I assumed things were different now he's back."

"Wanting a change is one thing, but actually leaving his career and starting out again—doing God knows what—is a massive step to take. His home is in L.A. His life is there. Sure, he's in therapy to help him handle all those emotions, and once he does, and realises he's a lot stronger than he gives himself credit for, then he'll have room for being creative again. Being an actor is a large part of who Jack is; he might wake up and realise he doesn't want to run from it all. That he might just want to shift gears a little bit."

"That doesn't mean he won't want you," Ally soothed.

"But let's be realistic. Long distance with a movie star wouldn't exactly work. We live two completely separate lives. The trip to L.A. made it clear that I don't fit in his world, and he certainly doesn't fit in mine. And what? We live our lives seeing each other in snatched moments of time while getting photographed every other week? No, thank you."

They would never have what her parents shared. A long and

lasting relationship. Marriage, children, a future...she would share none of those things with Jack.

"So what? You'll both just part ways?" Maddie shook her head. "You know I'm a cynic above all else when it comes to relationships, but hell, Sera, even I can see you two are gorgeous together. He's not Jack the movie star when he's with you."

"But that's who he is all the rest of the time. That's his life. It's not just a nine to five job and he can clock off. It's his world. And 'my Jack' and 'movie Jack' are separate people."

"But plenty of people make it work," Ally offered.

"And it sounds like you've just decided everything for him. Not cool, De Lotto."

Sera squirmed. That thought didn't sit well with her at all. But she couldn't allow herself to think about losing Jack. Her heart squeezed, a painful wrenching that wouldn't ease. Loving and losing him a second time would break her.

Because she cared. Damn it all to hell, Jack made her care. And when the time came, he would choose his career over her again. She wouldn't be enough. She wasn't all those years ago when he didn't even have a career. Why in the world would he stay now when he had his dream life?

Far better for them to feel the sting sooner, than to be ripped apart by their choices down the track. Sera cleared her throat. Pragmatism never failed her. "Pretending like we don't live separate lives doesn't help either of us."

"Oh, honey." Ally shook her head.

"We're not kids anymore, Al. And that's okay. Look, I don't mean for this to be a downer, so let's just get back to enjoying the pampering and talk about our outfits for tonight's party."

"One last thing before we do? I think you and Jack need to have this discussion so you can figure it all out. Together." Ally squeezed her arm, eyes serious.

"I'm just going to enjoy it while it lasts. But thanks for hearing me out."

"We've got your back, De Lotto. Always." Maddie nudged her.

They settled back to their pedicures and talked of the night ahead.

Sure, Sera's heart was a little heavier than it had been, but she supposed that was what happened when you were in a relationship that was fleeting. She didn't know what had come over her of late, but the joy at seeing Jack had given way to so many fears about their future.

Every day that passed was a step closer to saying goodbye.

CHAPTER THIRTY-ONE

*a*nd just like that, it was the big day. Her best friend was getting married.

Sera inspected her ruby red lipstick in the bathroom mirror of the gorgeous bridal suite of Hawdon Estate. The grounds were extensive, holding not only reception rooms, but accommodation for guests as well. It was chic yet homey, the perfect blend for Ally and Owen's big day. The perfect blend of them both.

Ally was getting her happily ever after. The very thought dispelled any nerves that had taken hold.

Sera was a sucker for a love story, and who wouldn't be with how they got together? After so much adversity, so much heartache, they were finally living their lives as a family. And celebrating that commitment by getting married was just icing on an already decadent cake.

Sera inspected her emerald-green eye shadow and adjusted the strap of her bridesmaid dress. Yes, they very much looked the part.

A little steadier, Sera stepped out of the bathroom.

"Ready for more photos?" Maddie waved the bridesmaid bouquets in her face. "This one's for you."

"Oooh pretty."

"Uh oh. What's wrong?"

Sera's smile faltered. "I didn't think anyone noticed."

Maddie patted her on the back. "Dear, dear, child. You may be banging the hottest, most talented actor in Hollywood, but an actress you are not. The stink was written all over your face."

"Great."

"That's okay, you've always been a terrible liar. And even worse at hiding your feelings. Want to talk about it?"

"Not particularly. And it's nothing I can really put my finger on. Just a lot of thoughts. It's kind of like being on one of those whizzy dizzy things at the playground, where you try to jump off but it's going too fast. I can't quite let them go, but I also can't seem to get a good grip on any particular thought. God, I sound mental."

"No, just like a woman who needs some time and patience to process it all. Or a good drink."

"Yep. So I shoved it all aside and focused on Ally and Owen, and that's cheered me up."

"You're such a softie."

"Thank you. Let's go look pretty for the camera."

They took photos together, then with Ally as she lounged around in her silk robe, getting ready. And when it was time for them to help her put on her dress, Sera knew she would have to reapply her make-up.

Ally turned, and Sera had to choke back a sob. She was exquisite in a strapless dress, with tiny beading and diamantes trailing down the bodice to the floor. It was simple, classy and a dress fit for any princess.

"Is it okay?"

"Owen is going to drop dead." Maddie dabbed at her eyes.

Sera's voice wobbled. "Ally, you're a vision."

Just then Charlie came into the room and took one look at Ally, then burst into tears.

Ally opened her arms and held her stepdaughter close.

Once they fixed their make-up, they continued taking photos with Ally's parents outside by the flower garden and near the bridge by the lake. It may have been sweltering outside, but the manager of the estate had everything on hand a bridal party could need in the summer. Sera placed the motorised mini fan in front of her face, enjoying the breeze.

She knew that on the opposite side of the estate, the men were getting ready, and her heart fluttered. Jack's presence back in town was food for every gossip magazine. And it had taken considerable effort for him to ask the press for privacy at the wedding, but even still, Sera couldn't help but peek over her shoulder. The high brick walls of Hawdon Estate would hopefully deter any nosey paps.

She allowed herself a little daydream as the photographer changed his lens. What would life be like with Jack? If she gave herself the chance to dream about making a future with him, would she always be looking over her shoulder? Would she have any privacy left?

Sera couldn't imagine it and didn't know how she could marry the two worlds together. Looking at Ally, beaming, talking to her parents—a big step in itself—she was able to find love with a man who was willing to wait, to give her the time she needed to figure it all out. But Owen wasn't like his Hollywood brother. His life fit into Ally's, and they had time to take things slowly.

Sera and Jack were never going to fit. No matter how much they connected, there would always be Jack and his lifestyle and Sera and her life. Separate.

She turned off her fan, suddenly cold. Did they even have enough of a foundation to make it work in the long run? There were so many qualities she liked about him, but there was also a lot of stuff she didn't know, traits she had just assumed were still there, even over ten years later.

People changed. Sera certainly wasn't the same girl, so why would she expect Jack to be the same guy?

When the photographer called out positions, Sera shook off her thoughts, definitely wrong place and time.

She'd deal with them when the need arose. Tonight was for frivolities and fun and she would make sure she had her fill of both.

If you had paid Jack a million dollars, he'd never have thought he'd be in this position: standing at the alter as a groomsman in his brother's wedding. Not that he didn't think Owen would re-marry, the guy was made for it. But being best man hit a little different now he was in his thirties.

Even though thinking about marriage still gave him the willies, seeing the way Owen looked at Ally, watching them together, made him a little less cynical.

Jack was tired of the false pretence of marriage; the way that every man and his dog in L.A. was divorced, in the process of getting a divorce, or had been divorced multiple times. It wore thin. The ones that did re-marry, did it for status, money, power, all the acrid-smelling reasons, even if they convinced them-selves it was for "love."

How many of those weddings had he been to that ended in disaster? He was tired of it. No, he was tired of that world. Not the same thing. Which was why his brother's relationship was refreshing. It was real.

When the string quartet began, Jack's heart kicked into gear. Looking at the end of the makeshift aisle lined with rich red rose petals, Jack saw Charlie first and he grinned.

He couldn't believe he was looking at his niece, now a

teenager, and soon becoming a young lady. If it hurt him, it must feel like daggers for Owen.

He gave her a high five and then grinned when Maddie walked down next. The green contrasted with her red hair, and he was sure he saw Gabriel sit up straighter.

When it was Sera's turn, Jack's heart stopped for a good minute before kicking off like a herd of wild stallions.

He couldn't move. Couldn't breathe. He was turned to stone, even when his body was trembling. There was a surreal quality to watching her walk down the aisle, like he was a part of and yet separate to it all. He was having some kind of out of body experience.

But fuck...that face. It mesmerised him more than he really understood. The logical part of his brain said it was Sera, just Sera beneath the emerald gown and the well-crafted make-up.

But it wasn't. She had been transformed into a golden goddess. Her dark curls were bundled up, her eyes defined and shadowed by the same shade of green that was her dress. Those lips. Jack's chest seized. Red, bold, and tempting him to kiss her until they died for want of breath.

He wasn't an overly romantic man. He was fond of grand gestures when it suited him, or when the person deserved it. But that was usually for show.

Right now, all Jack wanted to do was make the grandest of gestures. In private. Without prying eyes or expectant faces. The impatient bubbling in his blood was urging him to do something bold, to take all that flowing need and...What was it? What the hell was it that was making him want to slay dragons and climb mountains? To whisk her away so he could do it all with her safely by his side.

When she grinned at him, those eyes warming, that smile beaming, it was like a sucker punch to the gut.

Love. He was in love with Sera.

It dawned on him that it wasn't the first time either.

Well...fuck.

He didn't know what he would do with all this emotion. Labelling it, figuring it out didn't ease that rushing need to do *something*. In fact, it only made it worse.

But there was no need for immediate action. Not that he could anyway. He was stuck here and now, at his brother's wedding. *Focus, Jack.*

He breathed in deeply and watched as Sera stood beside Maddie. Her smile faltered and she raised an eyebrow at him. He winked, forcing a grin. Normally, having Sera close calmed him. She was his centre when he was spinning off axis. Not today. He was like a live wire, filled with energy.

"You okay?" Owen glanced at him. "You look more like the nervous groom today than a best man."

"Just afraid she'll run away with me, eh?" Jack grinned. "Still time."

Owen's light punch in the stomach eased the pressure. A fraction.

How could everybody be so relaxed when he was being consumed by his feelings? It was odd and almost laughable that he had just realised he was in love with Sera at the altar of his brother's wedding.

What he needed was the time to process it. He would park those feelings for now until he could figure them out.

Time...He just needed time.

Jack rubbed at his chest. Christ, ever since he first arrived, he'd been on a rollercoaster ride of event after event. All big, life-changing stuff. Therapy, filming, delivering a baby, Owen's wedding. And now this.

It was no wonder he was finding it hard to breathe. Just when he thought he would have some time to settle, to cruise, the universe threw another thing at him.

Love.

What the bloody fucking hell did Jack Davies know about love?

When the opening notes of the wedding march came on, Jack forced his mind to go blank. It didn't matter if he was a novice when it came to love. Or that he didn't know fuck about having a healthy relationship. He was at his brother's wedding. He would be present and enjoy the day.

Hell, maybe he'd even learn a thing or two.

The food was delicious, the wine flowing, and wherever Sera turned, people were having a great time.

It was by far the most fun she'd had at a wedding. It was also the most painful.

She watched the way Ally and Owen spun on the dance floor and she couldn't help but grin. Love. They all but radiated with it. And then she would remember. After today, there was nothing keeping Jack in town. Nothing keeping him with her.

Time was up.

But every ounce of her wished it weren't the case. Sera was frightened that wanting to be with him was outweighing her good sense. The sense that told her if she kept seeing him, she would be devastated when he left again.

Which he would. Maybe not next week, or even next month. But eventually, he would be sick of the routine nature of her life and want something more glamorous.

She was utterly torn and not at all comfortable with the feeling.

"Dance with me, De Lotto."

Jack's hands settled on her waist; his voice was close to her ear. She shivered, her body responding to his touch.

Sera's thoughts were heavy, her feet, aching, but it didn't matter one bit. She promised herself an evening without worry, and she would enjoy every minute of her time with Jack while it lasted. She placed her hand in his and followed him out to the dance floor.

And boy did that man dance.

Spins and twirls and a blur of movement as they enjoyed song after song with the rest of the guests.

But eventually her feet reminded her that she didn't wear heels very often. Which meant after a day of wandering about and an evening of dancing, she'd be hobbling about come tomorrow.

"I need to sit down."

"Walk with me."

"Are you crazy?"

"Always."

"Walking is the opposite to sitting."

Jack guided her off the dance floor then lifted her up.

"Put me down!"

He swung through the open doors of the deck that led down to the acres of garden below. The night was warm, the lights in the garden inviting, and Sera stopped protesting the moment he set her down at the bridge overlooking the pond.

"Better?"

"Much."

"Here, let me."

Jack lifted her leg and undid the strap of her shoe, massaging the soles.

"Before you ask, I left my flats in the room and have been so busy having fun I didn't think I needed it. That was before you went all Saturday Night Fever on me."

Jack grinned, undoing the strap on her other foot.

"If you went and got them, then I wouldn't have the pleasure of doing this, would I?"

Sera threw him an appreciative glance then moaned. "Oh, well, I suppose not."

"That good?"

"Divine."

She closed her eyes briefly, sighing at the pressure on the soles of her feet. It was exactly what she needed to ease that tight band of muscle around her arches.

Her feet were aching, she was slightly tipsy, but damn it, she couldn't stop smiling.

"Happy?"

Sera opened one eye, then noticing his serious expression, opened the other. Sitting up a bit straighter, she studied Jack's face.

Gone was the carefree, playful demeanour. She could tell he was going deeper. Her heart pounded.

"I am. Why do you need to ask?"

"Just a feeling."

"I'm happy to see your brother and my best friend in love and in an amazing relationship."

"And what about us? Our relationship."

"Am I happy in it?"

"Yes. About us. About the future."

Sera took his hand. Yes, he was very serious. And the light that she had let in suddenly dimmed. "Jack, this is a conversation for another night. When I'm not tipsy and tired." She had thought to have this conversation tomorrow, to have one last night together before saying goodbye.

He frowned, seemingly hurt by the lack of admission.

"Why won't you answer my question?"

"Yes, I'm happy with us."

"And the future?"

"I don't know what that means. When it comes to us, to our lives, which are very different, I look into the future and...I can't see it." Sera swallowed back the pain, throat tight. There. She'd said it. The truth they'd both been avoiding.

Jack shifted back. "What?"

"I wanted to speak to you tomorrow. I didn't want to talk about it at the wedding."

"No, let's get into it now given you've dropped a pretty big bomb."

"Jack, we both know that we didn't start this to have a long-term relationship at the end. You certainly never intimated that to me, and I don't think I've given that impression. You said it yourself you couldn't make promises."

"Things change."

Sera studied his face, surprised that he could want more. She hadn't expected that. He hadn't given her any indication that he wanted things to change at all. But reality tugged at her dreams, burying her feet in the ground.

"Do they, Jack? You live in La La Land. Your life is about making movies, taking pictures, modelling, travelling the world, going to exclusive parties—"

"So what?"

"So you're floating. You haven't figured out what you're doing. You could decide you want the quiet life this week and be gone the next."

"That's not fair."

"That's the truth. Whether you want to face it or not, you're not ready for commitment. You weren't then and you certainly aren't now."

And she couldn't settle for less than that.

"You can't still blame me for what happened over a decade ago."

"You're right Jack, that would be unfair. You walked out on our relationship without even giving it a chance. It was your choice to end it. You left for the bright lights, for fame, when I—"

She would have stayed. Sera closed her eyes, unable to admit it. How had she been so wrong about what they shared? It wouldn't be the first time.

"What?"

"It doesn't matter anymore, Jack. When it comes to you, nothing has really changed."

"That's crap and you know it. I'm in therapy, I'm getting my shit sorted."

"But that doesn't mean you can give me what I need!" Sera cried out, frustration and fear bubbling to the surface.

He reeled back as if slapped. "Ouch." Jack rubbed his jaw, blue eyes brimming with frustration.

"You're fun, Jack. The life of the party, a thrill-seeker, and that's all well and good. But when it comes to commitment...I need stability." Sera's heart bled for all the things she said now but never had the courage to before. But Jack needed to hear it. To understand. "Your life in L.A. is a far cry from mine here. We come from two separate worlds, with different expectations. You said yourself you'll be working on promoting your films for the next few years. Where does that leave us? You can't build a relationship on thin air. Do you expect me to wait two to three years until you're ready and have figured it all out?"

"We can make it work."

She cared too much for him to watch whatever they had dwindle down to nothing. She wanted it all: marriage, babies, dependability. The commitment that her parents shared.

And it cut her heart into a million pieces to accept that it wouldn't be with Jack.

"You can't just quit your life in the span of a few weeks or months."

"Why the hell not? It's *my* life. Don't you get it, Sera? I want to figure it out *with* you. This is going to take time and being with you again has shown me that I've wasted a lot of it with women I thought I wanted, in relationships I thought I needed. Until you."

"It's not the right time."

"Will there ever be a right one?"

Sera trembled. She had been so firm in her resolve for so long, but was he right? Would there ever be room in her life for him? Would there ever be a right time?

Jack's shoulders sagged. He rubbed his hand over his face, sorrow marking his appearance.

"Why are you really doing this, Sera? Why are you punishing me for what happened years ago? We both know I'm not that same guy. Why are you determined to push me away?"

"I don't know."

"What will it take for you to make that leap? For you to trust in us? In me?"

Sera didn't have any answers. She didn't know why she couldn't let it all go. Why she couldn't just follow him, to try to make something work.

Whatever it was, it was breaking her heart.

And then she knew. Like a silent ripple in the water, the thought grew, manifesting itself clear and true. She had always known it. Beyond it all, deep down inside, she didn't trust herself. Her instincts were wrong before, and Sera was fearful that they would be again.

She was afraid that keeping things light and loose wasn't possible. The more time she spent with Jack, the deeper those connections became. Sera trembled.

And if she was wrong again, if she trusted Jack and he ended up leaving...she wouldn't be strong enough to survive it.

"Jesus, Sera, I wasn't expecting this. I knew something was up since I got back, but I didn't think...I figured we'd work through everything together. When it all settled down."

"I won't ever lie to you about how I feel Jack. I will always be honest with you."

"Right now, I wish you weren't." He rubbed at his chest.

"You don't mean that."

"Don't I?"

"I've hurt you already. This wasn't what I wanted to do." She stroked his cheek, seeing the hurt etched deep in his face.

Sera willed her tears away. She wouldn't cry about what she couldn't change. It didn't help them at all. She needed to do this. To protect herself.

"And here I wanted to dance with you in the moonlight."

"We still can." And she drew herself up and then him, seeing his reluctance, but wanting, desperately to offer him comfort.

The slow, sweet music from the brightly lit mansion surrounded them.

It took a few songs for them to find a connection. For Jack to lose the stiff, stilted manner, to hold her close and lovingly. For her to relax.

A part of her hated what had come out of her mouth, but another part, the one hurt so many times before knew it was for the best. She held Jack close, feeling his firm body against hers, committing it all to memory.

Sera accepted the answer in her heart with resignation. It was a bitter, bitter ending.

Later, much later, when all the guests had gone home and the wedding party were tucked away in their respective rooms across the estate, Jack made love to Sera.

He took her in the moonlight, while his heart was full and his mind cluttered.

He showed her what he was too afraid to say. Through soft touches and fevered kisses, he travelled over her body, lingering over the bands of muscle, around the sweet curves until he lost himself inside.

There was a desperation in him to hold and cherish her.

One last, sweet time.

Jack loved her with an intensity that nearly broke him.

He would savour her and what they shared here because he understood that this was goodbye.

Jack kissed the tips of her fingers then her palm. When he looked down, her hazel eyes were filled with tears.

"Don't cry, Sera. Not tonight."

But the tears spilled over, and those small, capable hands drew him close.

Cinnamon and jasmine filled his senses. Earthy and floral. Steady and sensual. She was everything.

Emotion clogged the back of his throat, threatening his vision. But he wanted to see her, to capture this moment in his mind. To always remember.

Jack kissed her, slowly, lingering on her mouth, drawing out her need. Loving her completely.

How would he live without her? The thought was on a loop in his brain. It circled around his heart, cutting off oxygen until he couldn't breathe. Jack couldn't picture his world without Sera in it.

The pain was unbearable.

He had shown her his world, but it wasn't enough. He hadn't been enough. A decade too late.

So he wouldn't think. For the next few hours at least, while she was still his, he would make love to her and hold her close.

"Sera...don't leave. Don't go."

"Jack," she sobbed as he entered her. But still he yearned for more contact.

He kissed her now, with an intensity that was close to frantic. His desire, punishing.

Jack took his fill, torturing them both. He rocked over her, pinning Sera to the mattress, a frenzied desperation marking their rhythm.

She was flesh and blood, yet a phantom. His ephemeral lover.

And when Sera cried out, calling his name, Jack's heart shattered. When he followed her over, cradling her close, a single tear fell, marking the pillow.

When the sunlight filtered through their window a few hours later, Jack lay beside her, watching her sleep.

He drank in every detail, savouring every minute. The golden light on her warm skin, the dark sweep of her lashes, her glorious hair, wild and free. Jack absorbed it all, hoping she would sleep for hours still. He wasn't ready to say goodbye, not just yet.

He didn't think he ever could.

CHAPTER THIRTY-TWO

*S*era spent the rest of the holidays alternating between moping around her apartment and being dragged out by Maddie to this show or that restaurant. When Ally returned from her honeymoon, glowing and happy, Sera just wanted to burrow even further.

But she had forced herself to get back into a routine, to adjust to being on her own again. And every night her fingers hovered over her phone, writing phantom messages in her head that she would never send.

She had asked Jack to leave her alone, to give her some space. So why was she so disappointed when he did?

Why did it hurt that he left for L.A.? That he did the very thing she had expected him to do, the very thing she had wanted.

She had hurt him, she knew that as clear as the summer blue skies, but she was hurting too.

Sera was lying on the couch in her apartment debating whether to have another popsicle when the buzzer rang.

She glared at the intercom. Too hot to move. Then cursed when the ringing continued.

IDA BRADY

"What?" she hollered, seeing Maddie standing on the other side.

"I come bearing comfort food." Maddie held up a grocery bag, cheeks flushed. "Now will you let me in, it's hotter than Satan's ass crack out here."

"Who even says that?" Sera muttered, pressing the release button.

"You know, for a girl in the twenty-first century, you act like an old lady."

"You don't have to parade around on the beach half-naked just because it's hot out."

"Sure thing, Golden Girl."

"Is there a point to this morning's assault, or can I go back to my freezer for my third popsicle?"

"Why have sugared water when you can have premium ice cream?" Maddie pulled out three tubs. "I also brought chocolates, chips and booze."

"If there's not a Snickers bar in there, I don't want to know."

Maddie's grin was gloating. "Oh, ye of little faith."

Sera ripped off the wrapper and sank her teeth into the chocolate-nut-caramel combo then tossed it on the table in disgust.

"Still lost your appetite?"

"No, my appetite is there, it's just every bloody thing tastes like cardboard."

"Oh dear."

"But school is starting soon, so that'll be a nice distraction."

"And you haven't thought about speaking to Jack?"

"What do you care? You've never been a fan of us dating." Sera closed her eyes, wishing she could take it back.

"Crabby today, aren't we?"

"Sorry."

"It's true, I haven't been Team Jera."

"Ew."

"Better than Team Sack."

"Marginally."

"But I know that Jack was really working on himself, on making changes, because you mattered. Surely that's got to count for something, De Lotto."

"We live very different lives, Madds."

"So what? Look, have you at least called him?"

"I pick up the phone and don't have a clue what I'll say. I asked him to leave, so he's just respecting that."

"You know the ball is in your court, right? If you want to make this work, you need to find a way."

"I don't know what I want anymore, Madds."

Maddie was about to respond when the buzzer pealed yet again.

"What now?" Sera huffed, stomping to the intercom. She winced seeing her mother on the other end.

"Can't avoid her forever," Maddie called out.

"Whatever." But the heavy, guilty weight didn't dissipate.

When Sera opened the door a few minutes later, she was torn between shame and relief.

"Hey, mum." She fought against a fresh wave of tears when Maryam simply put her arms around her and held on tight.

"I'll see myself out," Maddie said, shutting the door gently.

"Walk with me, Seraphina," Maryam implored.

Forty-five minutes later, Sera lay flat on the grass of the local park, body slick with a light sheen of sweat. The heat was smothering, yet her mother looked fresh and comfortable.

"I know you've been avoiding me and your dad. We understand you didn't want to talk about it when it just happened, but *habibti*, you need to let go of this grief."

Sera sat up with a groan. "I'm surprised you waited so long to give me a lecture."

"Not a lecture. We thought you needed some space to figure it out."

"I did."

"But keeping it bottled up inside you is a poison, *habibti*. What exactly happened between you and Jack?"

"In short, I told him he didn't have what I needed to make a relationship work."

Her mother shook her head, but she felt the 'tch' of disapproval deep in her heart.

"To question someone's character—their worth—is a big deal, Sera."

"I know it." Her throat closed over. No more tears. She'd shed too many already over the past month. "It's for the best."

"For whom?"

"For Jack."

"Who are you to know what's best for him?"

"You're supposed to be on my side."

Her mother waved a hand in front of her face. "I'm supposed to tell you the truth. And if you don't like it, you at least need to accept it."

"That's not the way denial works."

"Relationships need honesty and time. You can't just walk away when it gets too hard."

"I'm not walking away." But there was an uncomfortable itch between her shoulder blades. She had accused Jack of doing the same thing, of not sticking it out when things got tough. "I'm ending something that we never should have started in the first place."

"Why not?"

"Because we live in two different worlds. I'm sick of talking about this. God, I sound like a broken record."

"You're sick of it because you don't want to be told you're wrong."

Sera huffed, "that's not true."

"Really? You would rather give up on something that brings you joy because you're the one who is afraid?"

Sera ignored the trembling in her heart. She didn't need to hear this.

"I want to forget about this. About him."

"You can't forget about the ones you love. It's not in your nature. Nobody can if they truly love someone. And I see it. I see you love Jack even though you fight to keep your heart protected. I see how you look at him, like he's given you a diamond ring and not just his time. I see that you love him and not the wealth he can offer you. I see it, Sera because it never left. It was there when you were with him at nineteen, and it's here now."

"That's not true." But her voice wobbled.

"I see it. Your dad sees it. So why are you pushing him away?"

"I couldn't lose him again." Sera flicked away the tears, angry at herself. "To put my heart out there, loving him for however many more months, or hell, even years, before he decided I wasn't what he wanted anymore. I didn't want what we had to die a slow death."

"Don't you see? You've already given him your heart, it's been his all this time."

Sera glanced at her mother, unwilling to hear the truth, but feeling it all the same.

"I won't be the reason he gives up his life, for him to just resent me down the line. Seeing him in L.A. showed me how important that work is to him."

"You're looking at it backwards."

"No, I'm not."

"And you're stubborn, so take it from one wilful woman to another, you're wrong." She squeezed her hand to soften the blow. "You must understand that it's not about whether it works or not, because when you love someone, you make it work. When you love someone, you compromise, no matter what."

"You sound like Jack."

"The man is right."

"Why is he right?" The fire leapt in her gut, making her sound defensive.

"Because he's willing to do anything he can to be with you. Isn't that enough?"

"What if I can't take him being away for work for so long? And everything falls apart?"

"This is your fears. It isn't about Jack at all."

It was like someone flicked an elastic band around her spine. The sharp twinge she felt at her mother's words made her sit up straighter, making her realise what she hadn't want to face before.

"I..." Sera couldn't find the words.

"Listen, when the boys were just babies, your father was given an opportunity to work nights, with triple pay. Marco couldn't have been more than three-months-old, and Omar was running around wild at not even two. I was on my own in a small apartment, and we were hoping to save to buy a bigger place. This place."

"And what happened?"

"I told Tony to take the job. It was the hardest year of my life, but we made it work, we found our rhythm. And every day I missed him so much I thought I'd explode. But I knew it wouldn't be like that forever."

"You were married, though."

"So?"

"It's different."

"Why do you have to have a piece of paper to prove the strength of your commitment? Whether you're married or de facto or lovers, you're in a relationship, making a commitment to be with one another. Yes, it might be easier to walk away, but I find that if the love is deep and intentions are true, walking away will feel like cutting off your arm. You won't be able to function the same way without it."

"I don't even know how he feels about me. He might not be in love with me. Hell, he might've moved on. And then what?"

"Don't worry about what isn't, focus on what is; plant that seed, water it, and watch how it grows. Understand?"

"I think so: all this is my fault."

"Some. But a relationship has two people in it, and for the love of God, you have to drop that guard."

"He said I was punishing him for leaving back then, and I suppose I've blamed him for a long time for choosing his career over us. For not even trying."

"You both made a decision to choose yourselves. That's not what he's doing here. You've been carrying that with you for a long time, Sera. It's time to figure it out, or you'll both miss out on having a future."

"Maddie said I'm attracted to orphans." Sera pulled up the green grass, throwing it off to the side. God, she sounded sulky. The look on her mother's face said she agreed.

"Sweet girl, you have a big heart. I've told you this before. Part of that is caught up in wanting to help people, to save them. And two people who have meant the most to you, in your life, have hurt you in some way. Elijah chose to listen to his brother, Jack chose his career, though I suspect there's more to it than that.

"Each of them hurt you because you loved them deeply. And you've not healed from either of those events. Not completely. It's what's stopped you from making a commitment to Jack."

Never in her life would she have connected what happened to Elijah with Jack leaving. But when her mother spoke to her, when she connected the dots, everything began to make sense.

Maryam continued, "so you feel if you encourage Jack to go,

you won't be responsible for making a mistake if it fails. It will be his choice again."

Sera's mind clung to the thread, understanding dawning. "Jack keeps telling me one thing, but I'm not wanting to believe him because it doesn't fit the image I have—"

"The image of a young guy who broke your heart. But you forget, people can change, Sera. Don't let those fears stop you from sharing something wonderful with him."

How had she made such a mess of everything?

"I do think you need some support to deal with Elijah's death. Professional help. It can't hurt to talk to someone again." Maryam ran a hand down her back. The familiar touch was soothing.

"I will. I think that's a good idea. I think I've just wanted what you have with dad that I didn't want to settle for less."

"And you never should. But your dad and I have had our hardships. Relationships take work, Sera. If you're with someone who is willing and able to work on themselves, to grow and learn, then that's a great start."

"You know, I've accused Jack of living in a make-believe world, but I think I'm the one who bought into this fairy tale idea of what it means to be in a relationship."

All this time, it was Jack who was dealing with reality. Trying to better himself, to manage his anxiety, where she had spent the whole time pretending, acting like it was okay.

Like she hadn't fallen in love with him all over again.

The warmth spread through her now, blanketing every fear she had. But with it came the painful reminder that Jack was no longer in her life. That she had been too late.

"You know, I've never watched one of his films? Not one."

Maryam smiled. "Why not? He's worth all the acclaim in case you're wondering."

"I told myself at first it was too painful." Sera gazed out

across the park, thinking about all the times she had convinced herself it was for the best.

"But then?"

She shrugged. "Then it became a defiant thing. Like, you chose your life in Hollywood over me. Stupid, I know, given we weren't dating for a long time."

"A few months can feel like forever."

"I suppose it did. I know I need to talk to Jack about how I'm feeling, but I don't know how to start. It's not exactly something I want to do over the phone, so far away."

"If you learn one lesson in your life, *habibti*, let it be this: life isn't neat. Sometimes working out the hard stuff, together, can strengthen your relationship. How else do you set boundaries or know what you need to work on if you don't meet challenges together?"

Sera froze, thinking it through. If she wanted to have a successful relationship with Jack, then she needed to not only have faith in him, but to show her strength, emotionally. She needed to choose him and everything that entailed.

"I think I've had a child-like view of love. I've wanted the end product, but not understood that a lot of hard work went into it. I feel so stupid."

"You can't see with your eyes closed. Don't blame yourself for not having the hindsight that only comes with experience, baby girl."

"Yes. You're right." Sera rolled her shoulders. "I owe Jack an apology."

"Trust in yourself, Seraphina. A woman who doubts her own mind can never be at one with it. Trust your instinct, it's like a muscle, no? You gotta work it to build its strength."

"Thanks, mum. I needed this."

"I'm just glad I could help. Now let's get out of this sweltering heat, eh?"

Sera thought about everything her mother said on the way

home. Even though it was difficult to hear, her advice had brought her a level of peace she hadn't felt in a long time.

Sera fell asleep on the couch that evening, emotionally drained. When she woke at 5 a.m., she didn't crawl into bed, nor did she go out for a morning run, either.

Sera sprawled out on the sofa with a tub of ice cream and turned on the television. She flicked through the range of movies on offer until she found one that sounded interesting.

Sera did something she had never done before: she watched one of Jack's films.

Jack wandered around his empty house, lost.

Since he had returned, all he could see was Sera: in his bed, cooking at the stove, wandering around the garden, filling his house with everything he craved.

A home.

But he knew it wouldn't be for long.

He had spoken to Gabriel a few times since Owen and Ally's wedding, Leila, too. Because he had plans bigger than just himself for once, and for the first time in a while, it made him excited.

But even through all that, was the sinking feeling, the disappointment that Sera wouldn't be there to share it with him. And he didn't want to live his life without her.

Jack continued roaming the house, seeing everything from a new perspective. He wasn't just going through the motions anymore, he was making choices, realising he was able to live and thrive in a conscious way. A healthy one.

Once he dressed, Jack made himself a coffee, opened his laptop and sat down at the kitchen table, ready for his appointment with Diana.

"How does it feel being back?" Diana was sitting at the desk in her office, the late afternoon sunlight filtering through her window.

"Like I'm wearing clothes a few sizes too small."

Her smile was warm, reassuring. "Sometimes change—even healthy change—can be uncomfortable. So, you've decided that you're going ahead with the move?"

"Yep. Plans are finally in place. I've been sitting on it for a few months, so it's not just a knee-jerk reaction." It had been brewing since he had returned to finish filming. Now, he would make it a reality.

"And what about all the work? How are you handling it?"

"Better than I expected. Though it's just doing interviews now, so I've had some breathing room, and time to say goodbye."

"Tell me, why has this film been difficult for you?"

"What?"

"You've had some time to process your parents' death, and you're making progress with managing your anxiety, so I think we can go a little deeper this week. You mentioned previously that you shouldn't have done this film, what was it that hit too close to home?"

Jack's sigh was deep. "Nothing gets past you, eh?"

"You need to explain it, Jack. To process it."

"To cut it short, the film deals with a son's guilt at being the cause of his father's death."

She paused, absorbing the information. "Okay."

"And so when I filmed that scene, the part where my character finds his father dead in the house, well, it hit a nerve. This film is all about how a son's addiction, his inability to take responsibility for his actions, affects the ones he loves the most. It's a little darker than my usual stuff, but I was drawn to it."

"And that shows to me that you were trying to process what happened with your parents."

Jack rubbed the band at his wrist. "I suppose so."

"How did it feel finishing the film?"

"A relief. I thought taking on the film would bring me closure. Boy, was I wrong."

"But it did, Jack. Everything has come about because you, in some unconscious way, decided you needed to deal with the grief. You just didn't have the tools to do it at the time."

"I can't seem to shake those feelings. Every time I think about what happened to them...I can't help but feel responsible."

"Can we dig a little deeper there, Jack?"

It was painful, still, to remember. Every single time he relived that night, it hurt. But the torment, his own condemnation over the years was what had drained him.

"I told you my parents had gone to the school over some stupid thing I did."

"Yes, and we discussed how you can't control what happens in life, the good or bad."

But he had. For so long he had carried the guilt with him, letting it fester, punishing himself in every way possible.

Jack steadied himself before responding. This bit hurt. "The thing I haven't told you, is that I was supposed to be there that night. At the school. I told them I would be a part of the conversation. To show some responsibility for my actions, and instead, I was losing my virginity, thinking it was all a joke."

"You had no reason to believe it wouldn't be okay." Diana leaned forward. "Jack, you've turned a minor transgression into a prison sentence. Were you responsible for the other driver losing control of their car?"

Jack squirmed in his chair. "No, but—"

"Was it your fault that your parents drove home via that route?"

"What? No."

"Or that your teachers chose that night to hold the meeting?"

"I get what you're saying, but it's not that simple."

"But it can be. Knowing that there are events in life we can't control, that bad things happen to us, can help up process it, to manage the guilt. Because you're not to blame, Jack. It's not your fault that this has happened. How do you know that you wouldn't have died along with them that night?"

Jack shivered. "What?"

"When we start thinking that way, we can lose ourselves in 'what ifs' and that's not healthy. That's your anxiety talking, Jack."

"It is, but it's something I'll never be able to get over."

"Letting go of the guilt and blame takes time. Life happens. Good and bad things in it, and we do our best to manage it all. But we're none of us in control of it. Taking these steps, accepting it, will give you some comfort."

The pressure, that vice around his body began to ease. He sucked in a deep breath. "I know it. But I'm finding it hard to accept."

"Why?"

"Because they're not here. I need them and they're not here. And I've only myself to blame."

"That internal self-hate is what has led you to all the destructive behaviours in the past, behaviours that you are now aware of...you might not see your progress Jack, but you're not the same man who sought therapy last year."

He felt it too, beneath all that guilt, he had noticed the changes in him, the way he caught a thought before it turned into a destructive belief. The way he processed his emotions. Everything was changing, in a good way. But there was still something missing.

"I know I have. But the one person that I want more than anything in the world isn't here to share my achievements with me. And it hurts."

"So what are you going to do about that?"

"Sera made it clear she doesn't want me. I know I glossed over our break-up when I last spoke to you, but Diana, she doesn't think I'm able to make a commitment." Jack explained what had happened in college and why Sera might feel wary of trusting him again.

"I want you to revisit the conversations you've had with Sera. Think about what it is she knows about your hopes for the future. What have you told her, shared with her that might show her you're not the Jack of the past, that you've grown?"

Jack rubbed the back of his neck. Had he been transparent? Or had he just expected Sera to go along with everything, without making her a part of those plans? "I'll have to think about that. I feel like I've been open with her." Hadn't he? "I have so many things I'm working on, and I can't imagine her not being a part of that, but I'm not going to start bombarding her with texts when she has asked me to keep away."

"Perhaps that open communication was what you both needed earlier on. But it's not too late. Start chasing after those plans, Jack. Nothing is stopping you. If you have things you want to achieve, independent of your relationship with Sera, then start achieving it. The rest will take time."

"Diana, what if I'm not enough for her?"

"You need to let go of the broken boy, Jack. The one who thinks he's unworthy and irresponsible. Challenge those beliefs because if you don't, it will consume you. Healing takes time. If you want to give this a chance with Sera, then you have to communicate. No more bottling up feelings. Show her your plans, and how she fits into your dreams." Diana paused. "You need to also accept that Sera's on her own journey and she might not want what you have to offer."

Jack made a strangled sound in the back of his throat.

"I'd rather stay cautiously optimistic."

"Then you need to make that leap. And if you're both

willing to learn and work through your issues together, then you'll find you can begin to trust each other to see it through."

Jack ended the video call a few minutes later. He still had a lot of healing to do, but he was no longer the cavalier playboy ready to drown himself in distractions.

He was facing his demons for the first time ever and damn it, he knew he was making progress.

Needing to face it, wanting to move forward, Jack walked into his study, and unlocked the bottom drawer of his writing desk. He took out the external hard drive and opened his laptop. With shaking hands, Jack plugged in the device and opened the file marked 'Dad.'

He played the first video that had come up, heart hammering in his chest.

The screen came alive with colours and sounds. His father was pretending to be a detective, and as always, Jack was his trusty sidekick, solving yet another case.

He studied his father's face, tracing the curve of his cheek on the screen.

And for the first time in a long while, Jack let the tears flow.

CHAPTER THIRTY-THREE

*T*he conversation he needed to have with Owen was well overdue. If it hadn't been for Sera and Diana, for the events over the past few months, he wasn't sure he would ever have spoken to him about it. But that said more about his own mental health than it did his relationship with his brother.

Part of moving forward meant he needed to let go.

Jack was back in Melbourne, and his plans were in full swing. He had taken the leap, for himself and for his future and he knew, without a doubt, that it was the right decision.

He arrived at Owen's place at the end of January, enjoying the blast of summer heat after a bleak Christmas and New Year in L.A.

"So, why the sudden visit and the serious face? You were cryptic on the phone."

"I wanted to chat in person. There are a few things I need to get off my chest that can't really wait." Jack was about to sit down but realised there was too much energy in his muscles for that, so he leaned against Owen's desk. "I'll just come out and say it: I bought a house. Here, in Melbourne."

"What?" Owen leaned back in his chair.

"I found a nice place, away from the bump and grind, because I'm moving back."

Owen's look said it all. "You're serious?"

"More than ever. I've been struggling for a while now. You know my mental health has been pretty shit, especially since the break-up."

"Have you spoken to Sera since?"

"She asked me to keep my distance, and I've respected that. But we can't avoid each other forever."

"But now you're back and buying real estate."

"Yep."

"Okaaaay."

"All of this." Jack gestured. "Filming, being back, your wedding, the break-up, has made me realise how much all the stuff with Mum and Dad affected me. How much I felt it was my fault."

"Jack, you know that's not true."

"I felt it was. If it weren't for me, they'd have not gone out that night."

"Not your fault that they were in an accident."

"I felt like it was. I was meant to meet them at the school, but I flaked. And that kills me. Knowing I would have disappointed them."

"You were a kid, Jack. They loved you, even when you were pulling pranks and messing around."

"I was old enough to know better, and that will stay with me for a long time. I've come to accept that I'll always feel a little guilty, but I'm working on that."

Owen rubbed the back of his neck. "Christ, I wish you would have told me."

"This is it though. I never wanted to burden you. You had so much on your plate. I couldn't do that to you. And from that, I guess I didn't realise how much I've held on to the hurt. For you not being there for me. For being there too much. For Mum and Dad dying."

Owen leaned forward. "Jack, why didn't you say anything before?"

"I didn't have the words. Or even a clue what I was feeling. But I do now, and I want you to know I'm grateful to you. I know it was tough being a teenager, with a new baby, then having to deal with the death of our parents. I'm sorry I wasn't there to help, but I was desperate to get away. A part of me didn't want to care and I was shit scared of responsibility."

"And I was distracted."

"Rightly so. But I'm letting it all go. The blame, the hurt, everything. I've been carrying all this guilt inside and I'm getting rid of it. I need to in order to move on."

"I get it. And I'm glad for it, Jack. I've carried a lot of guilt about not being able to do more for you back then. I saw you were out of control and I couldn't do a thing to stop it. Hell, I figured you needed to get it out of your system. But then it kept going."

"Charlie saved me."

Owen blinked. "What?"

"I remember holding her one day, when she looked up and laughed at something stupid I did, and that was it for me. I told myself I could either keep fooling around being a delinquent or I could figure out what I wanted from life."

"And you did."

"Yep. But Charlie, she saved me, made me realise I needed to stop fooling around and go to college, to follow those dreams."

"I think she saved us all back then." Owen cleared his throat. "Hey, they would be proud of you. Mum and Dad."

"Oddly enough, I'm proud of me too. And before you say anything, I don't just mean being an arrogant fuck. I mean deep in my soul proud. The real shit."

"I think I'm at a loss for words."

"Glad I could mess with your head."

"While we're on the subject of deep feelings, what's going on with you and Sera? Are you going to see her now you're back? Has anything really changed?"

"I bought a house here, I'm pretty sure that's a big move by anyone's standards. But in short, she doesn't think I'm cut out for long-term commitment. She figures I'll be caught up in L.A. and we won't be able to make it work."

"Ouch. Don't bite me for saying it, but isn't she right?"

"Here we go."

"Hear me out. You're back, and that's great. But what's changed for her? If she sees it the way I do, and let's presume because she's smart, she does, your career will drag you away from being together. If you're serious about her, you've gotta show her in all the small ways that count that you can be the guy that won't leave.

"You're making all these plans, but you've got to include her in them, Jack. Make her see that you're serious about this. It's not the big, grand gestures that will work with Sera. Just look at her parents, solid for decades now. That's her measuring stick."

Jack froze. "That's it!"

"Oh no."

"You're a fucking genius, Owen!"

"Jack—" he warned.

"Sera's parents! They're the key to all this. They'll know how to help me understand what she needs. They've been married for ages, and they know her better than anyone else. Yes!" Jack leaned down and grabbed his brother's cheeks, giving him a loud, smacking kiss.

Owen was right. If he wanted Sera to trust him, he had to help alleviate all those concerns she had about him and their future. Diana's advice rang through his brain: he needed to communicate with her, to tell her what he had planned.

Jack wanted Sera's faith in him, but more so he wanted to show her that they could do anything together.

He could only pray that she would listen.

When Jack visited Sera's parents' home, his mind was buzzing with plans for the future. He didn't know what would come of a discussion with Tony and Maryam, but somehow, the answer lay in talking to them about their daughter.

What he didn't expect was the blaring sounds of the radio upon his arrival. Jack walked to the side of the house and saw Tony, elbow deep in muck, gardening.

"Need a hand?" Jack closed the gate behind him and gestured to Tony's grubby attire.

"Jack! I have to admit you're the last person I would have expected visiting me today."

"I just got back a few days ago."

"You're in luck, I'm all finished. Wanted to have it done before Maryam got home, but I could use a cold drink."

"I'll grab a few from the fridge."

"Ciders, if you're interested."

"Always."

Jack popped the screw top lids and brought the bottles out to the yard.

"You've done a great job."

"Ah, keeps me busy."

"And your wife happy."

"That too. Seeing that look on her face is largely the reason why I do it. It's not just about her being happy; it's showing her that I understand this is important to her, and because it's important to her, I'm going to prioritise it. Even if it isn't to me."

Jack absorbed the advice. What was important to Sera? What

could he do to show her he was serious, that he cared? "I'm impressed."

"I'm sure you're not here to talk about this stuff. What brings you by?"

"Actually." Jack grimaced. "It kind of is."

"Glad we have the liquid gold. Take a seat."

Jack settled in the deck chair next to him and took a long swig.

Tony began before he could gather his thoughts. He was glad of it.

"Change."

"Huh?"

"The worst advice I ever received was 'I hope you guys don't change.' It was said to us by a friend at our wedding, and though it was kindly meant, it was the crappiest thing someone could say."

Jack laughed. "Why?"

"Change is inevitable in a marriage. In any relationship. You cannot stay the same person. There's illness and death and a myriad of stressors that will shift who you are, and sometimes what you believe in. But one of the most important parts in changing is that you give each other the room to breathe. If you're both evolving at the same time, it's too sudden and leaves you little time to understand one another."

"Here's the thing though, Tony." Jack lifted the bottle of cider to his lips before setting it down on the grass. They were leaning on garden chairs, watching the evening sun setting. If he wasn't so wired, if the conversation wasn't so important, he'd have almost relaxed into it.

But that buzzing, the busy bees working a hole through his gut were hard at it. Some things in life were better off hard won.

"She doesn't see a future with me. This is the problem."

"And what am I to do about the situation? Isn't that between you and my daughter?"

"You see, she isn't really listening to me, or more like she isn't willing to give us a shot. I was hoping you and Maryam could help me figure out how to get through to her."

"Son, I couldn't convince my only daughter to walk instead of run when she was just sixteen months old. I wish I knew the answer, but that's for you and Sera to work out together."

"Right."

"You can't make someone see that black is white no matter how many times you try to convince them."

"But she thinks we're from two different worlds."

"You are."

"To her, they may as well be separate solar systems. She doesn't believe we have what it takes to go the distance. To make it work in the long run."

"I wouldn't think she would say it if she didn't feel it. But this is down to the two of you, isn't it?"

Jack's heart sank. "This isn't exactly what I wanted to hear."

"You think my daughter picked up her honesty off the side of the road? You asked me for advice, and I'll tell it to you straight."

"I know it. I just don't know how I can make her see what I can see. To give her the hope she needs to keep going."

"She's right. Sorry to say it, Jack, but she is."

"What?"

"You lead very different lives and marrying the two will take a lot of hard work, and even more compromise. Seraphina has a life here she wouldn't want to abandon. She isn't the type of woman who would give up her career or her volunteer work and just be happy to follow you around the world. Now that might change over time, but you can't start a relationship hoping the other person will give up their own dreams."

"She wouldn't be Sera if she did. And I would never want her to do that. I get it."

"Do you?"

The moment of realization was like a one-two punch in his gut.

He understood now what she meant when she said they couldn't make it work. She didn't want him to give up his dreams any more than he did hers. But Sera hadn't a clue what he had been planning. She had no idea that his goals had changed over the past few months. How could she, when he hadn't told her?

It irked him to realise he had been looking after his own interests for a long time. But he wanted more. He needed to show Sera that her life was important to him, not just to alleviate her fears, but to create solid foundations for their future.

"I know what I need to do."

"When a man looks hopeful like that, there's not a person on this good, green Earth that can stop him."

"I do have hope. Because you know what, Tony, your daughter is a woman worth fighting for."

"This isn't some movie, Jack. I don't want you just chasing her and running on adrenaline because you think this will win you the girl. The thrill of the chase is temporary. This is real life."

"I want real. Shit, sir, I've been living in a land of make-believe for too long. It's not just about the chase; it's not just because she's rejecting a future, our future. It's because I can't live another day without her. I can't picture my life without her in it."

"So you're in love with her."

Jack fidgeted with the label on the bottle. There were few people he loved in his life, even fewer whom he told.

"If you can't admit it to me, you certainly need to admit it to yourself. She's a woman who wouldn't settle for less."

"I wouldn't want to give her anything less than my everything. When she's open to hearing it, I'll say what needs to be said. But she needs to hear it first."

Tony nodded. "I believe you." He raised his bottle, tapping the neck of it in congratulations. "I'll wish you good luck, son. And for what it's worth, I'm rooting for you. Love is terrifying just as it is exhilarating."

Jack's shoulders lowered. He leaned back in the deck chair.

"I'll take it."

This was exactly the conversation he needed to have. It centered him. All the other stuff wasn't important. Giving Sera the stability and life that she deserved was his number one priority.

He would do everything in his power to make her see that he couldn't live his life without her. Jack only hoped she would believe him.

CHAPTER THIRTY-FOUR

The start of a new school term at the beginning of February was a blessed relief. But after a restless night spent in her own apartment, Sera was feeling crabby and a little emotional.

Ever since her conversation with her mother, she was agitated. Things weren't resolved with Jack, and it left her feeling lost. There was a pressure around her heart, and a constant buzzing beneath her skin. In short, she was going out of her mind. Problem was, she didn't know how to change it.

Sera should have been focusing on the outline for the Year 10 Health curriculum, but her mind was filled with thoughts of Jack.

Checking the timetable, she noticed that Maddie had a free period. She needed some advice, or she'd never be able to concentrate.

Sera walked across the courtyard and into the air-conditioned comfort of Maddie's office, only to find it empty.

She turned, wondering if Ally would be free, yet knowing it really wasn't the time to have a crisis meeting about her love-life, when she ploughed straight into Jack.

His arms shot out, and the heat of his hands holding her steady, branded her skin.

Sensations, millions of them bombarded her, but all she could do was stare. His scent, that citrus zing, filled her now. And memories of that summer, long-ago, assailed her. It was a mere few seconds, but enough to set her pulse racing.

God, she missed him.

"*Jack*? What are you even doing here? When did you get back?"

"A week ago. I've learned my lesson." He tapped the visitor's badge on his chest.

Sera didn't know whether to laugh or cry. She couldn't breathe.

"I was going to contact you, but I've had a few things I needed to sort first. I just had a meeting with Gabriel."

"What? Why?"

"I can't explain right now. I think it would be better if I showed you." Jack stepped closer, and every inch of her body vibrated. His voice lowered and those expressive blue eyes turned serious. Heated. "Sera, I want you to know—"

"Jack?" Maddie sputtered.

Sera sucked in air, heart racing erratically.

"What the hell are you doing here?" Maddie juggled a bundle of photocopying, stacked high, then froze, eyes wide. "Oh...umm, I better put these down before I drop them."

But whatever it was Jack was going to say, whatever moment had hovered between them, now passed.

"I better go." Jack said when Maddie disappeared inside her office. "But I'll call you. If that's okay?"

"Yes. I'd like that."

His smile was slow but filled with warmth. Sera wanted to bask in it for hours.

"See you soon, De Lotto."

She watched him walk away, and everything she wanted to say bubbled to the surface.

"Jack, wait!"

Sera raced down the corridor, until she stood before him, uncertain, but hopeful. "I...I have no idea what to say to you." She pressed her hands to her stomach trying to remain calm.

Jack cupped her cheek, and the tender gesture made her want to fall into his arms, to tell him everything.

But she couldn't. Not here. Not now.

"I missed you, Jack." She bit her lip. "And I'm glad you're back."

There. She said it. No matter what happened, he knew.

"Christ, Sera. I've been lost without you."

He stepped in close, his breath caressing her cheek.

The shrill school bell echoed around them and Sera wanted to curse.

Jack jerked back, shaking his head. "Soon, Sera."

She watched him walk away, something akin to hope settling around her frantic heart.

Sera prayed her instincts weren't wrong this time around.

Sera knew that the best distraction would be movement. And since she had been avoiding socialising for a while now, she knew it was time that she visited Leila and her baby, SJ.

Sera looked down at the happy infant, now nearly two-months-old. She cuddled SJ close, breathing in her sweet baby smell.

While Leila filled her in on the promotion that William received at work, and their plans for their own rental apartment one day, Sera studied the young mum. Despite the evidence of sleep deprivation around her dark eyes, Leila was beaming.

"I heard about you and Jack. I'm sorry."

"How did you—" Sera shook her head. "Never mind. And thanks, but I'm not here to talk about Jack."

Leila shrugged. "Just saying. He turned out alright, ya know. And I'm not just sayin' it coz of the money. I know it was him who did it, even though it has no name. But if you ever see him again, say thanks, eh? It helped Will pay off a lot of our debt. Though I doubt we'll be on some fancy plane to America any time soon."

Sera opened her mouth, then closed it. Money? That was news to her. But when she thought about it, not so surprising. Jack always had a thing about looking after those he cared about.

She suddenly remembered how it had been Jack's lawyer that helped Owen win his custody battle. How had she forgotten? Or had she just been blinded by her own fears?

"Perhaps not right now, but you might travel one day with SJ and Will."

"I hope so. I want better for her than what I had growing up, miss. I guess that's what my parents wanted for me, too."

"Sometimes it's hard to see that when you're in it. And to be honest, there are issues there with your father that eventually you'll need to face."

"He doesn't want to see any of us."

"And your mum?"

"I send her photos, and she calls every now and then when dad isn't home."

"Do you want a relationship with them?"

Leila looked out the small window of the even smaller living area that was decorated with various baby toys and playthings. "If you hadn't taken me in, if we hadn't moved in with Will's mum, I know our situation would be worse. But I'm not sure I want any contact. At least not with my dad, especially not around my kid."

"Whatever happens, Leila, you have our support."

"Thanks. I'm not super religious or nothing, but if Eli was out there, floating around, I think he'd want you to be happy. He just wanted everyone to be happy, eh?"

Sera's throat closed over. She didn't know how to respond, but deep down inside, she knew it to be true.

It was time she stopped living in the past, because she knew without a doubt, that doing so meant she wasn't living at all.

CHAPTER THIRTY-FIVE

*I*t was a few days later, after a stilted phone conversation between them, that Jack picked Sera up from her apartment.

She had been a bundle of nerves ever since she had seen him at work. But every time she tried to pick up the phone to tell him how she felt, she was at a loss for words.

Sera knew that she was terrified he didn't feel the same way, that he couldn't love her. But she knew that she needed to tell him how she felt or risk losing him a second time.

They made the drive into the city in relative silence, save for some small talk. It was a relief when Jack was the first to break the ice.

"Would you have called me?" Jack asked after a while. "If you didn't see me at school, would you have ever contacted me?"

Sera glanced at him then looked out the window. "Yes. I wanted to. I was just afraid. I didn't know what to say, or how to begin, so I didn't do anything."

"Huh."

"Not the answer you expected?"

"No. But I appreciate the honesty."

"I'm sorry for hurting you, Jack. For not giving us a chance."

Jack rubbed his jaw. "I get it. I've been making plans in my head and I haven't explained everything to you. Not properly. Which is probably why you don't trust me. Not yet at least."

"Okay, this is leading somewhere."

"I want to show you something. And I hope it'll give you a bit of an insight into what I've been planning. Into how I feel about you." Thirty minutes later, Jack slowed down, driving through a set of opened chain link fences.

He stopped in the middle of a large rectangular patch of land. It was overgrown and in need of maintenance. In the far corner sat a dilapidated brick building that was once a factory of some sort in the city. Most of its windows were broken, and the façade was covered in graffiti.

"Ta daaahhhh." He gestured.

"Is there a reason why you've taken me to the dump?"

"It's hardly a dump; it's more of an abandoned plot."

"Are you planning on murdering me out here or something?"

"Tempting, but no."

She smacked him in the gut.

"I deserved that."

"Yes, you did. So?"

"Guess."

"Jack," Sera huffed.

"Okay, no guessing."

"Tell me already!"

"I'm building a brand-new arts and tech school. Here. On this big, ugly patch of land."

Sera stared at him, trying to understand. "Excuse me?"

Jack began to explain everything. In detail. His aim was to help educate some of the poorest kids in Melbourne with this school and create a bunch of opportunities for the community in the process.

Of all the things that could have come out of Jack's mouth, building a school for kids to explore an alternate pathway to mainstream schooling wasn't even on the list.

"What do you think?"

"Why are you doing this?"

"You. And Leila. And me."

"What about your career? You're not making sense."

"Walk with me."

They wandered the perimeter of the large, flat space. The overgrown grass tickled her calves and images of snakes and spiders flittered through her head.

"Well?"

"It was a conversation that I had with Leila, after Khalid's birthday, that sparked the idea. I saw how amazing you were with those kids, but it killed me that you had to teach them in some drafty, run-down room. When I asked Leila about what the community needed, she had a ton of ideas. And I knew, after teaching Maddie's senior drama kids, that I wanted to do something that was real. To help people. So I thought why not build an arts and tech school to cater to those kids who might want something other than the traditional school system?

"We'd target the South Row kids, help support them to stay in school. There will be scholarship opportunities for some of the poorest kids in the state, too, to give them a chance to achieve their dreams. You give them that chance every week when you tutor them, and I want to help you do that with a space for them to thrive."

It took a second for Sera to process it. She couldn't quite believe it all, but when she looked at Jack and saw the excitement in his eyes, she knew it to be true. Her heart soared. She hadn't seen him this animated in a long time. "Why didn't you mention this?"

Jack shrugged. "I thought we had more time. I wanted to figure it all out, to get my head around what it was I wanted to be doing before sharing it. There was a ton of administrative shit I had to figure out, to make sure I could actually get the green light to begin. I think, beneath all that, I was scared that I'd fail you in some way if it didn't get approved. I know I hurt you back then and I didn't want to do it a second time."

Sera reached out, needing to touch him. She squeezed his hand, her own shaking a little at what he was telling her. "I'm sorry I didn't have faith in you."

"I guess I just wanted you to trust me at my word, which I now realise was stupid. Especially given my track record. But I've learned a lot about myself lately, about what I want from the future. Look, I don't know if I'll ever return to the big screen. Maybe one day, but I think there's other things I want to do with my life, other directions I want to take for the time being that make me happy.

"I've been living life in the fast lane for a long time now. I never really slowed down long enough to evaluate what I wanted. I told Taylor that I was taking a break from the film industry. I needed to make it clear I wasn't accepting new scripts and that apart from promo work, I wouldn't be available for the foreseeable future."

"Jack, I didn't want you to give up what you loved and then regret it. Because of me."

"I get it now. I know what you meant when you said it, and I wouldn't want you to give up your dreams either. But Sera, that lifestyle was killing me. Therapy has made me realise that I deserve better than that. That I want more for myself. For the first time I'm seeing everything clearly."

Emotion seized her lungs now. She felt so very ill at the thought of how wrong she had been. "I'm so sorry."

"I am too. "

"I didn't mean to hurt you."

"I know you didn't. And I didn't want you to feel like you weren't important. Because you are. I'm rusty at this, Sera. But I'm trying to figure it out, to do what's right. I realised that a lot of my relationships have been divided; I've had my life and they've had theirs. I don't want that with you. Diana says I need to begin communicating with you rather than expecting you to just go along with everything I'm doing."

"Funnily enough my mother says I need to communicate how I feel too. I haven't been so trusting myself, and I know I was wrong to push you away. I let those fears and my own doubt get in the way of our relationship."

Jack brushed his hand along her cheek and Sera's body trembled. "I haven't told you the best bit though."

"There's more?"

"I'm also building a community centre. It'll be a brand-new building that has a library, study rooms, even an outdoor court for recreation and sports."

"You're building a community centre, too?" She repeated the words slowly. It was like she was in a dream, unable to grasp the meaning behind what she heard, but knowing it was vitally important that she did.

"Yep. For the South Row kids, and hell, any disadvantaged kid, to have a safe space to learn. This site is only a few blocks away from South Row, from that crappy ass library you used to teach them in. So the kids can walk here, shoot some hoops, learn a few lessons and head back home. Don't you see, Sera? This isn't just about my dreams, but yours, too. I did this, for you."

She was speechless.

"I don't know what to say. Thank you. I—"

She hugged him now, drawing him in, even while her mind was racing. She had forgotten his generosity, that spirit of kindness beneath the cool.

She had misjudged him in so many ways.

Sera stepped back trying to process what he was saying. The council had rejected their requests, but here was Jack buying an abandoned block in the city, so that she could teach kids in a space that would no doubt be warm and welcoming.

She tried to contain her feelings, but tears spilled over.

"Happy tears I hope?"

"Yes. So happy. Jack, you're amazing. Thank you."

"You're welcome. But Sera, this is just the beginning."

They walked back towards the car, but she was floating, in a daze. She was scared to ask the question that hovered in her mind since she he had returned. Now wasn't the time to hold back. "So how long are you in town for?"

"As long as it takes."

"For the school to be built? That could take a while."

"I'm okay with that. I need to consult a certain teacher on what a good community centre might look like. Leila has plenty of ideas, but I want a teacher's perspective."

"She told me about the money you sent her. That was kind."

"She needs it more than I do. And I hope she'll accept the job I'm planning for her once she finishes school. But that's for later down the track."

Sera's heart galloped. He made it sound like it was a long-term project, that his life, for the foreseeable future would be here.

With her?

She wanted it more than ever.

But once more the words dried up in the back of her throat. How did she tell him what was in her heart?

Jack opened the passenger door. "I've something else to show you."

Sera blinked, still in a daze. "A day of surprises."

"Best is yet to come."

They drove for close to an hour in the opposite direction.

Jack was staying. He would be here, building a school. For her. For the community.

For himself, too. A new goal, a new direction. It still hadn't quite sunk in. But there was so much she wanted to say, to help him understand.

When Jack stopped in front of a set of iron gates, nestled high in the mountain ranges, Sera frowned.

"Pass me that remote?"

She fished out a small device with two buttons on it from the glove compartment.

When Jack pressed one, the gates swung open. They drove up a winding path lined with overhanging trees until they reached a pretty white house nestled in the wilderness. Or at least that's what it felt like.

Sera glanced around and immediately loved the delicate porch that wrapped around the top floors, the stylish French windows and curling vines that framed them. Everything about the place screamed oasis, like something out of a storybook. It was perfect.

"And why are we here?" But her heart knew, somehow it knew what this meant.

"I wanted you to be the first to see it."

"Are you saying this house is yours?"

"Signed, sealed, delivered."

Her heart thudded in an odd, discordant rhythm. "You bought a house in the mountains?"

"I've always loved coming up here. And when this place came on the market, I wanted to buy it."

"But construction isn't going to take that long. What will you do when the school's been built?"

"Live in it."

"Here?"

"Well, I'll base myself here and travel when I need to for work."

"Jack..."

Sera closed her eyes and tried desperately to regulate her breathing. She couldn't speak, not when her heart was in her mouth.

Hope, the shining, wonderous joy of it, broke through any lingering fears.

"I know this comes as a shock, and you were sceptical about my choices, and I get it. You were right, I needed time to figure it all out. But I know what I want now, Sera. In my career, in my life. And through it all one thing has been constant. You."

She trembled. "I need some air."

Sera shoved out of the car and paced the driveway. She couldn't compute it. Jack was staying. He was building a school. He was putting down roots.

For her. Long-term.

"I can't breathe."

Jack steered her to the porch steps, settling her down. He gently guided her head between her knees until her breathing evened out.

"I can spot a panic attack a mile away."

When she sat up, her vision was blurry, her heart full.

Jack was staying. Committing. Building his life here. With her.

"You okay?"

"I don't know. It's just a lot to take in."

"I'm not doing this for a laugh, or as a reaction to what you said, though I do want to prove to you I'm serious about staying. Sera, I know I've been living fast and loose, but that lifestyle isn't what I want anymore. I want to build something real, with you. Only you. I don't care how long I have to wait or how hard it's going to be, I'm ready. I want to commit to you. And I don't want to wait another day."

"Jack—"

"When you were mine all those years ago, I was happy.

Then when I developed feelings for you, I told myself I wasn't capable of commitment. I couldn't lose you like I did my parents, so I pushed you away." He held her hands now, eyes serious, but steady. "Sera, you were the first person since their death that I loved, and I didn't know how to handle it. I didn't fully appreciate you. But I want you to be mine again. Trust me to do right by you."

"You—"

"I love you, Seraphina De Lotto. And I want to live my life loving you, only you. I'll wait as long as I have to, and I'll build as many schools as you need, until you give me that chance. I get it now. All your fears, all your concerns. Because I can finally see you. Generous and kind, stubborn and sweet. A woman with a spine of steel and a heart of gold.

"Your dreams are important, and I want to be the man beside you, watching you achieve them. There's so much more I want to experience in this life, but it all means nothing if I don't get to experience it with you."

Sera felt his words break down any remaining barriers she had in place. "I've been so scared of being hurt, of loving you again, that I convinced myself it was better to let you go before I fell for you." Tears welled now and she fought to keep her voice steady, to say what needed to be said. "But I don't want to let you go, Jack. I've never wanted to lose you. Here I was thinking you couldn't commit when it was me doing the running all this time. I was so afraid that I couldn't trust myself, that I couldn't trust in you, so I didn't give us a chance."

"What are you saying?"

"I don't care what you do with your life. I don't care what your profession is, or where you want to live, because without you, Jack, my life isn't full. It isn't rich and complex and every-thing I've been too afraid to let in. You've shown me what it is to do something even though you're afraid, you've taught me what it is to better myself, even when I couldn't see the way.

Damn it, Jack, I love you. Don't you see? I've never stopped." She pressed her hand to her heart afraid it would leap out of her chest.

"So you'll be mine? My leading lady?"

Sera laughed, tears flowing in wild abandon. "You bet, Hollywood."

Sera kissed him, and all the love she had suppressed, all the feelings she had been so afraid of, burst through. She was ready to make her own commitment now and forever.

When he carried her over the threshold, she squealed in shock and delight.

No matter what happened, she chose him.

She would a million times over.

CHAPTER THIRTY-SIX

"I could get used to this."

Sera lay in Jack's arms, relaxed and thoroughly sated after yet another round of reunion sex. She had to pinch herself a little at the sudden turn of events.

"It's funny how those split-second decisions change everything. I sometimes think about what my life would have been like had we not met that summer."

"Should I be worried?" Jack looked down at her, a dubious expression on his face.

"Not at all. When I first met you in college, I had a feeling that you were different."

"I bet that's what you say to all the boys."

Sera grinned. She missed the playful banter. Where once Jack would use it to hide his feelings, now his teasing came from a place of joy. There was an openness about him, an inner peace that wasn't there before. It thrilled her to witness it. "I knew you were meant for something bigger. You're compelling, Jack. It's what makes you such a great actor."

Jack felt her forehead. "Hmm...yes, as I suspected, delusional and drop dead gorgeous."

"It's true."

"I know you're a liar because you've yet to watch a single film of mine."

"Now that's *not* true."

Jack raised an eyebrow. "You've watched one of my films?"

Sera pressed her lips together. "Sss. *Films*, plural."

Jack's mouth hung open. The look of shock on his handsome face was well worth it. "You've seen more than one?"

"All."

Jack laughed. "That was a one-eighty. I had it on good authority that you were boycotting me."

"Don't trust your sources." Sera winked. "I could see as soon as I watched you on screen that it's in you. Having this break might be what you need, but you've an amazing talent, Jack."

"Keep talking, my ego is approving."

"I bet it is. So I guess what I'm saying is, if you ever decide to go back to making films, I'll support you. Whatever comes our way, I've got your back."

Jack pulled her in, a quick, hot kiss that sparked so much inside of her. When they parted, Sera couldn't seem to stop grinning. Her heart was full. Because of him.

"That means more than any award I've won, De Lotto, you have to believe that. I'm not always an easy man, but I'm making a promise to you, to stay and figure it out."

"I'm starting to realise that I don't want easy. It's funny, I've always seen what my parents had and wanted it so badly, forgetting about all the hurdles they've battled along the way. It's not necessarily been smooth sailing, but they've always worked through any problems, together. I think I forgot that happily ever after doesn't necessarily mean it'll be easy, and that's fine by me."

"Is this your way of saying I'm high maintenance?"

"I think I can handle it."

"Damn right you can. So you wouldn't object to marrying a high maintenance man then? A few babies down the road? Maybe a nice penthouse in the city? Because I want it all. You're my home, Sera. It feels like you've always been my home."

"You want to marry me?"

"I do. If you'll have me."

Sera kissed him and felt like she was floating high above the clouds. "I want marriage and babies and all the hard stuff in between, Jack. With you."

Love. It packed a punch, but isn't that what she always wanted? A love that left her breathless, giddy, and if she was honest with herself a little thrilled.

Because she was in love with Jack Davies, international movie star, and all-around good guy.

Her first lover.

Her last boyfriend.

Her future husband.

Want a spicy free bonus scene of Jack and Sera's reunion? Then type this link below into your device for your free download:

https://BookHip.com/ZNRAADJ

ALSO BY IDA BRADY

Teacher Chronicles Series

Before You Were Mine

When You Were Mine

If You Were Mine (Coming 2023)

To Tango with Love

A Sweet, Sexy, Scandalous Series

Sweet Spot

Sex and the Stage

Secrets and Scandals

SUBSCRIBE FOR ALL THE NEWS!

If you want exclusive access to giveaways, sales, and new release alerts first, then subscribe to my monthly newsletter, With You in Romance.

ABOUT THE AUTHOR

Ida Brady writes contemporary romance novels that promise humour, heartbreak and a happily ever after. With all the sexy bits! A lover of chocolate (milk or dark) and thunderstorms (the bigger the better), she's usually dreaming about her next cast of characters or what she's going to eat for her next meal. When she isn't trying to tame her intractable curls, she's running after her kids, usually with a book in hand.

Ida lives in Melbourne with her Irish husband and their out-of-control collection of books. She sometimes daydreams about having a huge library in her apartment but will settle for stacking novels in the kitchen drawers instead. In her past life, she taught VCE Literature and English to a gaggle of teenagers. While she misses their enthusiasm, she sure as hell doesn't miss marking papers. You might find her dancing the sexy Argentine tango in her spare time, which isn't very often these days. She loves travelling with her family, observing strangers at café's, and getting lost in a good story.

Want to hear more?

Visit: http://www.idabrady.com or sign up to my Newsletter, With You in Romance for giveaways and prizes!

Follow me on Tiktok, Facebook! and Instagram or leave a review on Goodreads.

ACKNOWLEDGMENTS

Wow...what a whacky tabaccy year it has been. Honestly, a lot of blood, sweat and tears went into getting this book ready for publication. But after a lot of hurdles (including a broken laptop at the final stages of editing, gah!) I finally managed to get this glorious book out.

And boy did I love writing Jack and Sera's story. I had initially intended for Sera to get together with some other dude, but when Jack rocked up in *Before You Were Mine*, I just knew he was meant for Sera. Swoon.

Anyhoos, on to the important bits, thanking all the wonderful people who made this happen.

To Team Brida: Brian, Adria, Niamh and Hugo. I can say I'm the luckiest woman in the world to have you all in my corner. All that love and support, not to mention sweet little hugs, have kept this sleep-deprived mamma going when some days it was just bloody tough. Love you all to the moon and back!

To Ally Blake, honestly, I can't gush enough. You have understood my book so well and offered me such wonderful feedback that I know that I couldn't have made it what it is today without your editing prowess. You're amazing, one day

I'll meet you in person for a proper chat and a glass of bubbly! So thank you a million times over.

To Norma Gambini, girl, you are a treasure! Honestly, your support and utter faith in my work over the years makes me want to cry happy tears. Your eagle-eye edits are the best, and I'm eternally grateful for all that you do. Thank you, soooo much!

To my family, as always for the love and support both near and across the wild Atlantic. I've finished all the Irish chocolate by the way...yep, I'll just leave that unsubtle hint right there. *ahem*

To Laurelle Cousins, my dear dear friend, I treasure your friendship and look forward to those days where we can chat. Cannot wait to give you hugs next time I see you, mamma bear. Honestly, you've been such an amazing support throughout this year, including my four horror months of being ill. Your kindness, care packs and genuine love is sooo very treasured. A big thank you for your wonderful feedback on this manuscript. You're just utterly amazing and I can't wait to finish your book now that this one is out!

To my wonderful writer friends, my Meetup girls, your advice, feedback and general support really makes me feel like I can do this. I wouldn't be where I am without your friendship and support, so thank you! Here's to another release, and hopefully another retreat down the track!

To my BETA readers, once again, your time, effort and insight make me feel super lucky to have you all in my life. Thank you for all the feedback, encouragement and support. Y'all ROCK!

Finally, to my readers. Whoever you are, wherever you may be, I hope that this novel gives you a chance to escape from reality, even if for a chapter or two.

With you in romance,
Ida Brady